THROUGH THE WATERS

The first of four ***Journeys of Faith***

By

Jeanne Brooks

THROUGH THE WATERS
The first of four Journeys of Faith
by Jeanne F. Brooks

Printed in the United States of America

ISBN 978-1-60791-091-6

www.xulonpress.com

What readers had to say about

THROUGH THE WATERS

"This was a very exciting book to read. I had a hard time waiting to read the next chapters... it was very touching... brought tears to my eyes."

—**Evie**, Tacoma, WA

"The story was not predictable as some stories are. It had twists and turns and kept me wanting more. I felt joy and many tears, but mostly it made me feel that my own relationship with the Lord is not what it should be. I have vowed to pray and talk with Him more after reading your story, and realize how easy it is to forget to put God first in our thoughts."

—**Wynona**, Bellevue, WA

"I can't wait to read the next book in the series. I really enjoyed this story with its ups and downs... it kept me in suspense."

—**Bobbie**, Sequim, WA

"...the way you describe smells, sites, feelings, is amazing. I feel like I know these girls already and I'm not even that far into the book... I'm reading it as fast as I can, I'm just so busy... So everytime I have a free second I'm grabbing a chapter. I really want to just sit down and read it though because it's really grabbed my attention from the get go..."

—**Telle,** Belleville, IL

DEDICATION

To Stan,
whose never-ending support has sustained me
through the years
To Terry,
whose personal experience was a life-defining event
for me and
To my mother
the best mom ever, and an inspiration and encouragement
in all I attempt

ACKNOWLEDGEMENTS

First and foremost, I want to give glory to **Jesus**, my Savior. Without His love to carry me through the trials of my life, I would not be here today. In everything I do, everything I attempt to do, I keep Him uppermost in my mind. As the scriptures say, His "strength is made perfect in [my] weakness" (2 Cor. 12:9). I hope and pray that the stories I write touch the heart of the readers in such a ways that their relationship with Him is changed for the better.

Secondly, I thank my son and his wife, **Stan and Chantelle**, for opening my eyes to the needs of young women reading Christian books. They shared with me the desire to see more topics aimed at the 'twenty-something' generation that still spoke to their spiritual life, and out of their suggestion grew the *Journey of Faith* group of books, of which this book is the first. Hopefully, in sharing the lives of these four young women, others launching their careers will be wiser in their choices and decisions and avoid the pitfalls and tragedies of these girls.

Thirdly, I want to say how much I cherish my lifelong friendships. **Chikako Nichols** took me under her wing when I was just 17 years old and living on my own; she was my supervisor in my first job out of high school, but she was so much more. She took time to mentor me as a young woman, guiding my decision-making and teaching me more than I even knew about life and being an adult. She even took me into her home when I was transitioning to leave for the military. Through her unique style of asking questions she made me think critically about my choices and goals and helped me realize my potential. Her encouragement gave me the strength to leave my hometown and join the U.S. Air Force and explore the broader opportunities available to me. Over the years, after I left my hometown, we maintained contact; I watched her children grow as I brought mine to visit and shared their development with her. She was always available by telephone when I had a crisis in my life, empathized with my struggle with depression, and sorrowed with me when my daughter died. Even my oldest granddaughter knows Chikako and is fully aware of her impact on my life. I brought Lauren to meet Chikako and, as she did my life, Chikako has begun to make an impression on Lauren, broadening her knowledge of the world and the cultures around her. Chikako had her own challenges, but she still made time to listen, and I pray I was as good a friend to her as she was for me.

My second lifelong friend I need to mention is **Carroll Henry**. Carroll showed up at church one Sabbath and our bond was immediate. She was tall to my short stature, dark to my fairness, and elegant to my ordinary. In the back of my mind, I think I yearned to emulate her because she represented everything I thought my husband appreciated about his culture; she was born on the same island that he was. Carroll was so much more; her spiritual intensity drew me into a fuller relationship with the Lord. Although I accepted Him as my Saviour at a young age, it wasn't until I met Carroll that I understood the relationship aspect. She mentored my Christian growth until I decided to be re-baptized into fuller relationship with Jesus. Beyond that time, we have maintained contact and the love of our friendship transcended the Atlantic Ocean and twenty-five years of distance. Although I have only seen Carroll a couple of times since leaving England, once when she came to be with me when my daughter died, and once when I attended her daughter's wedding, as well as two short visits while we were stationed in Germany, I feel as close to her today as I did in 1982 when I left England. I thank God for her loving spirit and hope that my friendship means as much to her as hers does to me.

I am weary with my groaning;
all the night make I my bed to swim;
I water my couch with my tears. Psalm 6:6 KJV

"When you pass through the water, I will be with you;
and through the rivers, they shall not overflow you."
Isaiah 43:2 NKJ

Prologue

"...Madeline Marie Galloway, Bachelor in Arts, Elementary Education with a minor in Early Childhood Development..." Maddie stepped forward, her freckles stood out on her cheeks and nose against her flushed skin. As she walked across the platform, she heard a few cheers from the audience, some from underclassmen friends, but then she caught her parent's voices in the midst. She flushed even more and smiled, so happy that her family had come to see this important event in her life.

Fragrant rose petals lay at the feet of students shifting in their seats, impatient for the ceremony to begin. Rose petals of every conceivable color lay on the floor decorating the recently constructed platform. Spring bouquets of a variety of flowers in baskets graced the VIP area on both sides. The perfume of the flowers mingled with other scents of spring – fresh cut grass of the football field and the earthy smell of fresh-turned fields from the farms nearby. Even the gardenia corsages worn by the girls and the carnation boutonnieres pinned on each guy added to the breath-taking atmosphere of the graduation.

Each student wore a neatly pressed graduation gown, the girls in white and the guys in deep blue. Their graduation mortar boards sported the white and blue tassel of their school colors. Drifting neatly over the left eye of each student, the bobble symbolized one final step remaining in the education process. Proud parents gazed up from the audience trying to catch the eye of their graduate and hoping to capture the moment on film. Meanwhile, each student avoided eye-contact with their parent, trying just as hard to avoid their cameras. Most students appeared nonchalant and disinterested in the events of the day while others were filled with awe at reaching their goal, finally, this the last weekend in May.

Memorial Day weekend began with a special Friday Prayer Service at their church. All graduates in the church family, from kindergarten to college, received the prayers of the congregation. The minister gave a sermonette praising the students for their successful completion of another milestone in life. He challenged them to continue in both their education and their walk with the Lord. Then the group encircled the children and prayed for the futures of each child.

The celebrations continued with an all day picnic on Saturday. The children competed in three-legged, egg on spoon, and potato sack races. The older students gathered in groups and watched with apparent indifference, yet each one recalled when they used to participate in the fun. The ladies of the church prepared fried chicken, hotdogs and served up lemonade by the pitcher. From morning until dark they played, laughed and enjoyed fellowship. For some it would be the last time they shared in celebrations with their church family.

Because so many came from out of town to see the graduation at the college, the church pews were filled to capacity for the Sunday morning Divine Service. It was a time where all students in the congregation were once again mentioned;

however, the worship did not focus on the students but proceeded with reverence and joy. And after church let out families gathered in front of the sanctuary visiting with friends they hadn't seen in some time.

The afternoon Baccalaureate Ceremony celebrated the academic awards and honors each student received as a result of their years of studies. By Sunday evening the young people were ready for all the celebrations to end. After so many services where they had to sit quietly and respectfully, they wanted to let loose and enjoy the summer break. Yet, the most important ceremony still awaited them: the University graduation and presentation of college degrees.

The Commencement Ceremony always landed on the Monday - Memorial Day. Sitting on the recently constructed platform in the football stadium of their college, were only those students who reached the pinnacle of their academic sojourn, those graduating from the University. Sweltering heat portended an unusually hot and humid summer, but those seated in their caps and gowns were not thinking about the heat. They barely noticed the Dean mopping his brow with his handkerchief.

The Dean introduced the University President, who also appeared noticeably overheated as he stepped out of the wings. He reached for the glass of ice water waiting for him under the podium. His keynote speech seemed aimed at the audience more than the graduates, who barely listened as he spoke. Each individual had his or her mind on the future. What was beyond this day? Did it entail more schooling, a higher degree? Or had they accepted a lucrative or interesting job offer somewhere distant where they would, for the first time in their life, be dependant totally on themselves?

The final speaker, before presentation of their degrees, was their classmate, Winston Braswell, the valedictorian of the class. He easily maintained his four-point grade point average in college, as he had done throughout his first twelve years of education. Everything came easy to Winston, not just academically, but in sports and even spiritually, it seemed. He didn't struggle with the issues typical teens addressed when away from their parents, and his example was evident to professors, as well as his peers.

Before he began talking, he introduced the Accapella Choir, to sing a song that he had chosen to compliment the theme of his talk. Members of the graduating class stepped off the platform to sing with their choir for the last time. Accapella was known for its camaraderie and cohesiveness because getting into it was so competitive. The choir also participated in competitions and won many awards. Several graduates teared up as they realized this was their last performance. Although the song began quietly, it grew to a strong crescendo in the end, with just a few shaky voices holding the last notes of *Climb Every Mountain* from the Sound of Music.

Winston held the attention of the audience, more so than his classmates, as he spoke clearly and concisely about the future of the Class of 2005. His reference text was taken from Isaiah 43:1 & 2 KJV, but he also used several popular songs whose words spoke of the journey ahead. "Jesus did not promise us it would be easy," he stated. "In Matthew 11: 29 He promised he would help to carry our burden, should we be willing to ask Him and depend on Him." Winston went on to talk of trials and hardships and some of the students shifted restlessly, not wanting to accept that their lives ahead would be anything other than wonderful, just as they planned. Finally, Winston asked the Honor Choir to sing *When You Walk Through a Storm.*

The Honor Choir was a smaller group formed out of the Accapella for more intimate occasions requiring a choral arrangement. This time none of the graduating seniors joined in because the next step would be the presentation of degrees. They had to be in their places to start filing across the stage when their name was called. The words of the song struck a sensitive note in many of the students, unlike the first selection. Its mournful, yet hopeful, tone emphasized the separation soon to take place.

Isobel, Ashleigh, Madeline and Taylor sat side by side, throughout the program, as they had done in various classes throughout the four years they spent together on this campus. As a unit, they held hands through the last words of the song, "you'll never walk alone!" Although each had a different train of thought, and each had a different life focus, they still maintained a bond like sisters. They became best friends during their studies at college, even though their interests were as diverse as their personalities.

While settling into the dorm in their first week of their freshman year, they found common ground with each other, quite by accident, on the first Friday evening on campus. The four of them were in the dormitory sitting room, while most of the other girls had already lined up dates or group activities. The TV was off, and they were just chatting, getting to know each other. Although it was Friday evening, they had each chosen to forego the usual college activities in lieu of a quiet social time together.

None of the foursome was interested in drinking or partying, and they each had only a passing interest in the guys on campus. For a variety of reasons, the girls had each chosen to postpone serious relationships until after graduation. After discussing how they planned to spend the weekend, they found a common bond in their religious upbringing and church school educations. However, as their friendships grew, and they spent more time together, the differences in their religious lives became more apparent.

Taylor ardently practiced her faith and spoke frequently of her close walk with Jesus, often giving Bible studies to curious students, or working with her local church neighborhood ministries. She seemed to have her feet firmly planted on the Rock, and to all who knew her, was the least likely to waiver in her beliefs. Sometimes she came across as overpowering in her zeal to argue the benefits of Christian life. Her home church was a lively mix of everything from former Pentecostals to A.M.E. The choir clapped and moved to their gospel sound and the church had an active lay activities outreach program.

Maddie, on the other hand, practiced her convictions through church attendance and youth group participation, but was less vocal about her beliefs. The daughter of missionaries whose worship and evangelism grew out of a Calvinistic, Presbyterian-type formality, Maddie was also more comfortable with traditional hymns and quiet preaching. She didn't proselytize or force her opinions on others; instead she lived her quiet faith daily. A shy, introverted, and plain girl, she chose a gentle walk with Jesus, an almost childlike faith guiding her every action. She had no desire to act in conflict with her beliefs and sought out friends of like mindset.

Like Taylor and Madeline, Isobel had attended Church Academy and was raised in the church, but she drifted from both attendance and involvement while at college. Her early life was tumultuous and it wasn't until high school that she heard the Gospel message. Throughout high school, while others took the long walk up the center aisle to take their stand for Jesus, she consciously avoided committing her life to the Lord, feeling it would get in the way of her social life. She longed for excitement and variety, while still avoiding risky behaviors purely out of fear, rather than conscience. She listened to the fear tactics of her aunt regarding pregnancy, STDs, and AIDS and avoided long-term or intimate relationships with the opposite sex. However, she was still curious about parties, alcohol and drugs, and even voiced interest in casual boyfriend relationships.

Ash learned about God from her grandmother who taught her the basics, like prayer at mealtimes and reading the Christmas and Easter stories at the appropriate season. She attended Christian schools only because her parents thought it looked good for their children to attend private school. Ashleigh had never had the "born again" experience, and knew nothing of a personal Saviour. To Ashleigh, religion was a ritual performed for special occasions, or for some, it was a weekly event, but it did not occur to her to read her Bible daily or to pray anything more than memorized prayers.

The four girls understood and accepted each other's religious differences and those variations in practice just as they accepted the diversity of their physical characteristics. They bonded quickly and formed lasting friendships which carried them through the ups and downs of the four years they spent at college. And now, with graduation finally here, they knew they would each be forced to find different support systems.

The University President stood to begin conferring degrees on the students. With him stood the Deans of each of the colleges within the university structure: the School of Business, the School of Allied Health, the School of Science and the School of Education and Liberal Studies. In the wings, the graduates handed a card to the President who stood at the podium on the side of the platform. He announced their name and one by one they stepped out of the shadows and shook hands with the President accepting the rolled paper tied with a black ribbon which represented their diploma. They moved along shaking hands with the Deans as they walked across the stage.

Cheers, catcalls, and applause greeted the students in varying amounts, depending on how many friends and family were in attendance. Some students acted silly, embarrassed by the attention drawn to them. Others tried to ignore the noise walking stiffly to the other side of the platform. A few took time to nod and gracefully acknowledge the recognition, lifting their beribboned paper in a gesture of pride.

The rest of the ceremony passed quickly until all degrees had been handed out, and then came the final congratulations from the various officials of the University. All the students stood together in one accord and prepared for the conclusion and the recessional to take them off stage. However, before they could march out, one last tradition had to be recognized. First, at the announcement of the President, all graduates formally placed their tassels over their right eyes. Then, palpable excitement mingled with fearful anticipation as they tossed their caps into the air at the close of the ceremony. Grabbing the nearest cap from the floor, they marched out much more casually than they had entered the ceremony.

Buzzing with the voices of parents and graduates, the stadium was at once a welcoming center where young people could introduce their classmates to their parents, and a farewell place to separate from those of like mind, and step out into the world on a new adventure. Screaming and squealing overrode the hum and buzz of voices as the girls jumped up and down in a group hug. Joyfully, yet tearfully, they looked into each others eyes, knowing this would be their last goodbye for a long time. They promised to get together from time to time just as all graduates promise their friends as they prepare to move on. Each girl knew, however, that they would not be able to keep that promise as a group. The best they could hope for was occasionally running into one another along their new path in life or seeing each other at class reunions every ten years or so.

Madeline and Ashleigh were joined by their parents. Ashleigh's family had enjoyed the weekend festivities with their daughters, and planned to stay to help them pack up for their various moves. Madeline's parents arrived late for the graduation, and she had yet to see them. Although she heard their cheers from the crowd as she walked across the platform for her diploma, she yearned to see their faces.

They had been in the mission field in Indonesia for the longest time, and Madeline only saw them sporadically during her years at the church boarding school she attended for high school. The past four years of college were spent without a visit from her family, and funds were too short for her to make the long trip to see them. As an Elementary Education major, Maddie hoped for a call to the mission field, also, although she knew it was unlikely she would be sent to the same mission as her parents.

Part One

Chapter 1

Tears clouded her eyes, as Maddie caught a glimpse of her mother and father pressing their way through the crowd toward her. Mr. and Mrs. Galloway made an almost comical pair, with her tiny, rounded mother barely reaching 4 feet 10 ¾ inches and her long, lean father, at 6 feet 4 inches, gently guiding Mama with his hand resting on her shoulder. All the same, it was that very contrast that caused all the loneliness of the last four years to well up to the surface in a groan as she rushed into her mother's arms. Suddenly, from both sides of her parents, her younger brothers and sisters popped out, reaching for her and squealing in delight. They hugged her and congratulated her on her graduation, each vying for the chance to hold her hand, or grab her cap and put it on their own head.

"I can't believe you all came for my graduation!" Maddie exclaimed. "How could you afford it?" Mama's red curls showed just a hint of grey at her temples that was not there the last time Maddie saw them, and Daddy no longer sported a thick, black mane. His hair shone silver in the sunlight, with a thinning on the top. Both had noticeable laugh wrinkles around their eyes, but the creases at the corner of Daddy's mouth gave him a solemn, almost sorrowful appearance.

"Well, dear," Mama started, "the church brought us back from the field." She hesitated, and looked toward Daddy.

"Uh, yes, well..." he began. "You see," he cleared his throat, and started again, "it's like this..."

Mama saw his hesitation, and decided to save him the trouble, "Your father has decided to retire from the mission field. We have come back to the States permanently."

"But, Daddy, why? You always loved the mission," Maddie protested, then saw her mother quickly shake her head in a signal to not question him further, and Maddie tipped hers in respect, as she had learned from childhood.

"Well, anyway, let's celebrate your graduation." Mama changed the subject. "Shall we go out to dinner, or have you already eaten?"

Maddie was glad for the chance to eat something other than cafeteria food. Ever since high school, she limited her eating out due to the tight budget she kept. They decided on Ryan's, a local buffet style restaurant, where they could eat as much as they wanted for one low price. Maddie was surprised at the new van her father drove, which easily fit the seven of them. Now 22 years old, Maddie was 9 years old when her first sibling was born; the four other children were close together in ages: Simon 13 yrs old, Samantha 12 yrs old, and the twins, Jamie and Jason 10 yrs old. They had the usual camaraderie seen in large families, jostling, teasing, and sometimes tormenting each other in the name of fun. Maddie watched them in quiet amazement, feeling like a square peg among them while they fit neatly into their round holes.

Once they each had their plates filled, and were seated around the table, they clasped hands, as was their custom, for family prayer. Daddy always led out, then closed after all the others shared their requests or thanks. When they were babies, Mama used to press tiny fingers together and teach them to say, "Ah-men" as soon as they said Mama or Dada. As they grew to the toddler stage, the children learned to repeat a brief memorized prayer, "Lord, we thank you for this food, for Jesus sake, Amen". But once they were old enough, they were expected to speak from their heart, and each unabashedly prayed aloud in this public place. Mama's prayer was always tender, listing the loved ones for whom she had special concerns, but also remembering to give thanks for their many blessings. After his final thoughts, Daddy used the Lord's Prayer to close, and they all joined in with him. Dinner conversation usually entailed a review of the day's events, and today's chatter was especially lively.

"Maddie, have you heard from the Conference? Or have you lined up a teaching position?" this came from Daddy.

"No, I haven't received a call to the mission field, yet, and yes, I have a job lined up. But before I share my information, tell me what is going on with you, Daddy. Where are you going to live? What are you going to do for a living? Tell me all about this sudden decision of yours... or was it not so sudden?"

Between Daddy and Mama, the story came out, how they missed her and worried over her for the past eight years, how they did not want to go through that with the other children, and had chosen to return for Simon and Samantha to attend Church Academy while living at home, rather than boarding. Maddie felt an unfamiliar heaviness in her heart, wishing they had made this decision for her years ago, then, with a deep breath, and a prayer for the Enemy to get behind her, she smiled and rejoiced with her siblings, that their teen years would be easier than hers.

Like her, Simon and Samantha had been home-schooled and completed eighth grade ahead of their age group. Moving from such a sheltered environment to the freedoms and temptations present at boarding school was challenging, even for a mature Christian youth. The fact that they were younger made that adjustment all the more difficult. Maddie quickly saw the wisdom in Mama and Daddy's decision.

Somehow, Maddie did not believe her parents were sharing the whole story, but she did not press the issue, knowing that, when the time was right, they would confide in her. Instead she focused on the meal and family chatter of her siblings, which brought overwhelming joy to her heart. They were so young when she left home for Academy and, although she had seen them on a few visits, she felt almost like a stranger in their midst.

As his Lexus scooted through Omaha traffic, Jim Buckley headed home contemplating the last ten years and what the future held for Suzanne and him as a couple. This Memorial Day weekend marked their tenth anniversary, which was indeed a landmark in this day and age, but at the same time signified a sad sense of incompletion in their lives. By this time, they both thought children would be noisily filling their home with joy, but so far, that remained only a dream. It wasn't from lack of efforts on their part; they spent the first five years totally immersed in each other, and praying for a child to come from their love.

When they accepted that conception may not happen without the help of a doctor, they consulted the best OB/Gyn recommended to them, to explore their options. Before writing off their chances to conceive naturally, the doctor recommended a variety of tests, each a bit more complex and invasive than the previous. As time passed, Suzanne seemed to lose hope bit by bit. Jim could see it in her eyes first, each time the doctor shared the results of a test. When it became more apparent that the problem might be with Suzanne's body, and not Jim's fertility, her posture started to drop. No longer standing tall and graceful, she took on the appearance of one carrying a heavy load on her shoulders, slouched and saddened. Finally, the doctor recommended they try artificial insemination or in vitro fertilization, both of which Suzanne rejected outright.

"I am not going to have you in one room and me in another when our child is conceived" She insisted, "and there is no way I am going to become a pin cushion, and allow some stranger to mix my egg with your sperm in a test tube somewhere!" Suzanne was adamant despite Jim's efforts to convince her that she would still have the blessing of carrying her child and giving birth. He couldn't break through the barrier her mind had built against what she perceived as artificial means of having a child.

Suzanne had long ago decided that artificial insemination and in vitro fertilization were man's way of playing God. Spiritually, she could not reconcile science with nature when it came to having a child. She could not accept the idea that she would not be like other women and conceive naturally. Instead, she prayed and searched the scriptures focusing on the stories of Sarah, Rachel, Hannah, and Elizabeth, all of whom conceived after protracted barren years and much pleading with the Lord to open their wombs.

Jim knew that if she could find someone to anoint her, she would try that. She would even seek a faith healer before availing herself of medical technology and breakthroughs which had helped so many women in recent years. He, too, turned to the Lord in prayer, placing his wife before Him, concerned for both her spiritual and mental health. He worried that Suzanne was so obsessed with pregnancy that she would fail to take care of herself, or would neglect their relationship.

To revitalize their marriage, he arranged a retreat weekend for them to celebrate their anniversary. Although many couples attending were barely holding onto their relationships by a thread, Jim knew theirs was still stronger than that. However, he also recognized the value in Christian counseling to overcome major obstacles before they became marriage-breaking stumbling blocks.

He hoped that Suzanne was ready to leave when he got home. The drive to the retreat was nearly three hours, so they would have to rush to make the 9:00pm check-in. He didn't pull into the garage, although he used his garage door opener to go through the garage and into the house. As he walked into the house, he saw their two bags near the back door to the garage, so he immediately took them out, placing them into the trunk, and then went back inside to find Suzanne.

Suzanne was not excited about this weekend; she only agreed to it to make Jim happy. Dressed in her khaki, Bermuda shorts, navy T-shirt with white trim around the v-neckline and short sleeves, and navy canvas mule-style tennis shoes, she looked ready to go boating. Her smooth brown hair curled gently under on her shoulders, with bangs just flicking into her eyes when she dropped her head. Her grey eyes looked dark and brooding when Jim found her standing quietly at the door of the nursery. She jumped and turned at the sound of his footsteps approaching her across the hardwood landing, and quickly said, "OK! I'm ready to go." in a light-hearted, too cheerful tone of voice.

Jim recognized the tone as her way of over-compensating for being off in a daydream. He chose not to mention his observation, instead just taking her hand, he led her to the car, opened her door and closed it gently once she was inside. Making small talk about her day and about his, he started the engine, backed out of the driveway as the garage door closed, and they made their way to the church's campground where the couple's weekend would be held.

Chapter 2

Later that evening, Maddie reclined on her parent's bed in their hotel suite, watching them as they got the other kids tucked in for the night. Even at 13 years of age, Samantha enjoyed a few minutes of special attention from her parents last thing in the evening, as did Simon, Jamie and Jason. It was a time to wrap up the days events, a time for each child to share thoughts or concerns with both their parents and with the Lord in prayer, as Mama and Daddy bowed with them beside each one's bed.

It had been so long since Maddie shared that intimate time with her folks, that once again, she had a sense of not fitting in with her family. Picking at the silky, floral bedspread, she longed to return to the tender years of youth, to the simplicity of childhood. If only there was some way to tell her brothers and sisters to not rush their years of learning and exploration; if only they could know ahead of time, that growing up held so much uncertainty. But then, while wishing for a life less complicated, Maddie still anxiously anticipated her own future. For years, she planned to be a schoolteacher, and now that dream was about to become reality. How many of her classmates could claim that their dreams were coming true?

"So, little girl, tell us about your teaching position," Daddy's rich voice interrupted her thoughts. "Will you be nearby? We plan to find housing close to the Academy campus or somewhere between there and this university, since Samantha and Simon will probably choose to go here like their big sister." Maddie could hear pride and a bit of a smile in his voice.

"Can I wait until Mama joins us? I really want to ask both of you for your advice." Although she had lived away from home for eight years, Maddie always deferred big decisions to her parents, and this time was no different; although it was her career choice, she still respected their opinion.

"Hey, honey," Mama walked around the corner to join them. "Now, what is all this about a job offer?"

The three of them sat cozily on Mama and Daddy's bed until the wee hours of the morning, discussing the opportunity Maddie had been offered. Although she preferred to work in a Christian school setting, this offer was in an underserved public school district, and Maddie felt she could make a positive contribution there. Ideally, she wanted to head straight to what she perceived as the safety of the mission field but, as Daddy pointed out, perhaps her mission field was not a distant land, just a different culture. And perhaps safety was relative.

"You know right from wrong, and are firmly grounded in your faith." Daddy reassured her. "Maybe you are meant to be a witness to your co-workers, maybe to the students. Whatever the plan, remember the Lord's promise in Jeremiah... The plans He has for you are for good, not for evil; they are plans for you to prosper..." Daddy always seemed to know the right thing to say when Maddie needed encouragement, and this was no different from the other times she had sought his advice. Mama, too, claimed promises on Maddie's behalf, and bolstered Maddie with her positive support. By the time they finished discussing Maddie's employment opportunity, she felt much stronger about her decision and less fearful for her future.

The dangers in Indonesia or the East Asia division may not be the same as those in the inner city, but risk existed wherever the word was being spread. Mama and Daddy shared insight into the last eight years of their time overseas and, unknown to Maddie, the pressure from the predominantly Muslim population of Indonesia had turned violent and threatening to the Galloway family. Then, too, they had been involved in the attempts to help after the Tsunami of 2005. Superstitious fears at the cause of such a devastating occurrence fed a deep cultural distrust of non-Indonesian services reaching out with assistance. Also, certain church groups implied that the tidal wave was evidence of God's judgment against Muslims, which only caused a wider chasm between the two religions, making the job of missionaries even harder.

"So is this what is really behind your return to the States?" Maddie asked pointedly. She knew they were holding back, and she was determined to get to the root of the issue.

Mama looked down at her hands, and Maddie just realized her mother was twisting a handkerchief, an old habit of hers indicating worry.

"Mama, you know I am old enough to hear the truth. And if you'd rather I don't tell the other kids, I can honor that request, too." Maddie implored her parents with her eyes, hoping they would realize she wasn't a child anymore.

Daddy nodded his head, affirming her statement. "You are right. You are an adult, now, and should be included in the difficulties the family faces as well as the good times. Your mother and I are grateful to have such a mature and understanding daughter." Maddie could see both pride and sadness in his eyes. Suddenly, Maddie noticed his eyes shimmering, shining with unshed tears. Mama noticed too, and saved him from saying anything more. None of the children had seen their father cry and she did not want this to be the first time.

"Maddie, dear, you know your father would never leave the mission field without a very strong motivation." She began. "I know you are smart enough to realize that Samantha and Simon's education is not that strong a motive, although we do worry about the boarding school situation for them. We are back because your father has not been feeling well for the last year or so…" she let her words sink in for a moment. "We made a trip to the Loma Linda Hospital about two months ago, and he had extensive testing. The results were not good. It seems Daddy has non-Hodgkin's lymphoma; it's a malignant problem in the lymph glands and needs extensive treatment. Right now the doctor's are not very optimistic, so we have made it a matter of prayer."

Maddie's eyes filled, but she gulped back the tears in an attempt to be brave for her parent's sake. Her father had never had so much as a head cold in all the years she knew him and, for him to have such a devastating diagnosis just when he was at the prime of his life, was heart-wrenching. Suddenly, it felt like the earth dropped out from under her, and that she should put her plans on hold to help the family through this crisis.

"Oh, no you don't" Mama said, looking into her eyes. "You are not going to try to solve this for us, and you are not changing your plans. I see that look in your eyes…" Mama always could read her heart.

"But what are you going to do? Is the church helping with the medical costs?" Maddie was aware of the fact that most missionaries had little or no health insurance, since it wasn't honored overseas in the mission fields so, when they returned to the States, it fell to them to buy into a plan.

"Well, unfortunately, we will be responsible for the costs. As a pre-existing condition, even if we got a health insurance at this time, it would not cover your father's current illness. Thankfully, we have a lot of friends willing to help, and various churches are having fund-raisers to build up a trust fund especially for your father's care."

Maddie and her parents talked late into the night, before Daddy took Maddie back to her dormitory. Mama and Daddy convinced her to carry on with her plans, but did welcome her help with their resettling over the summer months. She planned to pack her personal items over the next two days, then she would follow them to the town halfway between the college and the academy, where they had already been in touch with a realtor. They could not afford to purchase a home, but found several rentals from which they would choose.

Jim and Suzanne arrived just in time to check in for their private cabin some distance away from the main lodge. They drove along a dirt road leading up an incline to an isolated hilltop near the lake. The porch, with its two rockers, invited the couple to sit and gaze at the water, but mosquitoes were already biting, so they opted instead to get settled in.

Jim unloaded their luggage while Suzanne made her way inside to inspect the accommodations. The cabin was rustic, but quaintly decorated with quilts, afghan throws, crocheted doilies casually decorating the antique furniture. The bedroom held a tall, four-poster bed with steps to climb onto it. Curtains draped on each poster, the four of which were connected with cables to allow the curtains to close around the couple for even more intimacy. Out the window of the bedroom, a creek passed through an expanse of pasture bordered by trees, which allowed them to watch the migrating deer as they stopped for a drink of water or to graze in the field.

Jim drew Suzanne to the window, his arm around her waist, to watch the doe and her fawn. The deepening evening gave a solemn, almost mysterious feel to watching deer from such a close range. Suzanne appreciated the beauty of the scene, but also understood the psychology of Jim's efforts. Her heart only ached more as she watched, rather than feeling comforted by God's obvious control of all of creation. She turned from the window on the pretense of getting ready for the night, feigning a tiredness that she felt in her bones, although didn't manifest in her actions. She was always tired these days; just the effort of making it from day to day tired her. She knew this was a sign of depression, but hesitated to talk to the doctor about it, because she was so tired of hearing another word of discouragement, another diagnosis of failure on her part.

Both Suzanne and Jim found enjoyment in their time together at the retreat. Although the seminars seemed more of a chore than an anticipated activity, they did enjoy the quiet times... walking holding hands through the wooded, park-like environment, hearing the noises of the wild turkeys as they prowled along the creek in the woods, and even the quiet evenings in their cabin where, instead of separating to their individual spaces as they may have done at home, they found a companionable silence in sharing the warmth of a fire in the fireplace, reading their books.

The weekend proved to be a nice escape from their daily activities, but Jim was disappointed that Suzanne was not impacted by the uplifting spiritual themes at the various sessions like he was. He truly felt God's hand in the healing of couples, but soon realized that if both were not seeking help, only one of the partners may benefit from the hand of the Great Physician.

On the drive home, however, Suzanne seemed to open up. She was willing to discuss the options they had left, either artificial insemination or in vitro, and she told Jim she would consider in vitro. She had discussed this with one of the women who attended the weekend event, and realized that medical wisdom is one of God's healing gifts. Jim was elated to think that their journey toward parenthood wasn't over, but perhaps just beginning!

Summer for Maddie's siblings was freedom and fun, swimming at the public pool and getting familiar with the town and with other children with whom they would soon attend school. They had no idea that Daddy was ill; Mama and he made trips to Omaha for his treatments, while Maddie held down the home front. Once school started, Mama and Daddy could make the trek with the kids at school, protecting them from the knowledge of Daddy's illness as long as possible. It was harder to hide the truth from the children, especially Samantha and Simon. Josie and James were young enough to be carefree and blissfully blind to problems in their home.

The chemotherapy and radiation was taking its toll on Daddy, however, and his face was grey and gaunt. His gait was more unsteady, and he needed to rest more frequently during the day. He tried to maintain a brave front so the younger children wouldn't be frightened, imagining the worst, but both he and Mama knew his outcome may be just that – the worst.

Samantha was the first to ask Mama if Daddy was sick. From the start, Daddy and Mama agreed they would not lie, if any of the children asked outright, so Mama was gentle, but honest, with Samantha. She tried not to give a prediction of the outcome, choosing to tell Samantha only the minimum necessary about Daddy's illness. Samantha did not tell Simon or the younger kids, but she did talk with Maddie about her fears for the future. Maddie tried to encourage her, but also took the opportunity to ask Samantha to be strong and helpful in Maddie's absence.

Toward mid-August, Maddie prepared to leave her family once again. She truly enjoyed spending time with the family, despite the trials Mama and Daddy faced. She loved her brothers and sisters, and enjoyed watching how they interacted, how they had changed in her eight years away. Now saying good-bye was much harder. She wanted to remain with them, to help them deal with whatever was to come, but she knew Mama and Daddy wanted her to follow her dream of teaching. She packed up her car with as much of her possessions as she could, and with tearful farewells, she began her journey, stepping out in faith.

Chapter 3

Driving across the country from Nebraska to Illinois gave Maddie a lot of time to think and plan. Heading east through Omaha, Council Bluffs and Des Moines on I-80, aside from the cityscapes, the scenery was monotonous. Windows down and her hair blowing freely in the hot, dry wind as she drove across the prairie gave her a true sense of adventure. As she approached the Quad Cities area, the thought of crossing "the river', that great Mississippi she'd heard and read so much about, sent her heart racing like a child about to ride their first roller-coaster. Never before had she felt like breaking loose with a primal scream; never had she felt so free from encumbrances and restrictions. She also finally had a sense of adulthood and the responsibilities that also entailed.

Just three hours from her destination, Maddie decided to take advantage of the late hour and check into a hotel, so she could make the most of her crossing the river. She used the evening to sightsee, driving around through Bettendorf, Moline, Davenport and Rock Island, crossing and re-crossing the bridges over the muddy Mississippi. Seeing all the colleges in this area made her wonder why she had chosen a church school over the state school systems. Either could have prepared her equally for teaching, even for the mission field. Then she stopped to dismiss the enemy and praise the Lord, knowing that it worked out according to His plan.

Maddie arrived in Chicago full of hope and anticipation. Her hotel reservation already guaranteed her a place to stay, short-term, but she wasn't sure where she would live in the long-term. She hoped for help from the local church congregation in locating a family willing to rent a room to a single schoolteacher, if only temporarily, until she got her feet on the ground. Once checked into her hotel, she decided to explore her new environment, since it was still early in the day.

It was unusually hot and humid for late August and the air felt heavy whenever she took a deep breath. City pollutants added to the thickness in the atmosphere, although the occasional gust of wind gave a little relief. Totally new to the big city, always having lived in either rural Indonesia or on the college campus in small town America, Maddie was, at once, both disgusted at the dirty smell and overwhelmed at the awesome size of the skyscrapers and closeness of the buildings. Following a map she printed off of Yahoo, she found her way to the Cabrini-Green Housing projects and Sojourner Truth Elementary, the public school that would soon be her home away from home during work hours.

The turn-of-the-century brick row houses contrasted with more modern white and red structures, reflecting the continuous attempts to enlarge and improve government housing. However, all attempts to improve seemed to only add to the demise of the region, infamous for its crime in Chicago, just as Harlem and Bedford-Stuyvesant were known in New York City. Maddie saw people, sometimes whole families, sitting on the stoop in front of their door watching children play, barefooted and dirty. When she looked up, she could see ragged fabric billowing out open windows far too high above ground to be safe. Occasionally, a child peered out, causing her heart to drop, fearing they might fall from such heights.

Many apartments had plywood at the doorway, yet someone had worked it off enough to open, allowing squatters to take up residence and wires strung between trees or man-made structures held clothes drying in the dusty breeze. Men hung out in groups, some smoking, and some sipping from a bottle inside a brown, paper bag, all with a look of hopelessness in their eyes. Maddie had learned of these conditions in her Sociology class, and investigated Chicago's inner city situation fully before making any decision to accept the teaching assignment, but most influential in her decision was her father's advice. The harsh reality was worse than either she or her father discussed, and when Maddie could take no more, and the sun began to go down, she headed out to the safety of her hotel.

Her hotel was in the suburbs, Aurora, way too far from inner city Chicago to drive to work everyday so she knew it wouldn't be long before needing an alternate arrangement. She planned to take her father's advice to seek out the local church for help with resources and support, both physical and emotional. She valued the wisdom of the elders in the churches formerly attended, and knew this group would be no different.

Looking in the Yellow Pages, Maddie located the church nearest her hotel, and prepared her clothes for church the next morning. She lay on her bed and pulled out her devotional and Bible, but her mind wandered back to the sad conditions in the projects. Automatically, as she learned early in her Christian walk, she bowed her head and petitioned God on their behalf.

"Oh, Lord. Help me to serve this community. Help me to be color-blind, to be non-judgmental, and to love each child equally with Your love. Father, I long to be a mouthpiece for You, a witness to my co-workers, and shining light in such a dismal environment. Thank You for hearing my prayer. In Jesus name, Amen."

She turned in her Bible to the Gospel of Matthew and read the verse which had long guided her actions, "Inasmuch as ye have done it unto one of the least of these your brethren, ye have done it unto me." Maddie reread the verse, slowly, in context, to internalize the message. Then she said her evening prayers and turned in for the night, looking forward to a warm Sabbath fellowship with like believers.

She awoke the next morning rested and excited at the thought of attending church. While in college, she had attended a church near the campus, frequented by many students, both college and high school ages, but with a dearth of little children or elderly members. Now she looked forward to fellowship with the elders from whom she could draw wisdom, and interacting with little children who always reminded her of the simplicity of faith.

As a youth, before she left for boarding school, she had enjoyed working with the primary ages in their Bible classes, and working in the nursery, relieving the mothers so they could enjoy the worship service. Also, in the mission fields overseas, the one constant seemed to be the treatment of the elderly. Whether a family member, or a single or widowed member of the community, the elderly were revered for their knowledge, memory of historical events, and understanding of life in general. Their needs came ahead of the younger members of the society, and they were universally loved and respected.

After her morning worship and breakfast, Maddie showered and dressed in her church clothes, and grabbed her Bible on her way out the door. The nearest church was about 15 minutes from her hotel, but the sunshine and blue sky so captivated her attention, it seemed only seconds before she arrived at the parking lot. The familiar sign in front of the church welcomed her, along with groups of people congregating just outside the side and front doors. She parked and headed for the nearest door, not sure where her class would be, and asked the man standing at the door for directions to the class for young adults.

He directed her down the hall, to the left and into the first classroom on her right, where she found a class full of teens. She realized she had a youthful face, and was actually younger than most college graduates, but she did not expect to be placed with high school students. She quickly excused herself and looked for someone else to ask for directions. Explaining the mix-up, she fully expected to find a class of like-minded, twenty-something adults; however, this time she was directed to a class in the sanctuary which was mostly young couples. Settling into the pew, she decided to sit in on this class until she could talk to the pastor to find out more about the young adult picture in the church. That was her first disappointment for the day, but she wasn't about to let it ruin her whole day.

Although her class was not made up of other college-age singles, the discussions were lively and spirit-filled. She felt herself drawn into the dialogue through the skillful tactics of the teacher, which she appreciated from her perspective as an educator. She disliked classes where the teacher felt compelled to lecture, and even seemed annoyed at the intrusion of a question or observation by one of the class. Maddie felt her thoughts on the lesson added something for the class to ponder, and thought perhaps the Lord had worked it out for her to join this group for that reason.

Once Bible Study was over, the groups mingled in the foyer, and several individuals took the opportunity to introduce themselves and to meeting Maddie. She still wondered at the lack of single twenty-somethings, but at least she felt welcomed by the few who ventured in her direction. The visiting was short-lived; about ten minutes after classes broke, a gentle hymn sounded over the PA system, quieting the crowd and smoothly encouraging everyone to enter the sanctuary with reverence, to find their seats, and prepare for the divine worship service.

Maddie soon found herself totally immersed in the music and mood of the worship service. She added her alto to the church's voices singing praises and hymns, and then she listened intently to the sermon. The pastor appeared to be in his early thirties, and Maddie wondered briefly whether he was married, but quickly dismissed her curiosity as he presented his thoughts on the second coming of Jesus. She was so enthralled at the pictures he painted, that her spirit was revived and refreshed, as she had come to expect from her weekly church attendance. She no longer felt like a stranger at this new church, knowing they all shared in the glorious hope, and were in one accord in their faith.

After church, Maddie sought out the pastor, hoping for suggestions or leads on a room to rent from one of the church families. Pastor Green was still in the foyer, amid several men, "probably elders," Maddie thought. She hesitated and nearly did an about face, when they noticed her, and called her over. As she explained her situation, they all agreed to look into possibilities for her, and took her contact information, in the event that something came up.

Maddie had hoped for either a potluck or an invitation to the home of a member, but with neither forthcoming, she made her way back to the hotel. She ate a snack just big enough to stave off her hunger, and then changed her clothes into casual slacks and a light-weight top. She looked over a map and decided to head for the lake, Lake Michigan, for the afternoon, to enjoy the beautiful day and meditate on her upcoming job.

Several days passed and Maddie did not hear from the pastor, so she took the initiative to call him about the room to rent.

"Unfortunately, we have not located anyone with space to spare, Miss Galloway..."

"Please, call me Maddie."

"uh...Maddie, then. What we did find was a list of apartments in areas that might be safe for a single young woman."

He said that as if being single was a curse, or being young was a problem. Maddie tried to ignore the tone of voice and took the information from him. She thanked him for his efforts on her behalf and got off the phone. She set about exploring and locating the various apartment complexes until she found one close enough to her school to be convenient, but in an area that appeared clean and safe.

She decided to get second-hand furniture to keep her expenses down, and all she purchased initially was a couch and bed. Her closet had shelves which she used instead of a chest of drawers, and she planned on sitting on the couch to eat her meals. Fortunately, she did not have to buy appliances, since they were included in the rent, and before she knew it, she had settled in nicely, and checked out of the hotel. Using the few things she collected for her dorm room in college, along with a quilt passed down from her grandmother and the few items Mama gave her as "house-warming" gifts, she decorated her apartment in 'shabby, not so chic', but definitely with a homey feel.

Chapter 4

For one week prior to the start of the new school year, Maddie attended Teacher's Workshops along with her co-workers, most of them seasoned employees with the Chicago Public School system. She worked on getting her first grade classroom decorated with the usual colorful, carefully drawn, alphabet and sums, and organizing her files with the list of expected students in alphabetical order and color-coded according to the results on their kindergarten progress reports. Although she planned to give them all equal attention, she wanted a quick reference to remind herself of any special needs. Between all the preparations, whenever she had the opportunity, she got to know some of the other new teachers, as well as a few veteran elementary teachers she could use as a precious resource during her introduction to teaching.

There was Sadie Jones, a brilliantly dark-skinned young woman who had grown up in the projects, knew what the children lived with day in and day out, and wore a chip on her shoulder against the 'do-gooders' who came to do a year or two of 'charity work'. This was her third year and she had already seen several come and leave. In her opinion they were there just long enough to put a year or two of experience on their resumes, before moving on to better positions elsewhere. She resisted any attempt to draw her into the group, sitting on the periphery, just close enough to cast disparaging remarks at every chance in the conversations.

Then there was Kay-Leigh O'Brien, the red-headed little spitfire, determined to right every wrong and fight every battle for 'her children'. Like Maddie, she was totally new to teaching and enthusiastic to apply all she'd learned in college. She didn't let Sadie's negativism affect her spirited approach, and she didn't allow it to define her, either. She was determined to make the Public Schools in general, and this one in particular, better, by whatever means she could find.

Fred Dylan, another first-grade teacher, sat quietly observing the women. He had an air of nonchalance, yet he seemed to be sizing them up, looking for prey, for whatever reason Maddie could not discern. Good-looking, and seemingly quite aware of it, he worked his magic with the younger women as they came and went from the staff lounge, winking or half-smiling at each one. He rarely got together with the few other male teachers, who taught the older grades, preferring to mix with others who would see his students regularly in trade-offs at lunch or recess duties. He also had the advantage of experience; he had taught at the same school for the last five years. At 29, he had the confidence that came with age, while still holding onto a youthful charm with the opposite sex; his flirtatious behavior made Maddie uncomfortable.

Another young teacher intimidated by Fred's friendliness, was Lizzie Stephens. Sitting nearest Maddie during the various workshops, Lizzie was a mid-western girl, raised, like Maddie, in a Christian home in a rural locale in Southern Illinois. She seemed out of her element in this inner city school, but displayed a quiet strength in her questions and responses during the training sessions. Maddie and Lizzie hit it off right away; they seemed to sense the spiritual link between them, and were drawn together during lunches and breaks, at which time they compared notes on each other's lives.

By the time the Teacher's Conference and Training session came to a close, Maddie had earned a reputation as both friendly and helpful, always trying to work as an advocate for the underdog in any dispute, and aiming for peaceful coexistence with all of the staff. Always modestly attired in a mid-calf length skirt and neat blouse or sweater, Maddie tried to arrive each morning with a smile on her face, allowing the love of the Lord to shine from her heart. Without a doubt, she felt blessed as she took in her surroundings, and rather than looking at teaching in the projects with a negative attitude, she chose to accept it as her mission field, determined to search out opportunities to be a witness to both staff and children, without proselytizing or preaching.

Maddie's first day of classes at the rundown elementary school on the fringes of the Cabrini-Green projects started as expected. She arrived in a neatly tailored pantsuit, with a light-weight blouse under her blazer, so she could remove the blazer and keep cool in the warmth of the late summer heat. The children lined up outside according to their classroom assignments, some in raggedy shorts and T-shirts, while others sported the one new outfit their family could provide them for the school year; those whose parents had not checked ahead for their teacher's name stood to the side with their son or daughter, waiting to learn their designated classroom. Those in lines filed noisily into the school, laughing and jostling each other, each line directed by the hall teachers to their correct classes. Once inside the classroom, the children piled their personal items in cubbies with their names above them, and vied for seats, although they knew the teacher would probably reassign their seats before the day was over.

"Class, my name is Miss Galloway, and I will be your teacher this year." Maddie spoke firmly above the din of voices. She made eye contact with several children near the front and immediately fell in love with her first group of first-graders. She knew that teaching was in her blood and it wasn't what she did, but what she was.

She began by taking roll call and, as she recognized the name of a child previously noted to need extra attention, she reassigned them to a seat nearer the front of the classroom. Amid moans and groans of the dissatisfied, she negotiated seat changes until all children were placed where she felt she could best work with them. She knew that the process was dynamic, and would change more than once over the course of the school year, but for now, she was satisfied.

To start the day, Maddie decided to begin in the same thread she hoped to continue throughout the year. She had assumed that all public school children knew the Pledge of Allegiance and the National Anthem, but when she attempted both, she noticed many of the students mouthing along, pretending they knew the words. Only two kids actually knew both, with a couple who knew either one or the other.

Once that effort was over, and Maddie determined she must find a way to bring out their patriotism as a way of fostering good citizenship; she decided to let them work in teams of their own choosing, so she could observe how they grouped themselves. She had them play a game aimed at teaching the children tolerance of others different from themselves. She soon noticed the children grouped by previous associations, usually based on preschools or kindergartens they had attended together, which usually meant they lived in the same neighborhoods. Unfortunately, this also meant that they seemed to group based on color or culture, with the Hispanic kids in one corner and the African-American children together in another area. With only two white children in the class, as well as one boy of Arabic background, they were left to the sidelines, a group unto themselves.

Realizing that this type of grouping would not work with the game she had planned, Maddie tried an alternate approach. "Children, please come back together here at the front of the class, in two rows," she instructed them, knowing the two rows would again be somewhat segregated. "Now, we need three groups of the same size, so I want you to count 'one, two, three,' then start back again with one, until everyone has a number." The children complied, and soon she had them broken into three homogenous groups.

Amazingly, the kids seemed to adapt well to the new grouping, and the game proceeded just as Maddie planned. By the end of the first day, Maddie felt satisfied at her efforts, although she knew it was only a start, and she had her work cut out for her. Later, after the children were dismissed, she joined the other teachers in the lounge to discuss how their day had gone, and was pleased to know that hers and Lizzie's had the least conflicts and the best overall results. Lizzie and Maddie soon discovered they shared similar attitudes in teaching, and their friendship seemed to solidify immediately.

During the first weeks of school, their friendship proved more important than they might have imagined, as they supported each others efforts, at times against the opinions of more experienced educators. Lizzie took a firm, no-nonsense approach when communicating with the others, while Maddie was a bit more reserved and not so outspoken about her plans and goals for her class. She pondered things in her heart long before expressing them to others, purely as a defense mechanism she'd learned early in her lonely high school years. Unfortunately, that same reserve set her up as a target among some of the veterans who mistook her quietude for weakness.

It took several months of thinking on Suzanne's part, and praying on Jim's, but finally, in September, Suzanne made an appointment with the fertility specialist to discuss artificial insemination and in vitro fertilization. She needed to understand the differences and why someone would choose one over the other. The first seemed to replicate the normal process of conception, and she couldn't understand how that was helpful in their case. She had conceived, and even carried the pregnancy long enough for it to become a reality in her mind and body, but each had ended abruptly, suddenly, and without apparent cause. One process she adamantly opposed was surrogacy; if she could not carry their child to term, she did not want another woman doing that job. She would rather look into adoption than to pay another woman to act as an incubator for their baby.

Jim rested his hand on the small of Suzanne's back as he guided her into Dr. Pai's office fifteen minutes early, as requested. They signed in and were told that Dr. Pai was running a little late due to a delivery, so they took a seat in the waiting room with both expectant parents and couples waiting for their initial work-ups for fertility.

He noticed Suzanne's eyes quickly drop when she saw a woman with a tank top resting atop a visibly pregnant tummy, sitting across from them, her low-riders settled just below her abdomen, proudly exposing a distended tummy with prominent navel. It wasn't the visible skin from which Suzanne averted her gaze, it was the pregnancy itself. She responded the same wherever they were, when she saw a woman with child knowing, or at least feeling, she was unable to experience the same joy and anticipation.

Jim tried to engage Suzanne in small talk, but soon found she preferred time for quiet introspection to discussion; there would be time enough to talk once they were with Dr. Pai. He took up a magazine, having few to choose from, and noticing the title *Parent* Jim felt a familiar stirring in his heart. He knew he and Suzie would be great parents, all they needed was a chance, and hopefully, with Dr. Pai's assistance they would get just that. It seemed like hours, but in reality their wait only exceeded their actual appointment time by about 20 minutes.

"Buckley!" The nurse called to them from the doorway, "come this way, please."

Suzanne led the way, anxious to get out of a waiting room, and Jim followed her. Although today was a counseling appointment more than a physical, they were guided into an exam room. She automatically sat on the exam table, as she had for their many previous appointments. Jim took one of the straight-back chairs along the wall next to the desk. Following protocol, the nurse still took Suzanne's vital signs and informed them that the doctor would be in shortly.

By the time Dr. Pai arrived, Jim could see that Suzanne had worked herself into a nervous state. She always bounced her leg when nervous, or played with her hair, and this time she was doing both.

With a thick East Indian accent, Dr. Pai greeted them warmly and took her seat on the rolling stool. "So," she began, "you've come back to see me, again. Have you, then, decided you want to proceed with one of the alternatives we discussed last time?" Expectantly, she looked from Jim to Suzanne to see who was going to answer.

Together they started, looked at each other and nodded for the other to start, and then both began again and laughed. Jim said, "Honey, you go ahead… although we decided this together, you are the one it impacts the most, so you share your thoughts with Dr. Pai." He smiled and deferred to her.

Suzanne proceeded to tell Dr. Pai the considerations they had regarding artificial insemination and that they wanted to go with in vitro, to try to give the embryo a fighting chance at life. She also explained her resistance to any consideration to surrogacy, and Dr. Pai understood, knowing each couple had to determine for themselves how to deal with their fertility issues. Not everyone chose the same path, and she did not try to guide them, only advise them of their options.

By the time they left her office, Jim and Suzanne had enough information and a schedule to follow to start the process. The nurse took time to educated Jim on giving injections to Suzanne to regulate her ovulation and allow eggs to be harvested for fertilization at a specific time They were hopeful that within the next few months, they would be able to implant embryos and with the blessings of God, see a viable pregnancy result.

Chapter 5

As Maddie settled into her teaching position, and fell in love with her classroom of children, Mama and Daddy continued dealing with Daddy's illness. Shortly after Maddie left for Chicago, Samantha wasn't the only sibling to learn of Daddy's diagnosis. Simon soon realized that things were not normal in the Galloway household. He saw Daddy losing weight, his face gaunt and drawn, with a grayish hue and with dullness in his eyes indicating the weariness brought on by the chemotherapy. First, Simon mentioned his concerns to Samantha but she wasn't forthcoming; he went to Mama and asked her directly.

"Mama, what's up with Daddy?" he queried. "He doesn't look so good these days."

Mama took time to explain his father's condition to Simon, and tried to reassure him that Daddy would recover just fine, but maintaining a strong attitude was difficult for Mama. She, too, saw the changes in her dear husband and, although she never voiced her concerns aloud, she worried whether the treatment was worse than the illness. Every treatment left him sicker and unable to do his normal activities for several days, now stretching into nearly a week. He wanted to continue working for the church in some capacity, and for now that was as a volunteer, but she did not think he could continue helping much longer.

Mr. Galloway, on the other hand, was as determined as ever not to let the disease get the better of him. He claimed God's promise to not give him more than he could handle, and insisted on making himself available for the preaching plan, or to substitute teach at the academy. According to his faith, he believed he would be delivered from the cancer so he could glorify God and have a stronger witness. His optimism was contagious, and Mama hoped and prayed he was right.

Shortly before the Thanksgiving break, the doctor's informed them that his treatments had indeed worked, and that he was officially in remission. Mama was surprised, because his appearance seemed to say otherwise. He looked as though he had aged twenty years in the six months of chemotherapy. His oncologist insisted that that was par for the course. "He will start putting on weight before long, and you will wonder if he will ever stop gaining. We've seen this many times; as long as his blood work shows remission, we know appetite improvement and weight gain is just around the corner."

By Thanksgiving, just two weeks later, Daddy was already looking better. No longer vomiting from the chemo, his face filled out, and the grey around his eyes cleared. When Maddie got home on the Wednesday evening, she was pleased to see the improvement in her father. She couldn't have told her mother of her fears, but being so far from home during Daddy's illness worried her more than expected. In a way, she was fortunate, because she never saw him at his worst, and now his color was improved, and his eyes shone with the sense of humor she remembered from childhood.

The four day weekend passed too soon, and Maddie was on her way back to Chicago. This time, the weather was not so pleasant, and she drove with trepidation. Patches of black ice spotted the roads across Iowa, and once in Illinois, snow had fallen and drifted into the ditches alongside the highway. Thankfully, the IDOT had sanded and scraped the roads, and driving was not as treacherous as it might have been, but Maddie found herself questioning whether she should try to drive home at Christmas. Knowing how unpredictable the winter on the plains could be, she wondered if she should even try to go to Nebraska during the winter. They often got snowed in, and she did not want to find herself snowed in, unable to fly back in time for the January 3 resume date.

She also felt more secure in the knowledge that Daddy was in remission. Somehow, just knowing that took a huge weight off her mind, and allowed her to consider alternatives for the holidays. She had gotten used to spending time alone or with friends during the Christmas season, both while in high school and college, and had outgrown the need to receive gifts as evidence of her family's love. Instead, she thought she might invest her time in the needy; she wondered at the Christmas celebrations some of her children would have this year and, although she knew she could not solve all their problems, she considered how she might brighten the season a bit for each of them.

Saturday evening found Jim and Suzanne Buckley sitting quietly in the living-room, he in his recliner, she on the couch with her legs pulled up under her and an afghan tossed over her. Both were staring at the big screen plasma TV, but neither spoke as the television show droned on, they were not focused on the program. They each were deep in their own thoughts, unable to express the sorrow even to each other. The weekend began with such hope and promise, but too soon turned to sadness...

As the Thanksgiving Day weekend approached, Jim was full of anticipation for the future. With a four day weekend, he and Suzanne could spend some quality time together without concern for his job or her volunteer groups. He stepped with a lilt to his walk as he hurried to his car, stopping on the way home only once, to buy flowers for his precious Suzie. After years of trying to have a child, they finally opted for in vitro fertilization, and Suzie was to learn the results of the procedure today. Although this was their fourth implantation, Jim was certain that this time it had taken, after all, Suzie had missed her cycle, and had all the symptoms of pregnancy… moodiness, nausea and cravings. The yellow roses were symbolic of their hopes for the future with a home full of children and their friends.

Jim had planned the entire weekend, beginning with a special Thanksgiving dinner with her folks, and culminating with a picnic and boat ride on Sunday. He planned it down to the minute, wishing to show Suzie how much he treasured their time together, but also to introduce the playfulness of the zoo and parks, museums and carnival rides, all intended to celebrate childhood and family.

Jim pulled into the driveway of their beautiful suburban Omaha home, enjoying the site of the well-manicured yard and the welcoming décor on the front porch. The garage door rose in response to the remote control, and Jim pulled into a tidy, well-organized garage. "*Beautiful home for raising children…*" Jim thought, "*Yep! It's really nice!*" His heart pumped a little faster, realizing that Suzanne would already have heard the report from Dr. Pai's office. Now he wanted to hear her say the words.

He called out as he opened the door between the garage and the kitchen, "Honey, I'm home!" in a sing-songy voice reminiscent of some old-fashioned TV character. "Suzie? Suzie, where are you?" He walked toward the stairs.

Suzie stood at the top of the steps, a beautiful red dress skimming her slender figure, her thick brown hair falling softly over her shoulders, her grey eyes glowing and a happy smile on her face. She moved down the stairs gracefully, and glided into Jim's waiting arms, whispering into his ear, "Welcome home, Daddy."

He pulled away just far enough to look into her eyes in wonder and amazement, "You mean…?" and she nodded, leaning forward to kiss him, and finished his question with a statement, "I am pregnant! We are going to be a family, finally!"

After putting the roses into a vase, they went out to dinner at their favorite restaurant to celebrate. The ambience was emphasized by a piano player on the grand piano, alternating jazz pieces with the occasional romantic pop themes. Standing over her, looking lean and elegant in his khaki slacks and navy blue sports jacket, Jim took Suzanne's hand and pulled her to her feet, leading her to the small dance floor, where they graced the room with a smooth waltz, cheek to cheek, oblivious to the other patrons watching them. They made a beautiful couple, he with his thick salt and pepper hair, standing tall above her petite form, with his arms reaching down around her and hers wrapped around his neck.

Late in the evening, they made their way back home, each quietly content in the knowledge that they would soon trade the frequent nights out for sleepless nights in with diaper changes and feedings. For so long they had longed for just such an outcome, and now it seemed their prayers were being answered. Like Hannah in the Old Testament, Suzanne had placed her burden before the Lord, and left it there, fully expecting Him to answer it sooner or later. Jim had also petitioned the Lord on Suzie's behalf. As much as he yearned to be a father, even more, because he loved her so much, he longed for Suzanne's happiness to be fulfilled in motherhood.

Knowing Suzie's history of miscarriages in the first trimester, Jim withheld the natural expression of affection he would normally show to her. Instead, as they turned in for the night, Jim held her tenderly, gently expressing his love and awe for the fact that she was holding his child in her womb. He smoothed her hair and caressed her face, gazing deep into her eyes. The miracle of conception and birth never failed to amaze Jim, and this was all the more special, in that it was the result of their love, even if it was helped along by a lab and physician. They fell asleep in each others arms, happily sharing one side of their huge bed.

Jim slept soundly until nearly morning when he awoke to a keening, a wailing sound so pitiful, so sorrowful, he immediately knew it was Suzanne, and he knew the cause of her grief. He rushed to the bathroom and found her curled on the floor, her arms clutching her abdomen, toilet paper grasped in her hand but still attached to the roll. As quickly as her tears flowed, she pulled more paper to her face, forgetting to tear it off. Jim fell to his knees and wrapped his arms around her, crying into her hair as he joined her grieving. No words came to comfort her, and nothing he could do would ease her pain, so together they wept for the loss of yet another child.

They cancelled Thanksgiving dinner, opting to stay home, each seeking peace and quiet. The weekend passed quietly, with hardly a word passing between them aside from courteous responses necessary for basic communication. Jim tried to read, focusing his energy on work related subject-matter; Suzanne wandered between their bedroom and the nursery suite she had lovingly decorated in anticipation of her answered prayer. She alternated between spending hours sitting in the rocker, hugging the Winnie the Pooh quilt she had made for the crib, and curling in fetal position on one side of their king-sized bed with her face in the pillow muffling her sobs. Jim had no answers of his own; he prayed for understanding of yet another disappointment and returned to work after the holiday weekend determined to help Suzanne, to help them both, through this sorrow.

Chapter 6

Maddie threw herself into the holiday preparations at school. Although they were required to maintain a non-religious approach to the season, as long as Kwanzaa and Hanukah were both included with the Christmas preparations, the school board turned a blind eye to most celebrations, unless a parent expressed objections. This year Ramadan also fell near the holiday season, beginning in early January, so that complicated the equality issue even more. In the rare case where a parent objected to the teacher's approach, the principal merely instructed them to tone down their decorating for the benefit of agnostics, atheists, or various religions who may be offended, but they were never told to eliminate all holiday planning.

Lizzie and Kay-Leigh focused on Christmas more than the other celebrations, although they briefly mentioned each when discussing the season. Sadie, on the other hand, was totally into Kwanzaa, and felt her class of African-American children of the projects would benefit most from learning about African heritage, than getting distracted with other, 'less applicable', holiday celebrations. Fred seemed to feel that no observation was better than trying to please all, so his classroom had only cursory displays for each, in deference to the principal's encouragement for full participation by his teachers.

Although totally into the 'reason for the season' celebration of Christ's birth for herself, Maddie sought a balance between the three primary celebrations, especially since she had two Jewish children, several Hispanic Catholic children, a Muslim boy, with the rest African-Americans with varying degrees of religious and/or cultural observances. From her World Religion class in college, she was familiar with certain aspects of each and carefully thought out a plan to please everyone.

Avoiding the religious symbol of the nine-candlestick menorah, she chose pale blue decorations of dreidels and a plate with fake food representing the feast in one corner. Another corner held a small Christmas tree decked out with snowflakes, miniature musical instruments, and gingerbread figures. She also had a full corner display to show the seven-candlesticks of the Kwanzaa festival, as well as displaying the three focal colors and food used in the celebration.

In the fourth corner, Maddie took a unique approach of decorating using a primary element of each religious observance...the silver menorah, a nativity scene, a miniature mosque, and an unusual religious symbol of Swahili origin that she found in a specialty store downtown. For balance, she even added some for religions not represented in her classroom, such as Hindu and Native American. She drew the individual displays together with garlands of colored paper chains that the children helped make, each in colors of their own choosing and, in the end hers was by far the most colorful classroom, fully meeting the criteria of fairness and equal treatment.

The children joined in the decorating and learning process, enjoying the opportunity to share their own heritage with others, and finding equal satisfaction in discovering interesting facts about other cultures and religions. Not one parent complained about the classroom activities in Maddie's room, although a couple of the other teachers received negative feedback from parents via the school board and principal. Fred's lack of interest was an obvious magnet for parent's annoyance. Many saw the Christmas observations at school as the only way their child would enjoy the holiday, since home was unable to provide adequate decorations and activities, and when he failed to provide that, he failed their child.

Gossip about who was in trouble with the board abounded in the staff lounge. Although Maddie rarely spent time in the lounge, preferring the quiet of her classroom both while the children were at lunch recess, and after school, she still caught wind of the gossip. Kay-Leigh visited her class for the specific purpose of sharing juicy tidbits of news, and Maddie had trouble putting her off the subject without appearing rude.

"Have you heard?" she began in typical gossip style. "Fred's in trouble with the school board again!" She went on to explain the controversy and why parents complained. Maddie raised her eyebrows, but said nothing, trying to appear engrossed in her work. She did not want to encourage Kay-Leigh to spread gossip, but she also did not want to cut off her friendship by being to harsh.

"Yes, and he is mad! He is trying to say that the only way to avoid criticism is to have absolutely no decorations or celebrations in the classrooms."

This got Maddie's ire up. She knew how the children looked forward to all the various holidays, not just Christmas, and the fun of preparing for them...any excuse for a little party fun. From a financial perspective, she also understood the parents concerns for their kids. She knew what a hard choice it was for her parents to not see her at Christmas during her teen years, just because they didn't have enough money to buy her a ticket to their home in the mission field.

"Surely, they are not considering that...?" she questioned Kay-Leigh.

As Kay-Leigh started toward the door, she enigmatically said, "Well, you never know…this could end up at the Supreme Court." And with that she left.

Maddie sat thoughtful, wondering if to get involved, or to let matters run a natural course. As a Christian, she often struggled with whether to get caught up in political or social issues, or to let the government do its thing, and just do hers through her church involvement. This time she felt compelled to speak up, to voice her opinion on the whole matter, so she made plans to be at the next school board session, where both the parents and Fred (as well as one other teacher who received criticism) would address their positions on the matter.

A staff party was planned for the last weekend prior to the Christmas break; for political correctness it was called their 'winter event' rather than a Christmas party. This year's event, at a nice hotel near the downtown loop, was scheduled for the Friday evening, beginning with cocktails at 6:00pm, a sit-down dinner at 8:00pm, and dancing and partying into the night. Holding it at a hotel made it convenient for those that wished to overindulge yet not drive; they could book a room for the night, and not worry about going home until after breakfast the next morning.

Neither Maddie nor Lizzie were into parties, knowing they often turned out to be an excuse for drinking and eating excess, rather than a true opportunity for socialization; however, the principal left little room for declining the invitation, calling it a non-mandatory, although highly encouraged, social gathering. Maddie and Lizzie agreed to attend together, to keep each other company while appearing to socialize and mix with the more senior staff members. What they didn't anticipate, however, was the large group gathering and how difficult it would be to avoid separation.

They met in the lobby and laughed when they realized they'd dressed very similarly. Maddie chose a modest white blouse and a loose, flowing, black sparkling lammé skirt, while Lizzie wore a white sweater set teamed with a black velvet skirt. Neither favored a lot of jewelry, each wearing a tiny pendant on a chain and matching post earrings. Arm in arm, they claimed twin-ship and walked into the hall giggling like sisters. They chose a quiet corner to play the part of wallflowers, perusing the crowd's activities and enjoying their anonymity as they talked about their plans for the New Year.

"So, how's it going for the new girl?" Fred came up behind Maddie and startled her; she nearly dropped her cup of punch, spilling its contents onto the floor as she jumped back to avoid disaster.

"Uh...fine, I guess...I'm not much for this sort of thing," she tried to explain her discomfort, and looked with dismay at the mess.

"No worries. Here, you take care of that and I'll get you another one of those," he handed her some tissues with which to clean the spill, and then he turned his back to her as he ladled punch into her cup. "Now, let me introduce you around. I'm pretty good at these mixers," he boasted as he touched her elbow, gently leading her away from the comfort of Lizzie's companionship and into a group of teachers that Maddie had never met.

"Hey, this is another newbie...Maddie Galloway." He announced as they reached the edge of the group. Everyone seemed at ease with Fred, as if they were accustomed to his boldness. "Hey, Maddie." "Hi." "How ya doing?" They each greeted her then returned to their various conversations. Standing on the periphery, Maddie self-consciously sipped her punch, unable to enter their conversations about the latest vampire movie or a recent self-help book. She looked longingly at Lizzie, wishing she was still in their corner with her.

Fred must have noticed her discomfort because he moved to block her from leaving. Once again he took control of

Maddie's arm and guided her to a more secluded corner of the room. "We can get to know each other better here, don't you think?" Fred looked into Maddie's eyes with a look that bespoke of animosity, not friendship.

"I really need to get back to Lizzie," Maddie started to move in that direction, but Fred moved smoothly into her path.

"I'd like to get to know you, even if you don't want to make my acquaintance," Fred insisted. "I need to talk to you about the trouble I am having with these parents. I want to pick your brain about how I can make the peace. After all, I hear how everyone seems to sing your praises on how you dealt with this whole holiday issue."

Maddie paused, wondering if she was reading Fred wrong. Another final gulp of her drink helped her postpone her answer to his query giving her time to reflect. Perhaps he really did want her advice; maybe she could help him understand the children of Cabrini-Green a little better. "What can I tell you? You've been around these parts more than I have... and besides, we have different approaches to teaching..." Fred interrupted her, all too quick to take offense.

"Whadya mean? You think you teach better than me?" His speech suddenly betrayed the fact that he had already overindulged with drinking. "You know whachoo are...a goody-two-shoes, that's what!" The pitch of his voice rose gradually as he spoke, pointing a finger toward her chest.

Maddie was sure, now, that she wanted to leave his company and return to Lizzie, who was still standing alone in the corner where Maddie left her. However, she felt very lethargic and suddenly puzzled at her surroundings. The room looked as if she was seeing it through a fish-eye lens, with distortion and curves, and everyone was moving in slow motion. Reaching out to stabilize herself, she felt an arm around her waist and leaned into her assistant. She glanced up and saw a distorted caricature of Fred's face and realized he was helping her away from the crowd and toward the lobby, and then she collapsed against Fred, her legs like Jello, unable to support her weight. She could not get her feet to understand the instructions that her brain was sending, and her peripheral vision began closing in like entering a dark tunnel, with only a pinpoint light at the end getting ever smaller.

After Thanksgiving, time dragged for Jim and Suzanne. They did not discuss the miscarriage or the fact that the fertility specialist was not optimistic about trying in vitro again. By this time, with multiple failed embryo implantations, they were both discouraged, and Suzanne's depression was all-consuming. Each time tests pointed toward a successful outcome; however, for an unknown (or only God known) reason, the embryo implanted for a very short time, and was then expelled as a miscarriage, just as it had in their efforts to conceive naturally. Suzanne had been through about as much as she could tolerate both physically and emotionally.

Suzanne also felt herself drifting spiritually. She was wondering if the Lord had forgotten her, or why He seemed to be saying, "No" to her heart-felt pleas. She tried to read her Bible, but felt that ritual rather than desire motivated her actions. Even sitting in church, hearing how the family of God was praying for her and Jim, fell short of comforting her. It sounded hollow to her; her heart felt cold. She understood why Eli took Hannah for a drunk when she prayed in the temple, because sometimes her own brain felt befuddled; she walked around talking to God under her breath at inopportune times.

Finally, after the Christmas holidays, with the arrival of the New Year, Jim felt it was time for a fresh start for them, as well. Jim sensed Suzanne's plight, although they did not talk of her spiritual struggle. Somehow, the subject was too personal to bring up, and Jim was working his way through his own issues. His faith did not waiver, his trust in God's unfailing grace still warmed his heart, but he did question God, frequently. His prayers were full of why's, confusion over the turn of events reeked havoc with his intercessory prayer life that was once his strength. Rather than promising to pray for others, he found himself focused on Suzanne's sorrow and his own helplessness.

Finally, he decided to speak with their Pastor about his concerns. Pastor Gary was a sensitive, kindly older man who had seen more than enough grief in his lifetime, both personally and as a comforting minister. He listened to Jim, asked a few pointed questions about Suzanne, which showed Jim he had been observing her distancing herself from the membership. Then he made a suggestion which surprised Jim. Rather than rationalizing the miscarriages and encouraging hope for another trial of in vitro, Pastor Gary suggested adoption.

"Could you see yourself and Suzanne raising another woman's child?" Pastor Gary got straight to the heart of the issue.

"I don't know...I never considered not having our own..." Jim started to reply.

"Think about the question carefully before you answer," Pastor Gary cautioned him. "If you truly want to be a parent, does it matter if the child is your own blood? There are so many unwanted babies out there, although not as many in our country since abortion became a popular method of birth control. But, every now an then we hear about a Christian girl in trouble, who doesn't think she can raise the baby, but wants the child to go to a Christian family of her same faith."

Realizing he had Jim's attention, he continued, "Occasionally, I hear of these cases so if you like, I can keep my ears open. These are usually open adoptions, meaning that you get to know her, and she is kept in the loop as the child grows, sometimes only through letters and photos, but sometimes as a family friend, so the child knows her as his birth mother. Just think about it, and pray about it. Ask Suzanne, and let me know."

Finally, Jim saw a ray of hope shining out of all their sorrow. Perhaps this was the answer he was seeking; maybe Suzanne would consider adoption now that their options were limited. He drove home listening to his Christian music and felt a burden lifted from his heart. Adoption? A baby of their own to raise; a little one to help them become the family they longed for. After all, weren't they all adopted into the family of God? If he placed this option before them, who were they to turn it away?

Chapter 7

When everything cleared, she found her body unable to respond to commands, as she lay on what felt like a bed, and stared at the ceiling. A bed? She must be in one of the hotel rooms. She couldn't sit up; she couldn't even turn her head to look around. She'd heard of girls in college going to parties and things getting out of hand; occasionally, one would claim rape, whether resulting from too much alcohol or drugs, she didn't know. However, in trying to make sense of her situation, she realized she had been slipped a date rape drug, and her heart began to race with terror.

"Oh, good, yer awake. I had to help you up here and it wasn't easy. You get mighty clumsy when you've had too much to drink." He laughed. "I was afraid you wouldn't be up to enjoying this as much as I will…" Fred leaned over her, his breath heavy with alcohol, and his eyes vicious and angry, his lips smiling an evil smirk, totally devoid of emotional connection. "Now, let me help you…"

Maddie's eyes widened as she felt his hands against her chest and realized he was undressing her, and she could do nothing to resist. He slowly unbuttoned her blouse as if savoring the fear in her eyes, and then removed it. Next he reached behind her, his body nearly laying on hers as he unfastened and removed her bra. She tried to protest, she wanted to hide her breasts from his evil gleaming eyes, but she couldn't move her arms or even get her lips to cooperate as she tried to say no to this monster. He moved on to her skirt, stockings and underwear. She closed her eyes and prayed hoping God would intervene and put a stop to the madness. As he started to violate her, hot salty tears streamed down her face, ran down her neck and wet the pillow under her head. Fear, embarrassment, and pain held her hostage as she continued praying throughout the ordeal, until he was finished with her. Once again Maddie passed out, this time from the pain of having her virtue stolen despite her prayers for God's help.

When she awoke the second time, she was alone, only able to move slowly at first because of the pain. Her head was still fuzzy, although her memory of the awful event was sharp. She felt soiled and wanted to wash herself, but she couldn't risk Fred's return; finding her clothes in a pile on the floor, she got up as quickly as she was able and hurriedly got dressed.

Gathering her purse, she saw the clock registering 3:00am, and suddenly realized what this would look like to the rest of the staff that attended the party. Oh, what must Lizzie think of her, if she saw Fred helping her out of the conference hall and onto the elevator? The agony of it all felt like a weight on her heart. She could hardly take air into her lungs. How could she even return to work after the holidays? She made her way out of the room, down the hall to the elevator and to the lobby, watching carefully for prying eyes, but not encountering anyone else from the school.

She asked the concierge to call a taxi for her, and when it arrived, she gave the driver her address, without a backward look at the hotel. Quietly, she pondered her situation; she had no time for the small talk the taxi driver attempted. What should she do? Who would believe her? It was her word against his, and he was obviously more astute to the ways of the world than was she. Suddenly, she felt very small, very naïve, very stupid. How could she have been so gullible, to take a drink from him, when the warning signs had already signaled her? What was she going to do? Over and over that same question resonated in her brain.

Another thought troubled her...she was no longer untouched by a man, as she had always intended to be on her wedding night. She longed to be the pure virgin to present to her husband, someday. All her hopes for the future seemed in jeopardy. How could she think any man of God would want a tainted wife? She knew from listening to Christian young men at college that, although guys might date women who had been around, when it came to choosing a wife, they all wanted a virtuous woman without a past. They didn't want to wonder whether their bride was innocent and unsullied.

As soon as she got inside her apartment, she went into the shower and scrubbed as if trying to erase all traces of the evening. Her skin glowed, reddened from scrubbing and toes and fingertips wrinkled from staying in the water so long, yet she still felt unclean. Unaware of how long she stood under the water, she suddenly began to shiver, and realized the water was running cold. She turned it off, and quickly covered her nakedness with her bath towel, ashamed to look into the mirror for fear of seeing the change in her body. Suddenly, as if the effect of the drug were returning, lethargy and sleep attacked her, and she climbed under her blankets, covering her head and blocking out all light.

Welcome exhaustion overtook her body and mind and, thankfully, she rested totally oblivious to memories of the traumatic evening. Morning dawned just as it had every other morning in her life; sunshine brightened her room through a space between the curtains, but Maddie sensed a terrible darkness enveloping her. She realized her nightmare was not part of her unconscious hours; it was a reality with horrible results. Maddie's whole world was suddenly upside-down, and she had nowhere to turn, nobody in whom she could confide her deepest fears and sorrows. She pushed her face into her pillow, trying to block out the daylight and the memories; however, her thoughts, once awakened would not rest, and she found herself longing to retreat into permanent sleep.

The ringing of the phone broke through her yearning, waking her mind to the truth. Maddie looked at the clock... three o'clock again, this time it was after noon.

"Hello?" tentatively, she spoke into the mouthpiece.

"Maddie? Is that you? I've been trying to reach you all day! Why weren't you answering your phone?" Lizzie's frantic tone reflected Maddie's mood.

"I...uh...that is...I didn't hear the phone. Guess I was wiped out after the party last night."

"That's just it. What happened to you last night? I saw you being led around by Fred, and the next thing I know you were gone. Did you leave without me? Did he say something to upset you?" Lizzie's rapid fire questioning left Maddie exhausted trying to keep up. Lizzie never seemed to consider the possibility that Maddie had left with Fred, and Maddie couldn't get a word in edgewise. In the end, Maddie was left with no response whatsoever.

"Maddie? Are you all right? What is it?"

"N...nothing, just tired I guess," Maddie knew Lizzie would never understand, "I'll talk to you after the holidays, 'k?"

"OK, if you're sure you are all right."

"I'm just tired, that's all. Bye, now." Maddie clicked the receiver before Lizzie could interrogate her further.

Fatigued, Maddie fell into the nearest chair and pulled one of her mother's hand-knit afghans around her, and thought of her younger years when a hug from Mama made everything better. This time she knew nothing would ever be right again.

Unlike the other lonely times in high school and college, Maddie found difficulty in prayer and reliance on her Friend, Jesus. It wasn't that she doubted His existence; she questioned her lack of protection. Wasn't a strong spiritual life, a total reliance on the Lord, supposed to place a hedge around the believer? She knew about Job and Daniel, as well as many others who experienced trials. She knew Jesus had his own struggles in the wilderness and in the Garden of Gethsemane. Somehow she could not reconcile all of it in her mind; it was too much to think through right now. All she wanted was to sleep, and wake up from this nightmare.

Throughout her vacation, Maddie remained in her apartment. She did not venture out to the stores, not even for groceries. While in the apartment, she longed for release from her tormented thoughts... what should she do? How could she go back to the school and teach, knowing she would see Fred on a daily basis? If she didn't go back, how would she support herself? She couldn't run home to Mama and Daddy; they had enough on their minds with Daddy's illness and raising the younger children. It would be difficult, to say the least, for her to find another job halfway through a school year. Besides, she did have a contract to honor.

Maddie felt like an inflated life raft, drifting on an ocean with a slow leak allowing air to escape and without even an oar to propel it toward safety as the raft shriveled under its occupant. She considered her options: quit work, take family medical leave, or try to continue on as if nothing had happened. The first was totally unacceptable and went against Maddie's independent up-bringing. The second seemed plausible, although she did not know whether she met the criteria involved in the process. The third option was her least favorable, and would only happen as a last resort.

Christmas Day would have passed without a notice by Maddie, if Mama had not called. "Dear, we hadn't heard from you?" Without asking, Mama's voice inflection asked the question if Maddie was alright, "Maddie?"

Maddie didn't know how to answer her mother. If she said nothing was wrong, Mama would recognize the lie in her voice, but if she told her of her problems, Mama would want her to come home for comfort, and Maddie felt she would only be a burden to her family.

"Mama, I am just going through some adjustments," Maddie responded noncommittally. "I just thought I should deal with this in my own way."

"I can understand that, sweetie, but it is Christmas, and I know you are alone. Are you really OK?"

"Yes, mother," the impatience in Maddie's voice was uncharacteristic, especially when talking to her parents. Any other time, she would have seen it as disrespectful, but for now, she just needed space.

Mama did not question her further, but wished her well for the holidays, and reassured her that she could call anytime. Maddie was glad that the phone call was short; less time on the phone meant less lies to cover her lack of interest in what used to be her favorite time of year. Maddie resumed her cocooning, isolating herself from the world, not even catching the news to stay up on world events.

On the day before school was to resume, Maddie went to her doctor. She did not share with him the horror of that night two weeks before; she just explained she was under stress and needed to take her sick leave for mental health time, and he readily agreed. She took his letter to the administration office at the school district headquarters determined to apply for medical leave.

"Excuse me. Is the Superintendent of Schools available?" Maddie asked at the front desk.

"Do you have an appointment?" the receptionist asked without even looking up. She seemed bored with her job, but very interested in her game of Solitaire on the computer.

Trying to keep her voice steady and assertive, Maddie replied, "No, I just need to talk with her." She placed her trembling hands to the desktop in an effort to steady them.

"Well, you can't just waltz in here without an appointment, you know," still she didn't look up.

"Now, look," Maddie's voice raised in pitch a little, "Emergencies are not something we plan for and can make an appointment for! My name is Madeline Galloway. I am a teacher at Cabrini-Green Elementary School. Will you please check to see if the Superintendent can spare a few minutes, now?" Her voice cracked even as she tried harder to maintain a semblance of control.

The young girl jumped up and glanced back over her shoulder with a look of annoyance as she knocked on the Superintendent's door. She slipped inside and returned within minutes. "She asked if you'd take a seat for a few minutes, Ms. Galloway." Her emphasis of Ms., saying it more like Mizzzzz as if in an attempt to put Maddie in her place.

Maddie sat down and looked at the clock; it was 10:30am and Maddie was well aware that lunch began at 11:00am, so she watched as the minutes ticked off, ready to grab the Superintendent as she left for lunch, if necessary. Maddie tried to focus on what needed to be discussed, how to avoid talking about the real problem, but stating her need for some time off. Her mind wandered as she considered how to approach the Superintendent until a voice roused her from her thoughts.

"Miss Galloway?" Dr. Harpin had stepped out of her office looking impatient as if she had already called Maddie several times. "Please come in. I only have a few minutes..." Maddie looked at the clock and saw it was just five minutes until 11:00; she missed part of what was being said. "...so we have just a bit of time, I'm afraid."

Maddie quietly followed Dr. Harpin into her office and sat in the nearest chair facing her desk. Before Dr. Harpin sat down, Maddie blurted out, "I need medical leave!"

Dr. Harpin's face reflected her surprise, but then she consciously gathered her bearing and looked down at a folder on her desk. "Well, I see you have only been employed in the district since August, isn't that true?" She looked at Maddie over her reading glasses without raising her chin more than an inch.

"Yes, but I really need some time off… I have a letter from my doctor…"

"Well, Miss Galloway, you should know that FMLA is not authorized unless you've been employed for at least a year, and even then you must meet some strict criteria."

"But… my doctor…"

Again, Dr. Harpin cut her sentence off, "I am sorry, but the only thing I can suggest is to take a leave of absence; however, there is no guarantee you will have a job when you return. We can't just hold positions open for people who want to take off at a whim!" Again, she glanced up over her glasses and, trying to sound sympathetic, her voice fairly purred. "Now, surely there is some way to deal with your problems without taking off from work?"

"Well, I do have about ten days of sick leave accumulated, which would give me two weeks…"

"There, see how easy that was? Take your two weeks and come back to work feeling better. We will get a substitute for your class and everything will work out just fine."

Maddie looked down at her hands clasped in her lap to prevent them from trembling. Anger and hurt boiled together inside her like a cauldron of poison. She now understood the expression 'going postal', because she felt on the verge of losing control. Not that she would hurt anyone, unless maybe herself, but she could feel a flush creeping up her neck, and hot tears welling to the surface as she fought back the urge to scream at Dr. Harpin, at anyone within hearing range.

"Miss Galloway, did you hear me? I must leave now that we have resolved your little problem. Stop at the desk to fill out the paperwork for your sick leave, and we will see you back in two weeks." She opened the door dismissively and Maddie got up without acknowledging the plan set before her. She stopped at the desk to do the sick leave paperwork, and drop off a copy of her doctor's letter, but did not allow herself to be brought into the small talk with the receptionist. Instead, she was circumspect as she handed the forms to the girl, keeping her head down.

Maddie remembered a saying her father used in a sermon, "Your eyes are a window to your soul" and her eyes momentarily met the large, mascara and eyeliner enhanced brown eyes of the teen that quickly looked away. Maddie wondered, 'had she seen into my soul, seen my pain, sensed my hurt? Or was she just unwilling to have her own soul searched by an older, wiser and sadly more damaged female.

Leaving the district office, Maddie headed straight home. She had no desire to stop, not even for much needed groceries. Her apartment held a semblance of safety which allowed her to relax, to retreat. She slipped into a routine of sleep, bathroom, water, sleep. Her weight dropped dramatically and her face became gaunt. Even though she ate little, she found herself vomiting daily, which she attributed to nerves. She avoided phone calls, and did not answer a ring on her call button downstairs two days later. Whoever it was, they were not important enough for her to allow them into her sanctuary.

Chapter 8

Several days into her sick leave, Maddie found herself staring at her bedroom wall. She lay curled in fetal position, her recent favorite for sleep, but sleep evaded her. It seemed she had slept herself out. Each time she closed her eyes, they popped open and her muscles ached from lack of exercise.

She studied the rough plaster finish on the wall, searching for a pattern, longing for sameness. Her mind cried out, "Oh, God!!!" from the depths of her gut, as the reality of her life grabbed hold of her. This time was different from the others that sent her running to the bathroom with nausea. Instead of trying to rid herself of the memories, she carried them to the Lord. At first she couldn't find words to express what was on her mind; she just kept repeating, "Oh, Lord... oh, God... Dear Jesus... Father God." In her thoughts, she claimed and called out every name she could think of for God the Father and Jesus, her Savior. Then she found her voice and, in a prayer as heartfelt as the Psalms of David, she called out to God for help, understanding and peace.

A sense of relief swept over her as Maddie realized that she still could call out His name. The distance between herself and her Lord had seemed too far to breach over the last few weeks, but with that one guttural outcry, she knew He was still listening. She fell back on her faith and hot tears of gratitude ran down her face as her heart continued to share her unspoken grief with the Lord. She prayed until she felt His presence embracing her.

Lo, I am with you always…

Reassurance bathed her in peace and Maddie suddenly knew that she could deal with whatever was to come her way. She had long ago placed her life in God's hands and was once again hearing His voice as clearly as if he sat in the chair beside her bed. The tranquility that Maddie knew so well throughout her lonely years in high school and college returned and she fell into a restful sleep.

When she awoke a couple of hours later Maddie felt more refreshed than she had from all the sleep of the past three weeks. She got out of bed and decided to shower and go out of the house.

With me all things are possible…

Again, God's voice spoke to her heart as her strength built, and she showered, got dressed, and went downstairs to check her mail. The mailbox was stuffed full and a post-it note stuck on the front told her to check in the rental office for additional mail that could not fit into her box. Maddie was energized with a strength she knew came from above. She even found herself returning the smile that greeted her in the rental office.

"We were wondering what had happened to you… thought maybe you went home for Christmas and forgot to come back?" The apartment complex manager's voice held a question even as he smiled and handed her the mail. "Glad to see you back among the living, though."

"Thanks, Mr. Zelinski. I just needed a break, so I was hiding out in the apartment. I didn't think anyone would be worried about me…"

"Not worried? What are we supposed to do when the mother of one of our tenants calls up checking on her?" He looked at Maddie intently, still not asking what was really on his mind.

"I'm so sorry, Mr. Z. I didn't know she called. I will call her right away to set her mind at ease. Thanks again, Mr. Z." Maddie waved as she headed out the door. She did not want to engage the landlord any more than necessary, because she could not answer his questions; she barely had answers to her own bewilderment.

Maddie carefully considered what to say to Mama before she called home. She still did not think she should tell her folks about her traumatic experience, but just reassure them that she was doing well, and not to worry about her. She also realized that, since Thanksgiving vacation, she had not asked her mom for an update on Daddy's illness.

"How selfish! And how self-centered!" Maddie thought. "Sure, I have problems, but Daddy's is life and death. How could I not ask about him?"

"Hi, Mommy?" As in other stressful times of her life, Maddie reverted to her childhood name for her mother.

"Maddie, my girl, are you alright?" Mama sounded the same, Maddie thought, as if Maddie's horrors should have made a change in Mama's voice.

"I'm just a little homesick, Mommy. How is everyone there? How is Daddy? Are the twins doing OK in school, and what about Sam and Simon? Give me all the news…"

"Now, slow down, Maddie. How can I tell you anything if you don't come up for air?" Mama's voice had a lightness to it that easily lifted Maddie's spirits. She could hear a smile in Mama's voice, too. "Everyone is just fine…Daddy is still in remission and looks good, although he is a bit tired these days. As a mater of fact, he is napping right now, I'm afraid, so you won't get a chance to talk to him. The kids are all great, off to soccer and other school activities…they stay busy, but they miss their big sister. How are you doing?" Mama never was one to stand on ceremony; she always came right to the point whenever she had a concern about her family.

As delicately as possible, without sounding overly cautious, Maddie told her mother that she had been a bit down over the holidays, but was doing fine now, "leaning on the Lord, just as you taught me, Mama." Maddie wanted to let her mother know that she was still strong in her faith, that the big city had not corrupted her little girl.

The more they talked, the more relaxed both Maddie and her mother became. It was just like the old days, when they could talk for a long time, not paying attention to the cost of a long-distance phone call. They never seemed to run out of conversation fodder. It was different when Maddie talked with Daddy. They had a cordial, but somewhat formal communication style, although Maddie was sure of Daddy's love, just as much as she was of Mama's. Maddie always chalked it up to his rigid Irish upbringing. His family was not demonstrative when it came to love but, while living, they could always be counted on to be there for a family member in rough times.

Maddie and Mama closed their conversation with promises to talk more often, and even though she had not told her mother about the rape, Maddie innately knew her mother would have understood. Maddie peacefully settled back into her chair with the afghan once more wrapped around her shoulders. Without a doubt, she knew she could face returning to the classroom, and the possibility of facing her attacker, with a sense of confidence. With a deep sigh, she smile up at the ceiling, "Lord, you always know what I need to feel grounded. Thank you!" And with that prayer, she felt at calm and in harmony with God's will for her life.

Chapter 9

Her two weeks of sick leave went by much too fast, but through the grace of God she found strength to return to her classroom. Surprisingly, at least to Maddie, the children had missed her immensely. They made Get Well Cards for her during one of the art classes, and the stack of multi-colored, folded construction paper cards sat on her desk to welcome her back. All the children sat quietly at their desks with their hands folded. It was as if they thought that she needed quiet in the classroom, although she never restricted their cheerful early morning banter before.

"Miss Galloway," one of the boys who had been more troublesome than the rest raised his hand high from the back of the classroom.

"Yes, Jorge," Expecting his usual behavior, her voice held an air of reserve.

"Miss, Galloway, we were wondering… are you gonna die?" His voice broke on the last word of his question.

Maddie looked around the classroom to all the children still sitting quietly, expectantly, as if afraid of bad news, but trying to prepare themselves. "Now why would you ask that?" she replied.

"It's just that… always before when a teacher stayed away… I mean… they were either fed up with us, or so sick they were dying, so we…" He bowed his head, embarrassed by the water filling his eyes.

"I was just really sad, and needed a rest," she replied gently. "I appreciate your concern, but I am back now, and we are going to enjoy the rest of the school year together, OK?"

In unison, the children clapped and cheered, and Maddie smiled as she turned to the blackboard to write down assignments, which was greeted with groans and the rustling of papers as they got ready for the morning lesson. The morning passed without incident, and Maddie wondered at the ease she felt slipping back into her role as teacher. Somehow she thought returning would be a lot harder, but she had yet to see Fred, or encounter all the questions from the rest of the staff.

"Hey, girl!" Lizzie rushed into her classroom just after the children were released to the lunchroom. "I was getting worried about you… what happened? Did your dad get worse or something?" Obviously, Lizzie had imagined all sorts of scenarios regarding Maddie's prolonged absence.

"It's a long story, Liz. Too long to get into right now, but I will share it with you sometime later, OK?"

Lizzie seemed satisfied with that for the moment and began happily chatting about all the events of the last two weeks. Her less than favorable report on the substitute teacher reinforced what some of the class had already told Maddie. Evidently, she wasn't creative or relaxed, but rather taught in a strictly regimented manner, attempting to control the classroom with rigid rules and promises of punishments.

Maddie finished tidying her desk, pulled her lunch from the bottom drawer of her desk, and together she and Lizzie headed for the staff lounge. As they approached the door, Lizzie warned her, "Don't be surprised by anything… there have been all sorts of rumors about your 'sickness'… some not too nice, either."

As they opened the glass door with STAFF ONLY painted on it, the noisy chatter heard as they approached suddenly hushed and all eyes seemed to follow them into the room. Maddie tried not to meet any of the stares, and Lizzie led the way to their usual table by the window. Once they sat down, conversations resumed, whispers replacing the otherwise boisterous voices, and Maddie knew they were talking about her, but not one had courage enough to ask about her health, or the cause of her absence. It seemed they found more fun in gossiping and building their own suppositions than hearing anything near the truth.

Lizzie leaned forward and gently touched Maddie's hand, "Don't let them upset you... it's none of their business... they will soon find someone else to gossip about."

Maddie knew Lizzie spoke the truth. Then she heard a voice, deep in her heart, yet as real, and as calm and reassuring as Lizzie's.

I will not give you more than you are able to bear...

Sitting tall with her shoulders straight, she smiled at Lizzie and opened her lunch. Quietly, she inquired as to how Lizzie was doing, made small talk about the school and some of her special children, and by the time the lunch hour passed, all conversation and activity seemed back to normal.

One thing still bothered Maddie. She had not seen Fred, and Lizzie had not mentioned him. She hesitated to ask, either, because it would seem out of character to show any interest in his activities, since they had not been friendly before the Staff party. However, by the end of the day, her curiosity was assuaged. During the afternoon recess, she overheard several of the teachers talking about Fred's sudden departure to a school in Texas. Evidently, it was a move planned long before the winter break, after his trouble with the school board, but he had kept it quiet, and left without so much as a farewell.

Relief mixed with surprise flooded Maddie, her heart raced and a flush spread up her neck as she realized that Fred had probably planned his attack and escape long before the actual event. She had no way of knowing differently, but was just happy he was no longer a force to be reckoned with. She praised the Lord for removing that issue before she even thought to ask; she was in awe of his omniscience in knowing what she needed to recover from the trauma that night had inflicted on her heart.

Suzanne continued to struggle in her spiritual life; never before had her faith been tested as now. She continued to pray for a child and reread every passage in the Bible relating to women who were 'barren' until God saw fit to bless them with children. She read about Sarai/Sarah who was over 90 years old when she gave birth to Isaac. Rachel's story of yearning for children while her sister, Leah and both of their handmaidens presented Jacob with sons touched her heart, because she saw the birth of many nieces and nephews over the years. When Rachel finally had Joseph and Benjamin, she rejoiced, and praised the Lord, but her faith was tested as she waited for God to bless her. Then in the New Testament she saw Elizabeth and Zechariah who were 'advanced in years' when they were given John to be the forerunner of the Messiah.

Trust in the Lord, with all your might, and lean not on your own understanding…

Suzanne came to understand the need for patience and faith, however difficult. She also wondered at all the alternatives they had tried; were they contrary to God's will as when Sarah gave Hagar to Abraham or when Zechariah questioned God's ability to make it happen? Perhaps she and Jim should be more patient? After all, they were still young, not near the end of her reproductive years. Her heart's voice spoke to her, and peace filled her spirit.

I know the plan I have for you, it is a plan for good not for evil…

Of course, God had a plan; she just had to be patient enough to wait for it. Suzanne continued to wonder if she could be satisfied if God answered, "No" to her requests, but as she spent more time in the Word, she became convinced that it would all work out the way He planned it, and ultimately that would be for her good.

Jim noticed the change in Suzanne's enthusiasm for church, and the sparkle return to her eyes. Their marriage once again blossomed and they found joy in spending time together. After several weeks of improvement, he saw the opportunity to broach the subject of adoption with her. He knew it would be a bitter pill, if she never had her own children, but the more he thought about offering a Christian home to an unwanted child, the more convinced he was that this was the path God had set before them.

One evening, while sitting on the couch in front of the fireplace, they watched the flickering glow of the fire as it consumed the last remnants of wood. Jim's arm rested comfortably across her shoulders, and Suzanne had her feet tucked up under her as she leaned on him, her eyelids drooping off and on during their conversation. Jim pulled away and looked deep into her eyes as she was suddenly roused from her restful state.

"What is it?" she asked, sensing a change in atmosphere.

"I was just wondering… what would you say… would you ever consider… I mean…"

"Jim, don't beat around the bush. What's on your mind, now?" She encouraged him with both her strength of response and the look in her eyes.

"OK, here goes... would you ever consider adoption... I mean bringing another person's child into our home to love...?" Jim anticipated an immediate negative response, and was surprised at Suzanne's smile.

"There was a time when I would have been angry at you for even suggesting this," she answered. "But the Lord has been softening my heart, and I realized he answers prayers in many ways... yes, no, or wait a while. I'm not sure if adoption is the answer, but I will pray about it, and wait until I hear His voice. Is that enough of an answer for you?" She looked at him tenderly and his heart melted.

"I am so blessed to have you as my wife!" he exclaimed. Helping her to her feet, he hugged her. "I am able to wait as long as you need, and I, too, will pray for His leading. After all, we don't know God's plan for our lives; we need to walk beside Him, not run ahead of Him." and then together they walked toward the bedroom.

Chapter 10

Maddie enjoyed being back in the classroom. Her qualms subsided immediately after hearing that Fred had left the area. Putting the horrid event behind her was easier without facing him each day, and before long, she slipped back into the routine of teaching, and her friendship with Lizzie grew even stronger. They shared a certain level of spiritual commitment, although from different denominational angles, which anchored their alliance. They even began having Bible studies together during lunch, away from the prying eyes of the other staff members, usually in one of their classrooms.

Aside from her frequent calls to her mother, Lizzie was Maddie's most dependable sounding board. They talked about subjects from current events to family issues of their students to personal details of their social and church lives. Both struggled with balancing the desire to find Mr. Right with the conviction that their Heavenly Father knew what was best for them. If singleness was their lot in life, both women were willing to accept that as God's will.

Maddie finally found her niche at her church, teaching the Cradle Roll class. She also began to form friendships with other young adults, although they were the parents of her little students. There were few singles in her church, so she attended the occasional event catering especially to the young unmarried members that other churches in the area hosted, but she had yet to meet any young men with dating potential. She wanted to wait on the Lord for a clear sign of 'rightness' and not try to force a relationship that was not blessed.

Lizzie, on the other hand, was still seeking a church family with whom she felt at home. She attended multiple churches, maybe one or two times, decided they weren't lively enough, or they were too loud and energetic. Or she attended just long enough for the church people to no longer call her a visitor, and then stop because they were 'unfriendly'. She complained if there were too many children in the service, or if the church population was too old. Once Maddie tried to convince her to give one church a better try, pray about it and be open to finding a niche where she could serve the Lord; perhaps that group would become her church home, but Lizzie continued her negative approach.

Maddie's favorite of Lizzie's complaints was that all the guys seemed to be on the prowl at the youth conference, looking for a 'good Christian wife', which was exactly what she and Lizzie wanted to be. They were both hoping and praying for a mate who sought them out first of all because they were God-fearing women, and secondly for whatever other qualities they found attractive. Yet, Lizzie seemed put off by any social event that placed single women and men in close proximity and in an environment conducive to initiating a relationship.

Maddie finally convinced Lizzie to attend church with her and to spend the weekend, like a slumber party, so they could talk and just be themselves outside of the school. She looked forward to a casual girlfriend evening, playing Scrabble and pigging out. It seemed Maddie was doing a lot of that lately, pigging out, that is. Her appetite had increased tremendously over the last month, once she knew she wouldn't have to face Fred everyday, and she was putting on weight as evidence of her binging.

The excitement of a weekend for the girls resulted in a giggly Friday in the lunchroom. Maddie and Lizzie were both assigned to Lunchroom Detail, supervising the children as they ate, so they were on opposite sides of the lunchroom, but that did not prevent them from signaling messages to each other. Trying to maintain their composure for the rest of the day was difficult, but somehow they got through the day, and left the school arm-in-arm, just like a couple of schoolgirls.

Lizzie followed Maddie to her apartment and they quickly got into the spirit of the weekend. While fixing dinner of salad and soup, they chatted about their respective students and shared concerns for special kids in their classes. After dinner, Lizzie settled onto the overused, second-hand couch, wrapping in Maddie's afghan and, with her quilt around her legs, Maddie curled up in the old chair. Together they chose to watch an ancient favorite on the movie channel, not that they paid much attention to the story; they already knew the ending, so the movie became backdrop noise for their girl talk.

"Do you ever wonder if you will meet Mr. Right?" Lizzie posed the question to Maddie after they shared their lists of criteria for the perfect guy.

"Sometimes," Maddie looked up, "but I try to trust God to bring the right one along, if he is out there."

"Well, yeah… I mean me too, but it is so hard, sometimes. I just want to be dating someone now. Sometimes I wonder if I am being too picky or come across as too straight-laced."

"Remember what the Bible says in Psalm 37, '*Delight yourself also in the LORD, And He shall give you the desires of your heart. Commit your way to the LORD, Trust also in Him, and He shall bring it to pass. He shall bring forth your righteousness as the light, and your justice as the noonday. Rest in the LORD, and wait patiently for Him*'. I have to constantly remind myself of these promises, or I would really get worried." Maddie's confidence and faith impressed Lizzie.

Their conversation ran quickly from one subject to another, from comparing shopping preferences to movies. They found they had more in common than they thought, but at times the differences stood out rather starkly. When their discussion turned to politics, Maddie found that Lizzie supported the death penalty and women's rights to abortion. Just the idea that a fellow Christian could uphold those two ideas stopped her in her tracks.

"Don't you see those two issues as murder?" Maddie asked, totally puzzled at Lizzie's stance.

"No. I think if someone kills another, he should be put to death. It's only fair!"

"But, what about forgiveness? I mean, once they're dead, they can't repent. Doesn't that mean we prevented them from an opportunity to be forgiven, to accept Jesus as their Savior?"

"I don't see it that way," Lizzie replied, "they already made that choice, and had plenty of chances to ask forgiveness." And, from Lizzie's tone, Maddie realized that she did not have the wherewithal to change Lizzie's heart on that issue.

"OK. I'll leave that one alone. Maybe you are right; I just don't agree, but that doesn't mean I am right either."

Lizzie softened a bit; she realized her reaction was a bit out of proportion for the discussion. After all, they were just two friends comparing notes on various issues.

"So what about the abortion issue?" Lizzie looked at Maddie.

Looking back at Lizzie, Maddie's face paled. Suddenly, her heart felt heavy like a brick dropping into her stomach; brackish water filled her mouth as a wave of nausea overtook her. She ran for her bathroom, closing the door behind her, she vomited into the toilet and clutched her arms around her stomach.

"Maddie? Are you alright? Are you having a relapse or something?" Lizzie was outside the door knocking. "Is it something we ate? Maybe too much grease?" She was trying to come up with some reason Maddie would be overcome with an unsettled stomach. "Did I upset you with my arguing? Or the question about abortion?"

"No, Lizzie, I'll be out in a minute." Maddie wondered how she could explain to her friend the reason for her sudden flight from the room. "Don't worry, I am fine."

Lizzie paced for a few minutes, then sat onto the couch and wrapped the afghan around her shoulders, shivering as much from concern as from a chill in the air. Maddie finally came out of her bathroom, face flushed and eyes a bit glassy, but otherwise composed. Lizzie looked up at her expectantly, but Maddie wasn't talking; she just sat down in her chair as if positioning herself for an argument.

"I'm sorry if I upset you..." Lizzie started.

"No, I told you, I'm fine. Don't worry yourself. I just need a minute and then I'll try to explain." Maddie swallowed hard, but could not move the massive lump forming in her throat. She cleared her throat a couple of times, swallowed again, and then looked Lizzie straight in the eyes.

"I think I am pregnant!"

Lizzie stared at her as if she had not heard, so Maddie said it again.

"I think I am pregnant, Lizzie."

"But Maddie," Lizzie protested, confused, "when we met, you told me you were a virgin, too. You said you didn't mess around!!"

"Lizzie, listen to me. This is hard enough as it is, without you making assumptions."

"Oh, so now you are going to tell me it was immaculate conception!" Lizzie's sarcasm hurt Maddie, and she wondered how wise it was to share such a personal thing with Lizzie.

"Lizzie! Just shut up for a minute! I need to tell someone before I burst!" Now Maddie was close to tears. "I was raped..."

"What? When? How? Who?" Like bullets, Lizzie's questions fired at Maddie, "Don't worry, you know there is the morning after pill that can prevent pregnancy; we just need to get you in to a doctor right away..."

"Stop, Lizzie. I got sick because I just realized that I've missed two periods!"

"But that's impossible, if you were just raped..."

"I didn't say it just happened. If you would listen long enough, I could tell you," by this time Maddie was near exhaustion trying to counter Lizzie's energy. Her voice softened to just above a whisper, "remember the staff party before winter break?"

"Fred? What? You mean he...?"

"Yes, he raped me, after he put something in my drink..." Resignedly, Maddie told Lizzie the whole story.

Chapter 11

Maddie felt such relief at finally sharing her burden that she failed to take into consideration their differences in values. Despite the fact that they were both Christians, Lizzie had strong feelings on certain issues, abortion being one of them. She spent the evening trying to convince Maddie that an abortion was justified, and that she still had time to 'resolve the problem', as she put it.

"But Lizzie, it isn't a problem... it is a baby." Maddie tried to reason with her.

"Right now it is just a bunch of cells, what they call a fetus. Doctors don't even call it a baby yet." Lizzie insisted.

Maddie could not believe that Lizzie was so poorly informed. She pulled out one of her science books from college and turned to the section about sexuality and reproduction. Looking through the pictures, she found the various pictures taken of a baby in the uterus of its mother throughout the pregnancy; the earliest was at eight weeks gestation, just about where she would be at this time.

"Look, Lizzie. This says, '*At eight weeks gestation, this fetus is able to kick and straighten his legs, turn them round and move his arms up and down.*' It shows the baby with all its parts already."

Lizzie looked at the picture for a long time; she did not seem convinced.

"Lizzie, can't you understand? It's all over in the Bible, like Psalm 139, where it talks about God knitting us together in our mother's womb. And Job asked, 'Did not He who made me in the womb make him, And the same one fashion us in the womb?' (*Job 31:15*). How can you still believe it is acceptable to terminate a pregnancy?"

"But those are all in the Old Testament, Maddie. They didn't have the understanding of Christians of the New Testament. Jesus taught differently, didn't he?"

"Lizzie, Paul and John, the Baptist, and Jesus all talked about being consecrated for the Lord's service while we are still in our mother's wombs. I can't argue anymore about this; I just need to think."

Their discussion had taken them into the wee hours of the morning and Maddie was beyond tired. She could hardly keep her head up, so as Lizzie made her bed on the couch, Maddie went to her bedroom, fell into her bed and closed her eyes. Before sleep overtook her, she began to pray, asking God to guide her through yet another trial of her faith. Her last thoughts were wondering how He could let this happen; why would a good God allow such a tragedy to fall on one of His faithful servants? Was it because she had not trusted Him after the rape, because she questioned His will for her life and did not depend on His word for guidance? Before she heard the answer to her questions, she dozed off into a fitful sleep.

Maddie awoke to the smell of breakfast. Looking at her bedside clock, she saw it was nearly 11:00am. She never slept that long under normal circumstances. Then she remembered the conversation of the previous evening, and lay back onto her pillows. Well, now was as good a time as any to face Lizzie, but Maddie was sure she would just have more of the same arguments.

Maddie took a leisurely shower, refreshed herself with a spritz of after-bath cologne, and dressed in a casual pair of denim, jean capris and a multi-colored, tie-dyed T-shirt layered over a white camisole which showed below and at the v-neckline with a little lace. She pulled her hair up into a clamp allowing some to drop over it in the back, and liked the effect. 'No make-up today,' she thought, 'just relaxed and comfortable'. Then she headed out to the front room which doubled as her dining-room.

Lizzie looked up from the stove. "Thought I'd make us some pancakes and eggs, hope you don't mind me taking over your kitchen," she looked appreciatively at Maddie's outfit. "Hey, I like that…is it new?"

"No, I don't have money to splurge on new stuff right now. I am saving up… well I *was* saving up, that is, for my summer vacation. I wanted to do some traveling. Guess that won't be happening, now."

Lizzie looked up, but said nothing. She came over to the table with a plate stacked with beautiful, huge pancakes and a bowl full of scrambled eggs with a spoon in it. On the table was the Mrs. Butterworth's syrup, a tub of margarine, two tall tumblers of orange juice, and a pot of coffee. Lizzie had already set the table for the two of them, including a single, fresh flower in a vase of water. Maddie wondered where she found the flower, but let it go.

"This is beautiful, Lizzie. It's sweet of you to fix us a special breakfast!"

Lizzie smiled and motioned for Maddie to take her seat. Then she sat at her place and folded her hands for prayer. Maddie followed her lead, bowed her head and heard Lizzie give thanks.

"Dear Lord, thank you for your many blessings; thank you for this food; thank you for this new day, and especially for the new life growing inside of Maddie. Help us, Father, as we work through the days ahead that, whatever the choices are, they will be to your honor and glory."

Maddie looked up in surprise, wondering at Lizzie's apparent change of heart.

"Yes, Maddie, I have changed my stance on abortion. I stayed awake after you turned in. It seemed the Lord had some work to do on me, and so I wrestled with Him over the abortion issue until I couldn't argue anymore. He won out in the end, and I realized that the baby is real and created by Him. I want to help you in whatever you decide on this; I will be your listening ear and confidant, and I promise I won't share anything with anyone until you are ready to make this a public issue."

Her long speech surprised Maddie, but it also pleased her to know that she didn't have that battle to fight anymore. She needed someone in her corner, and was glad that Lizzie would be there with her.

"Thanks, Lizzie, it means a lot to me to know you will help me, because I am still so confused. I went to sleep questioning God, wondering why He let this happen. I was out sick, in January, more because of my spiritual struggle than any physical illness. Oh, I did have morning sickness, although I didn't know that was what it was, but I was more distressed at the actual rape, and why it happened to me. Then I realized, I was not immune to the results of sin in this world, and I began to trust God, again." Maddie paused, "Guess we should eat before your wonderful breakfast goes cold; we can always talk later."

"Right! We have a bunch of things to do today, so we will need our energy."

Maddie wondered just what was on Lizzie's 'To Do' list but, at that moment, her hunger took priority, so she took a huge bite of the fluffy, golden pancakes drenched in syrup. She did not care about calories or fats in the meal; she just wanted to fill her hollow stomach again. After last night's episode, her tummy growled incessantly all night, interrupting her rest.

Lizzie, too, seemed to enjoy breakfast with abandon, washing each bite down with either a sip of juice or coffee, and hurrying so she could get to the dishes before Maddie even finished. Obviously, Lizzie had the day planned and Maddie was content to let her take the lead rather than fighting with choices herself. After weeks and months of loneliness and weariness, Maddie was happy for someone else to lean on.

"Finished? Good, I'll be ready in a jiffy; just get yourself ready for a busy day." Lizzie cleared plates from the table, including Maddie's as she took her last bit of food onto her fork.

"You're not wasting any time, are you?" Maddie laughed at Lizzie's energy as she ate that last bite and got up from the table finishing off her juice. Lizzie promptly took that glass from her hand, too, and Maddie went to her room amused by Lizzie's industrious behavior. At work Lizzie was always a bit more organized than Maddie, but she'd never seen such a hyperactive side to Lizzie before. It was enough to almost make her feel tired just watching Lizzie rushing.

She brushed her teeth and made sure her hair looked OK, then found a pair of flat shoes for walking. She wondered if to wear socks since, according to Lizzie, they would be walking around, but decided on footies that didn't show above the shoes; she liked the clean look with the capris as she inspected her reflection in the full-length mirror.

Lizzie had finished washing up, even down to putting dishes away, and was waiting patiently by the front door with her shoulder clutch tucked under her arm, with her car keys in her hand. Maddie's eyes on the keys indicated her surprise, since Lizzie had said they would be walking, but Lizzie was quick on the uptake and answered her unspoken question.

"First we are driving somewhere, and later we will be walking about, so let's get going."

"Where are we going, Lizzie? You have to give me something, some idea at least!"

"OK. I thought about it long and hard, when I woke up this morning. While saying my prayers, I realized we are making a big assumption, right now. You are assuming you are pregnant because you've missed two periods, but that can happen with severe emotional stress, too! So I came to the conclusion (with God's leading, I'm sure) that first of all, we need to do a pregnancy test, so we are going to the nearest drug store, buying a couple and going back to the apartment to either confirm the pregnancy or find out it is a false alarm. We need to do several, just in case of a false reading the first time, or different results on first and second tests, so we need at least three packages, OK?"

Maddie stood nodding in agreement as Lizzie finished her speech, and felt breathless as Lizzie, herself, finally stopped and came up for air. They headed out the door, with Lizzie taking the lead, and made their way to the parking lot and Lizzie's cute, little red Beetle. For a 1979 model, it was really well-kept and in great condition. Maddie never rode in it or anything like it, and was surprised at the comfort and ease Lizzie had in driving and parking it in city traffic.

Lizzie had obviously explored more than Maddie, because she headed directly to a Walgreen's pharmacy. Together they went inside and Lizzie walked up to a store-worker and asked for the home pregnancy test kits. Maddie hadn't even considered taking a test; she assumed she was pregnant when the realization of missed cycles hit her last night. Now she wondered if she could be wrong. Maybe it was all a false alarm, and she could go on with getting back to normal. She knew she would have been too embarrassed to ask for the kits, and, for once, she was grateful for Lizzie's assertiveness.

Making their purchase was also painless as Lizzie played the role of customer, not caring if they thought the tests were for her or not. She was all about business, today, and Maddie was like an appendage, watching as the whole transaction happened and they were soon out of the store, heading back to her place. They opened the first kit and read the instructions carefully. Lizzie had purchased different kits, to avoid any discrepancies that might be common in one brand. "*Trust Lizzie to consider even that possibility. I would never have thought of that,*" Maddie thought to herself.

She took the sticks to the bathroom and Lizzie got the timer out of the kitchen. She came out of the bathroom expecting immediate results, but Lizzie told her they had to wait several minutes, according to the directions in the package. Lizzie set the time as soon as Maddie came out of the bathroom, and they waited.

Chapter 12

Together they stood looking down at the three plastic sticks. The wait seemed interminable. Maddie's heart raced in her chest until she felt it would take off on its own. It was even hard to breath; the anticipation was nerve-wracking. Lizzie stood beside her, holding her hand; she squeezed Maddie's hand as the results began to show in the windows of the sticks.

The first one showed one dark colored band in the triangle and another faded line in the circle - was that really there or was it a shadow? The second test was supposed to show plus or minus signs – definitely a plus, but what if that was one of those false positives they'd read about on the instructions? The last test left no room to wonder – the word 'pregnant' seemed to jump out of the window as they stared down at it.

Maddie looked at Lizzie with tears pooling in her eyes. She could not find words to express her grief; her hopes were dashed, and her fears realized.

"Oh, honey," Lizzie embraced her like a mother comforting her child, "I'm so sorry I gave you false hopes, but you had to do the test to be sure."

Maddie nodded her head resting against Lizzie's shoulder, as her tears wet Lizzie's blouse. Together they grieved for the lost possibility now obvious to them, and for the reality that Maddie now faced. They stood that way for several minutes when suddenly Lizzie took Maddie by the shoulder and pushed her to arms length, looking her straight in the eyes. She was dead serious when she spoke.

"Now, look here! This is not the end of the world! We knew this was a possibility, even the most likely result of all this! Now, the question is what is your next step going to be?"

"What do you mean," Lizzie looked puzzled, "I thought you understood that I am against abortion."

"No. No. No. I'm not talking about that kind of step... I am talking about how we can help you have the baby without it becoming a Federal case at both work and with your family and friends back home. After all, have you thought of their reaction? The nice missionary's daughter goes off to the big city to work and comes home pregnant, claiming to have been raped."

"But I was..." Maddie began protesting until cut off by Lizzie.

"I know, I know... I wasn't saying you weren't. I'm just saying what other people might say when you show up there, if you go home. People can be cruel, you know."

Maddie had not gone so far in her mind as to consider whether to go home to her folks and raise the baby, or try to do it alone here in Chicago. The only options she had looked at were those about whether or not to even have the baby. That was as far as her mind allowed her to think. Now, Lizzie was bringing up new concerns, and suddenly her legs went weak again, and her stomach churned.

"Whoa, girlfriend!" Lizzie took her arm and led her to the couch. "Don't go getting all shaky and faint on me. You gotta pull it together and start thinking like a grown woman." She moved to seat Maddie before her legs gave out.

Maddie sat down on the couch, pulled her knees up to her chest and hugged them tightly. She avoided eye contact with Lizzie, because that would mean more discussion, and for right now, she just wanted to absorb the fact that she was actually carrying a baby inside her. When it was just the fact of her no longer being virginal on her wedding night, it was bad enough. But to have a child before marriage... what kind of Christian young man would even consider dating her, let alone marriage? How could she introduce a child to a prospect for a lifetime commitment? Then her mind went off in another direction.

How would she even take care of a baby? How could she teach and be a mother... alone... without family support or a husband to share the load? Was she prepared for that kind of responsibility? Could she shoulder that burden and honestly give the child all they needed in terms of love and attention? Could she love the result of a rape, the product of an attack? Just the phrase sounded so impersonal, so void of love. Was it possible to see the baby as hers alone? What if it was a boy who looked like his father? She would see her attacker daily for the rest of her life!

As these thoughts paraded through Maddie's mind, Lizzie sat quietly waiting until she was ready to talk. She didn't force conversation, but occupied her hands by looking at a book from the end table, looking up occasionally to see if Maddie had unwrapped herself. Exhibiting more patience than she felt, Lizzie finally broke the silence, clearing her throat.

She spoke softly as she began, "Maddie, are you OK?"

"Hmmm?" Maddie looked up at her, vacantly, still in her own thoughts.

"Are you OK? I mean, are you ready to talk?"

Maddie lifted her head to look at Lizzie, her sorrow evident in both her eyes and her posture. She maintained her protective body language, with her arms hugging her legs even more tightly as she made the effort to answer Lizzie.

"Oh, Lizzie...I was so hoping..."

"I know, honey. I know." Lizzie went to Maddie's side and wrapped her arms around her shoulder, comforting her as one would a child. "We can get through this, together... with the help of the Lord." Lizzie's statement of faith helped Maddie's resolve. She realized that she wasn't alone, even if she lost her job, or if her family pushed her away, which she doubted. She would always have Jesus to help her through, and Lizzie had just promised to be there, too.

"Have you thought at all about whether you can be a single mom to this child?" Lizzie posed the unspoken question. "I know you can give a child love; I've seen that at school. But are you able to love a baby that resulted from... well, you know? I mean, have you thought about counseling to help you deal with the rape? If you just brush it under the carpet, it won't go away; it will just fester in your heart like a poison."

"I don't know..." Maddie was facing thoughts she hadn't considered. She was so glad for Lizzie's level-headedness.

"Even if you deal with all that, between now and the baby's birth, are you really ready to provide a home for this little one? In every way possible? Can you be both mother and father to the child? Suppose it is a boy... will you be able to love him if he looks like...?"

Maddie's face reflected horror at that thought. She hadn't considered the possibility, or probability that the child would be a daily reminder of that horrible evening. She believed in unconditional love, but was she capable of giving it when push came to shove? Could she truly allow the love of the Lord to rule in this case? She didn't know, and wasn't sure how she could be sure.

"Liz... I don't think I am ready to raise a baby, as much as I love children. And you raise some valid points. I need to pray over this, I really need to put it before the Lord." Maddie hung her head as if ashamed to admit her shortcomings, even to herself.

Lizzie moved around the apartment, tidying things that didn't need it, and adjusting the curtain at the window, and then she turned around and asked Maddie a direct question.

"Look, Maddie. What does your gut tell you about raising a baby, not just this baby, but ANY baby at this point in your life? Are you ready for the responsibilities both emotionally and financially? Spiritually, I don't doubt you and Jesus could work this thing out; but can you envision the next five years, until the child is school-age? How will you manage, on your income, in a little apartment like this, to provide all that is needed for an infant and toddler to grow and learn?"

"I haven't given it a lot of thought yet, but I'm feeling like the Lord is steering me toward placing the baby for adoption." Maddie looked up to see Lizzie's look of approval.

"Honey, I think that is a brave thing to consider. Now, let's stop here and place it in God's hands." She lifted her hand to Maddie and they clasped hands in petitioning the Father on Maddie's behalf.

"Dear Lord in heaven. We are told that where two or three are gathered, You are in their midst, and right now it is just Maddie and me. We ask you to help Maddie as she considers the journey ahead, to be strong and faithful, to continue to lean on You, and accept Your nudging and prodding, even when it goes against what she may wish. If she is to raise the baby, or if she is to put it up for adoption, is a decision not to be made lightly, but we know that You have it all under control, and will help carry her burden. Now we place it in Your capable hands, and ask that, until the decision is made, You will give Maddie peace and the joy of anticipating bringing into the world, a new life that You have created for a very special purpose. Don't let us lose sight of Your unfailing grace and love, and help me as I try to be the Christian friend she needs during this time. In Jesus name we pray. Amen."

Peace filtered into their hearts like the sunshine beaming through the sheer curtains, softly warming both Maddie and Lizzie and they looked up at each other in wonderment, amazed that a simple prayer could work such a miracle for both of them.

Chapter 13

Suzanne and Jim stepped into the New Year with a new sense of purpose. On a spiritual level, they were more in sync and they seemed to be moving toward the same on the emotional level, although Suzanne continued to experience low periods. On occasion the temptation to sink into self-pity was overwhelming, sending her into a spiral of sinking emotions. Could she really wait patiently for the Lord to answer their prayers for a family? Did she have the strength to endure this trial?

Jim, on the other hand, had no doubt that God was working in their lives. He knew in his heart that they would have the family they'd dreamed of. When Suzanne was down, he tried to encourage her and lift her spirits by reminding her of His promises, until one day, the unexpected happened.

Without the help of in vitro or injections, Suzanne was pregnant. At first, they tried to ignore the signs of morning sickness and moodiness as a virus or some temporary illness, but when she missed her first period, both wondered at the possibility. Was this the miracle they had prayed so hard for?

Suzanne scheduled a visit to the OB/Gyn for a pregnancy test, rather than trying one of the home kits. She wanted to know for certain, as early as possible, so she could do all within her power to protect this child. She felt like Hannah of old, crying to the Lord to fulfill her role as a woman, and finally having that opportunity. After the blood was drawn, Suzanne went home and prayed fervently for grace to accept the results if they were negative, all the while asking God to let it be positive.

"You are definitely pregnant!" the nurse gave Suzanne the news over the phone the next day.

Jim came rushing out of his office when he heard the whoop Suzanne let loose on hearing the news. Knowing without being told, he lifted her up as he kissed her and swirled her around before placing her gently on her feet. His forehead furrowed as he realized what he had done.

"I'm sorry, honey. Are you OK?" He wondered if he might have hurt her.

Suzanne smiled and touched her hands to her tummy. "I'm just fine." She answered, "Better than I've been in a long time!"

That evening they went out to celebrate with dinner at their favorite restaurant. The waiter assumed they were newly-weds because of the way they looked at each other in awe. He offered to bring champagne which they declined, knowing that alcohol wasn't recommended during pregnancy. They were determined to do everything in their power to protect the health of their unborn infant.

Before they went to sleep that evening, they took time to pray together, thanking the Lord for the blessing of life, and praying for a safe pregnancy and delivery for Suzanne. As Suzanne nestled into Jim's shoulder to sleep, her heart was full recognizing her blessings and reveling in her joy.

For the next several months, her first trimester, Suzanne fretted anytime anything seemed out of the ordinary. Although the doctor only required monthly visits, Suzanne seemed to find her way into his office weekly on one pretense or another. Any bout of indigestion or episode of sniffles took her in "just to be sure". The doctor and his staff were sympathetic, understanding how concerned she was considering the outcomes of previous attempts.

Both the doctor and his staff were thrilled when Suzanne finally reached the point of 13 weeks gestation, where they could say she made it past the first trimester without incident. Ultrasounds confirmed a healthy baby growing inside her, and when they were able to listen to the heartbeat for the first time, Suzanne and Jim both cried and hugged each other. Their joy was contagious and the staff rejoiced with them. As they left the office, they were presented with a tiny bouquet of carnations in a baby's bootie planter, and they carried it home as carefully as they would their child, since it symbolized a breakthrough in their progress toward parenthood.

Chapter 14

"Maddie, your father has had a set-back," Maddie knew before Mama spoke the words that the call was about Daddy. A phone call from Mama on a Sunday morning never meant good news. The family was usually caught up in preparations for church and getting out the door. Talking on the phone could wait until the afternoon when everyone was rested and visiting.

Maddie had not talked to her parents about her own problem, needing time to work through it in her own mind. She did not want to burden them when they already had so much on their plates. Now, hearing the weariness in her mother's voice, she knew she made the right choice. She would have to keep it to herself until their life was quieter, more ready for another change. And, until she could talk to them, she had Lizzie and her relationship with Jesus to sustain her.

"How bad is he, Mama? Do I need to come home?"

"At this point it is just a matter of more chemotherapy," Mama replied. "I don't think your coming home would make much difference. If he takes a turn, I'll be sure to let you know, OK?"

Maddie relaxed a bit, knowing that Mama would not tell her to stay put if Daddy were in imminent danger. She also relaxed because it gave her more time to sort through her own emotions regarding her pregnancy and plans for the future. She and Mama talked a bit longer, discussing what led up to Dad's return to the hospital, and what his prospects for recovery were. Of course, Mama was optimistic, as usual, and was praying for his full recovery. On the other hand, Maddie was more realistic. Having seen her father's gaunt appearance the last time she was home, she knew he did not have a strong constitution, like before, and that the cancer was taking a lot out of him.

"Have you told the kids, yet?"

"Yes, they all know Daddy is sick. I had to tell them since he is spending a week at least in the hospital."

"And how are they taking it?" Maddie wondered about her brother, Simon, especially, since he would try to take on the roll of 'man of the house'.

"Oh, you know Simon...ever stalwart and dedicated to keeping us all going. And the other kids are hanging in there, sometimes feeling guilty when they laugh, thinking they should not enjoy life with Daddy so ill. I have to constantly reassure them that Daddy would not want them to sit around all sad and depressed."

Maddie loved her mother's intuitive way with the children, how she seemed to read their thoughts by their actions. She had not developed that skill and doubted she would be as good a mother as Mama was, making her even more certain that she was not prepared to raise a baby alone. Her thoughts drifted as Mama kept talking until she heard her pause as if waiting for an answer.

"Hunh? I'm sorry, I missed what you asked."

"I just said it is about time to get off this phone... Maddie, dear, is there something you need to talk about?" Again Mama's intuition kicked in.

Not wanting to lie to her mother, yet not wanting to burden her further, Maddie struggled for a minute before responding. "I've got a lot of things on my mind right now,

Mama, and I was just daydreaming a bit. I love you, Mama, you're the best!"

With that Mama seemed temporarily satisfied, but would not get off the phone until Maddie promised she would call if she had any problems. Reluctantly, Maddie agreed, knowing all the while she was holding back already. After the phone call, the Galloway household went into full-speed getting ready for church and Maddie did the same in Chicago.

Mama went to visit Daddy at the hospital that afternoon and came away encouraged with his bright outlook. He was cheerful and rosy-cheeked, almost like before the illness had attacked him the first time. It always amazed her how he seemed to bounce back so quickly once they plied him with the necessary chemicals to kill the cancer cells.

In the weeks following his return home, he continued chemotherapy three times a week, and the long drive was hard on both Daddy and Mama. The early positive response to the treatment faded, and the doctor's became more concerned about his blood count.

"I'm sorry, Mrs. Galloway. It isn't looking good this time. He just isn't responding as we had hoped." Mama could see that the doctor was accustomed to bringing bad news as he kept his emotions out of it and was all business.

"What about experimental treatments? I heard the Mayo..."

"We have tried all within our current protocol, and do not have authorization for experimental trials and studies. We are limited here."

"Well, send him to Mayo, then, or somewhere where he can get other treatments." A sound of desperation in Mama's voice made it high-pitched, almost whiney.

"Mrs. Galloway," in his most patronizing tone, the doctor took her arm and led her to the sofa in the waiting area, "please understand. If I thought it would do any good, I would have already requested his transfer. Unfortunately, your husband's prognosis is grave, at this point, and I do not think there is time to apply for an experimental, trial study of new medicines. He only has weeks, at best. I am so sorry."

Mama's hands went to her face as tears flowed down her cheeks. She cried into her hands, sobbing as the realization of the future hit her. Raising four children on her own had never been her plan for her life, yet, now she must plan for that eventuality. How would she tell the children and Maddie? How would her husband take the news? She was heartbroken, despondent as her heart cried to the Lord for comfort.

Chapter 15

Despite the change in her father's health, Maddie threw herself into her job. Her friendship with Lizzie blossomed and through it Maddie found the strength to face her dilemma and her grief over Daddy's illness. She wondered at her mother's strength to face the future without Daddy and wondered if this was a message from God for her to move back home, despite Mama's protest.

"Lizzie, I have never heard you talk of your family." One day while they were sipping lattes at the local coffee shop, Maddie became contemplative. "Why is that?"

"I didn't come from much, you know." Lizzie seemed uncomfortable with the change in topic. As long as they discussed Maddie's issues, she was in her element… helping others; but, once the subject turned to her, her discomfort was obvious in both posture and defensive demeanor.

"No, I don't know. If you are talking money… well, neither did I!" Maddie replied gently.

"No. I'm not talking about money, although there wasn't much of that either. I mean, my family wasn't 'all that', as the kids say. In the town I grew up in, folks were proud to be poor, so not having much was no big deal. Everyone in the town was proud of being 'rednecks' and made no secret of their dislike for outsiders. But, it was inside our home, if you can call it that, that things were really bad. My daddy drank too much, and both he and mom smoked like chimneys. When daddy was sloshed, he could get mean, and that usually meant the razor strop across our backsides and mom never did anything to help."

"Oh, Lizzie, I'm so sorry. I didn't know."

"Nobody does, 'cause I just don't talk about them. I ran away when I got into my teens, and daddy tried to touch me the wrong way. I had been going to church with one of our neighbors, and just committed my life to Jesus, when he decided I was a 'goody-two-shoes' and decided to take me down a notch."

"Lizzie, you don't have to say anymore..."

"Yes, I do... I mean, I know all about you, and you didn't know about me... what kind of friendship is that? A bit one-sided, wouldn't you say?"

"I just don't want to open old wounds..."

"Anyway, he was too drunk to do what he tried. He fell down when I pushed him away, then just passed out from the booze. It was too close for comfort, and it let me know I needed to leave. So, I packed a few things, said good-bye to my little sis, my two brothers, and my mom, and then I caught the Greyhound to Belleville, near St. Louis. My pastor had arranged for me to stay with a church family so I could finish high school, and after that I went to SIUE to get my teaching degree... and you know the rest... here I am."

"Have you ever been back? Or have you talked to your mom at all since you left?" Maddie could not comprehend life without her family, even though she had been away at boarding school and college for so long. She still felt a close connection to them, especially now with Daddy so ill.

"No. I sent a graduation announcement for high school and another for college, but both were returned to sender, with my daddy's writing on the front. So I guess he hasn't forgiven me, and I just pray he isn't bothering my little sis... she should be about twelve years old now."

"Wow! That is quite a burden to carry, and not share with anyone. I am honored that you value our friendship enough to talk about it." Maddie was humbled at the thought that she was the first to hear Lizzie's story.

"Now, back to the subject we came here to talk about in the first place. How are you doing? What did the doctor say at your last visit? And, what have you decided... you said you came up with a plan, so 'fess up."

"Well," Maddie started hesitantly, "I am doing just fine. The doctor gave me a good report this week, and even let me listen to the baby's heartbeat. The ultrasound shows the baby is most likely a boy, unless that was a thumb or something..." she giggled a bit, then bit her lip as if chastising herself for feeling happy.

"Does that change the way you feel... I mean about whether or not to adopt him out?"

"Well, that's the next thing. Like I told you, I have come up with a plan. Since I'm not really showing much, and my baggy clothes hide it pretty well, for now, I decided to stick out the school year, if I can. I know unwed pregnancy can be an issue of morality for a schoolteacher, but I want to try to keep it quiet and avoid that, until it is too obvious to hide."

Lizzie pressed her for more information, "What about your folks? I know you don't want to add to their problems, but when will the right time come to tell them? Or do you plan to hide it from them altogether?"

"Oh, no, I couldn't do that, Lizzie. I have to tell them eventually. Maybe over Spring Break, if Daddy is doing alright. Or, if not, I might wait until school gets out in May... I will still have two and a half months to go, so it isn't like I have the baby, and then tell them."

Lizzie thought for a minute, and then she smiled. "Yeah, that sounds good. Do you feel God answering you about whether to place the baby for adoption or not?"

"I truly think the baby would have a better chance at a full life if I give him up for adoption, and I feel God leading me that way. I talked to a Christian counselor..."

Lizzie's eyebrows raised in surprise, because she had no idea that Maddie had decided to seek counseling about the rape and pregnancy. She was pleased that Maddie did, though, and had noticed a sense of peace about Maddie over the last couple of weeks.

"...and I agree with her."

"Wait, I missed something. I was so shocked that you mentioned a counselor that I missed what she said to you."

Maddie smiled, patiently. "Liz, she suggests talking to my pastor when I get home, and see if he knows anyone seeking to adopt. That way, I could be sure he was going to a Christian home, at least. And possibly, if they agree to an open adoption, I can get reports on how he is growing, how he does in school..."

Maddie did not dissolve into tears and easily discussed the adoptive process, and Lizzie realized that their prayers were being answered, slowly, but surely. As they encouraged each other spiritually, Lizzie knew that she and Maddie would be friends for a long time as a result of this shared trial.

Chapter 16

Spring arrived in all its glory and seemed even more glorious to Jim and Suzanne. In preparation for their baby, Suzanne and Jim began to decorate their nursery with everything they could find that told the story of Samuel, the long awaited child of Hannah, in the Old Testament. This was an uncommon theme for a nursery, so they often substituted decorations meant for another theme, to represent parts of the story of the child dedicated to the Lord's service. Suzanne shopped for various items in the Christian bookstore, some from felt board stories, others from children's books, which she reproduced and found ways to add to the nursery.

Jim was the one who suggested the name of Samuel for their little one, when he saw the ultrasound indicating the probability of a boy. If it had been a girl, he thought, it would have been a lot harder to find a Biblical name, because daughters were not as treasured in those days, having no part in the worship rituals or ruling leadership of Bible time society.

With the room nearing completion, Jim brought home a glider/rocker with ottoman to complete the furnishings. In light wood with soft green cushions, it blended nicely with the pastel artwork Suzanne had painted onto the wall in murals. She used the felt characters to create a mobile to hang above the light oak, round crib, which represented the baskets used for infant beds in the Old Testament. Every detail was thought through carefully, from the gauzy fabric of the curtains, imitating the veil in the temple, to the depictions of Hebrew life on the murals: women around a well, children playing nearby, and men sitting in groups discussing the Law and the Prophets.

He loved to come into the room and watch the gentle sunsets filter through the windows in the evening, after a long day at work. He imagined coming home to Suzanne with Samuel nestled at her breast, sitting in the chair he just bought her. Breathing a prayer of thanksgiving, he headed into the kitchen where he heard her preparing dinner.

"How's everything with my beautiful mother-to-be?" Jim whispered into her ear as he wrapped his arms around her from behind, and gently touched the round mound of their son, growing in his mother's womb.

She turned into his embrace and faced him, and he did not loosen his wrap around her.

"I am doing just fine, and you, my fine father-to-be? How are you after a long day at work? I heard you bringing something in, but couldn't leave the stove unattended to help…"

"You weren't going to help anyway!" Jim exclaimed. "There is no way you will lift anything heavier than a spoon, until our son is born, do you hear me?" He was firm, but not harsh in his instructions. After all their past efforts, he wanted nothing to go wrong with this pregnancy.

"Yes, dear, I understand. I will be a good girl." and she timidly dipped her head in mock submission as she turned back to the stove, "Dinner will be ready in just a few."

She understood his concern and, although their joy and anticipation grew by leaps and bounds once they got past the initial trimester jitters, their focus continued to be protecting the pregnancy. As she moved into the second trimester, they knew the baby's survival, if born early, was much improved. They tried not to think in terms of viability, but it was hard not to when so many previous efforts had failed. The doctor told them that some babies are able to live after 20 weeks gestation, but after 26 weeks was even better, so Suzanne looked at each doctor's visit as one more step toward a surviving baby.

Despite the warming weather brought on by the changing season, Mrs. Galloway had a hard time enjoying the blooms of new life in their garden and on the trees. The mood in their home was one of quiet resignation, and the children went about their tasks as if afraid to make noise or act normally. The worry in their eyes was magnified in her heart. She saw her beloved husband's condition continue to decline despite the chemotherapy, and knew that this time the Lord had plans that did not include a miraculous healing.

After all the years of serving the Lord, and preaching about the joy of being reunited with Jesus when he returns to claim his own, Mr. Galloway, too, knew that he would soon meet his Savior. His only regret was that he would not see his children grow to adulthood, but he trusted God to provide for them in the future. He had done as much as he could; now it was up to the Lord.

"Should I call Maddie and ask her to come home for a while?" she asked her husband one day when he seemed especially weakened from his treatment.

"No, my dear, she has her work to do. There is nothing she can do for me here."

"Maybe if I ask her to just come over Spring Break…?"

"If it would help you to have her here, go ahead. But don't feel like you need to ask for my sake. Maddie knows the Lord. She knows my relationship is holding me up right now, and that the doctor's are doing what they can." He took his wife's hand between his and patted it gently. "My dear, I know this is probably hardest on you, but you will need Maddie far more when I am gone than now," and he looked into her eyes with the same love she remembered from their courtship year.

She never could resist that gaze; tears gave evidence to the melting of her heart. They embraced and held each other for several minutes, cherishing the time they had left, and then she pulled away and looked at him sternly.

"We WILL get through this!" she said determinedly. "He has not brought us this far to fail us now!" Although it sounded like she was insisting on a miracle, she really was asking for the strength to survive the loss of her best friend. She did not want to let her husband down, either, by showing weakness and frailty, when he needed the encouragement. And with that attitude, they continued day by day, into the spring, praising the Lord for each new day they shared together.

Chapter 17

Spring Break was scheduled later than in previous years, this time in early April, and thus far Maddie had had no questions to answer at work. Occasionally, someone mentioned that she had really filled out, or suggested joining them at the gym after work, but not one indicated the slightest suspicion that she could be pregnant. The children were a bit more observant, or maybe just more honest, and several times mentioned her expanding tummy. Just two days before the school break their questions became more direct.

"Miss Galloway, why are you getting such a round tummy?" The tiniest little girl in her class spoke in a soft voice, barely above a whisper.

"Yeah, it looks like Santa's belly... are you eating too much sweet stuff?" The class clown strutted around making his stomach stick out, rubbing it and patting his head.

"That's what my mommy says I do... eat too much..." A chubby little boy with wide open brown eyes, and deep dimples smiled at her.

A mix of little voices joined in the discussion and question, as Maddie considered how she would answer the queries. Maddie wanted to keep her secret from the children; she did not think they were old enough to understand and, even if they were able to grasp the idea of her being pregnant without a husband, too many questions would come from sharing her secret with them. Then again, she did not want to lie to them. That went against all she believed as a Christian.

Clapping her hands for attention, she quieted them down with her peaceful demeanor. She smiled gently at the class and avoided directly answering the questions by opening a discussion about what is polite to ask someone and what isn't. First she talked about how her Mommy and Daddy taught her to be nice to others, especially to older people and those who looked different or were handicapped. Gradually, they joined in the discussion, sharing what they were taught. When it was obvious they were distracted from the original questions, she brought it back to a similar topic.

"How many think it is OK to tell someone they are getting fat?" Only a few raised their hands, while others looked around as if scared to say yes or no. "So, how many think it is NOT OK?" and a few raised their hand again, while some still did not commit. "How many just don't know?" Nearly all the children raised their hands.

"Sometimes we say things that hurt another's feelings…?

"Oh, Oh, I know!" Chubby little Marky jumped up and down with his hand raised high. "Just like when the kids call me slow or stupid!"

"That's right, Marky. Comments like that really hurt your feelings, don't they?"

His big, brown eyes pooled with tears as he remembered how he felt. He nodded and lowered his eyes, sitting down in his seat much quieter than before. Some of the other children looked sad, too, because they knew who had said hurtful things to Marky and some of the other kids.

"So from today on, let's try to only say nice things to each other, OK?" The class nodded in unison. "And whoever has the absolute best behavior will get a Good Citizenship badge at the end of the school year." They all cheered, each determined they would be the one to win the badge.

In the Staff Lounge later, Lizzie and Maddie sat together eating their sack lunches. Maddie told Lizzie about the questions and how she had handled it, and Lizzie openly approved. They spoke softly for fear of others hearing their conversation. Curiosity was rampant among the other teachers as they saw Maddie and Lizzie spending more time together. Some even made ugly insinuations about their relationship, which they chose to ignore. After all, if two women could not be just good friends, what was the world coming to?

"Maddie Galloway? Miss Galloway?" The school secretary announced over the intercom. "Please come to the office at your earliest convenience." Then the page was repeated.

"*What now?*" Maddie thought. "*Did someone finally figure it out? Lord, help me.*" She packed up her lunch; suddenly, she had no appetite. Passing the other teachers, she left the lounge and headed down the hall to the office. Once inside, the Principal motioned for her to come into the inner sanctum of the Principal's Office, closed the door, and instructed Maddie to take a seat.

She sat in the nearest chair, unsure if her legs would carry her to the pair nearest the Principal's desk, so the Principal sat opposite her in the other armchair. She looked at Maddie with compassion in her eyes, and a hint of a tear in the corner. The empathy reached out to Maddie and proved to be her undoing.

"I'm sorry I didn't say something earlier..."

"Don't worry about it, Miss Galloway. It probably wasn't something you could easily talk about."

"I...I... m-mean..." Maddie stammered. "I j-just..."

"Miss Galloway," she reached her hand out to Maddie's knee, "Maddie? May I call you by your first name?" Maddie nodded. "I lost a parent not too long ago to cancer, so I do understand."

Maddie looked up in surprise. "You mean...?"

"Yes, your mother called to say your father is gravely ill, and asked if you could be released early for Spring Break to come home before..." The obvious was left unsaid.

Shaken and surprised, a flood of relief washed over Maddie when she realized this meeting wasn't about her situation at all; it was about her father's illness. "So he hasn't died?"

"No, my dear, but perhaps you should take the rest of the day to pack and get on the road, or catch a plane, or whatever, so you can be home with your loved ones during this time of crisis. We will subtract these two days, or day and a half, from the time allowed for bereavement, which is normally two weeks, but can be extended under certain circumstances. Just play it by ear, and keep us informed."

Maddie was still dazed as she left the Principal's office to find Lizzie and let her know of her change in plans. Lizzie assured her that her prayers would follow Maddie as she went home, and were with the entire family, too. With that, Maddie went home, got her suitcase that was already packed in preparation for the school holiday, and rushed to O'Hare Airport to reschedule her flight for the next available one home.

Chapter 18

Maddie called Mama just before the flight to Omaha boarded, only to hear that her father's condition was worse than even she'd imagined. He was on a morphine drip, according to Mama, the medicine made him sleep, so he was rarely awake enough to talk. Maddie regretted not taking time to go home at Christmas, despite her personal issues. Although they had assured her that he was doing well at that time, now she felt guilty and robbed of a last chance conversation with Daddy. How she wished she could hear words of wisdom from him one last time.

The hour and a half flight from Chicago to Omaha seemed an eternity to Maddie, although it was really quick and uneventful. Just taking off and reaching cruising altitude seemed as long as the flight itself. Flight attendants barely got the beverages passed out before they were collecting trash preparing for the landing. As soon as the plane touched down, Maddie had her cell phone out to call Mama again.

"No, honey, there's been no change. Come straight to the hospital, Room 310, then we can talk a bit more."

Maddie rented a car, threw her bags in the trunk and made her way to the Cathedral District. Her father was seeing the best oncologist on staff, and getting the best available care, yet Maddie wished for more. After seeing Rush-Presbyterian, Cook County and the myriad of hospitals in Chicago, she wondered if her father's outcome might have been better in a bigger city. She found parking without difficulty, and hurried to her father's bedside, where Mama, Simon, Samantha, Jason and Jamie all sat quietly.

"Mama?" tentatively, Maddie entered the peaceful setting.

"Oh, Maddie, dear. I am so glad you made it safely." Mama threw her arms around Maddie's neck, and suddenly the dam holding back her tears of worry broke. Maddie felt strange in the role of comforter, as she patted her mother's shoulder. Leaning back and looking Maddie in the eye, Mama seemed to question Maddie silently, and Maddie's face flushed. She realized that Mama was aware of her rounded tummy, hidden under her baggy sweatshirt and jacket, and there was no way she didn't feel that kick the baby gave just when Mama fell into her arms. Mama's hand lingered on Maddie's abdomen just a brief moment as she moved out of the embrace.

Unable to broach the subject in the hospital room of her dying father, and in the presence of her brother's and sister, Maddie looked away toward Daddy. His gaunt features with pale skin stretched tightly over the cheeks gave the impression of a figure in the wax museum. He seemed peaceful despite his emaciated condition, and for that Maddie was grateful. She reached out and touched his skeletal fingers, noting how blue the veins stood out against his white skin. Her heart broke, knowing he was really dying.

She needed air, or at least some space to catch herself, before she fell apart in front of Mama and the kids.

"Have you eaten, yet?" Maddie looked at her siblings, sitting in silence.

Simon was the first to respond, "Not since lunch…"

"They bring me a tray when they bring your father's, even though he isn't eating much, anymore..." Mama answered quietly, seemingly in her own thoughts.

"Well, then, let's go down to the cafeteria and get something... if that's alright with you, Mama?" Maddie's eyes met Mama's as she silently pleaded for patience.

Mama nodded, took her seat next to Daddy and picked up her knitting as she looked at Daddy and frowned a bit, then looked down at her hands. The click of knitting needles working followed Maddie and the kids down the hall as they headed for the elevator.

"Hey, sis, when did you gain all that weight?" Simon never was one to beat around the bush.

"Yeah, Maddie," Samantha chimed in, "what's up with that? You are really getting chunky!"

"Oh, you know, living on my own, not eating home cooking, not enough exercise... guess it's all catching up to me." She was grateful for the elevator, because everyone stood facing the door, and she could avoid direct eye contact with her brother.

Jamie and Jason were oblivious to the goings-on around them, content to talk to each other in their 'twin-speak'. Evidently they had their own issues and concerns, and Maddie was just as happy to leave them alone rather than draw any more attention to herself. They went through the cafeteria line, picked out what they wanted, and found a table large enough for the four of them.

When they returned upstairs, they were shocked to see a rush of activity at the door of Daddy's room. Mama stood in the hallway nearby, her arms wrapped around her and trembling a bit. Her cheeks were wet and tears glistened on her eyelashes and in her eyes.

"He's gone, I think..." she looked toward the room where the nurse was now clearing up. She turned off the monitor and the IV machine, although she did not remove the IV from the port that had long since been placed under the skin allowing easier access to give him medicines. Once his sheets were straightened and everything tidy to her satisfaction, she came out and told them that they could spend some time in the room, if the wanted to.

They filed into the room, one by one, until Maddie, with her arm around Mama's waist, helped her face the reality of their loss. Maddie suggested they say a prayer, and each in turn spoke a few words, asking for strength, courage, and wisdom for the coming days of planning a funeral and saying that final good-by.

Chapter 19

After spending a short time at their father's bedside, the children went to the waiting area to give Mama a chance to be alone with Daddy. Maddie, Simon and Samantha sat together in a companionable quiet, while Jason and Jamie sat across the room, talking about something totally unrelated to the loss of their father. They seemed to be relatively untouched by Daddy's death; perhaps the permanence had not hit them yet.

Mama came out some time later with red-rimmed eyes and rosy cheeks. To Maddie, Mama seemed to have aged greatly in just the few short months since Maddie had seen her. The fiery red of her hair had been replaced by icy silvery white, and her formerly smooth complexion was now creased and wrinkled. Was it really only five months since she last saw her mother? Perhaps the changes were normal, but they were accentuated by the stress and grief they were experiencing.

It also struck Maddie that her mother appeared fragile and vulnerable; while visiting with the undertaker, Mama was unwilling (or unable) to make the simplest decision. Maddie chose the suit for Daddy to be buried in; she picked out the casket; she even designated which cemetery they would use and added a second spot next to Daddy's for the future. Mama accompanied her to all the meetings, but sat silent, with only the occasional nod of her head to finalize the plan.

Thankfully, the church stepped in and helped plan the actual service. Since Daddy had served the church for so many years, many church leaders from various parts of the country would be in attendance. To provide enough travel time for everyone, the funeral was set for the following Friday, almost the end of Maddie's Spring Break. She realized, while seeing Mama through the process that she could not bail on her and go back to Chicago. She would have to ask the school to find a substitute for the last six weeks of classes.

She was torn because, on one hand, she did not want to return to answer questions about her growing abdominal girth. On the other hand, to stay in Nebraska meant disclosing the full story to her mother and family sooner than planned. Since Mama already had suspicions, it was bound to come out, but Maddie had hoped to make the adoption arrangements and then tell Mama of the whole plan.

"Dr. Harpin," Maddie addressed the Superintendent of Schools with a problem for the second time in one school year, "I'm sorry to ask, but I need a leave of absence for the rest of the year, due to the death of my father. I know I don't qualify for FMLA, but I am needed at home…"

"Miss Galloway, you know how hard it is to find a substitute at any time, but especially toward the end of the school year and for such a long period of time. Your principal explained your situation, but I am afraid we cannot hold your job for next year, if you choose to leave us in the lurch this way."

Maddie's heart dropped, but she knew she was doing the right thing. After all, she wasn't even sure what her plans would be beyond the pregnancy and adoption. She knew her mother needed her right now, and she was sure she would need her mother later, so her response to Dr. Harpin was not what she expected to hear.

"I understand, Doctor, and I hope you will keep me in mind for any future position..."

"I'm sorry, Miss Galloway. You did not fulfill the terms of your contract, and I would not count on a future position, or a positive recommendation at this point. Good day, Miss Galloway." and with that the phone conversation was terminated.

A sense of relief washed over Maddie, feeling that one burden was lifted, although she would have to go back and clear her apartment. Lizzie would help and Mr. Z. would understand her vacating early. Her rent was paid through May, so she had time to make those plans.

The congregation of Mama and Daddy's church was a wonderful support to them for that week between Daddy's death and his burial. They provided casseroles, baked goods, deserts and snack items, and everyday someone came over to wash the casserole dishes and take them to their owners, so the Galloways did not need to concern themselves about those details. The mothers of the church who had children around the same age as Jamie and Jason invited them along on various activities with their kids, so they would stay occupied, and those with teen-aged children invited Simon and Samantha on teen outings several times that week.

During one quiet spell, when all her brothers and sisters were out of the house, and it was only Maddie and her mother, Maddie went into Mama's room to talk to her. She found Mama on her bed with her Bible study material and Bible spread out in front of her; her hands were clasped and eyes closed as she prayed. Although her lips moved, no sound came out, and Maddie was reminded of the story of Hannah praying, when the priest thought she was drunk. Mama must have sensed Maddie's presence, or she'd heard her approach. Either way, Mama paused and lifted tear-filled eyes to her eldest daughter.

"Tell me, daughter, tell me what has happened." she inquired so gently that Maddie nearly fell into her arms as she had when she was a little girl. She held back, though, knowing that this was not the time to fall apart. She needed to be strong for her mother, because hearing of the rape and pregnancy on top of her recent grief was going to break Mama's heart.

"I'm pregnant, Mommy," Maddie fell back to her childhood name for her mother. "I'm so sorry..."

"Explain to me what happened, dear. I know something dreadful happened or you would have called us with joyous news, rather than coming home hiding it."

With that said, Maddie proceeded to tell Mama all about the attack and all that she'd been through since. She reassured Mama that Lizzie had been a good Christian support for her, and she discussed the prayers they'd said together regarding how to handle the pregnancy. Despite her sorrow for Maddie, Mama told her she was proud of her for choosing to give life to the child rather than seek an abortion. She vowed to help Maddie the best she could, and together they prayed for peace and strength to endure whatever the outcome once the church learned of her pregnancy.

The funeral service felt like a joyful celebration of Daniel Galloway's life. Many stood to say beautiful things about the impact he'd had on their spiritual growth, and how often he had gone out of his way to help others, even from far away in the mission field. Several choirs sang his favorite hymns and the pastor used Daddy's favorite Bible verse from John 14:1-4 to share with those in attendance Daddy's hope for the resurrection. The pastor took time to reassure family and friends alike that this was not the last they'd seen of Daniel Galloway; if they made their calling and election sure, they would see him again when Jesus returned in the clouds of glory.

Chapter 20

After a few weeks passed and life began to return to a normal pace, Maddie made an appointment to talk to the pastor of Mama and Daddy's church. Her mother was well aware of her decision to give the baby up for adoption, and supported her in that choice. When Maddie had explained the circumstances surrounding her conception, Mama recognized how hard it would be to raise the child that resulted. She told Maddie how their pastor had been instrumental in placing children in adoptive homes in the past, and thought he might be able to help her. He was known for keeping confidences and Mama assured her that he would not judge Maddie, especially once he heard her story.

Maddie waited outside the Office of the Pastor, contemplating her future. She had about three months left before the baby came; she needed to decide what she was going to do. Mama needed all her resources to take care of the other four children and did not need the burden of an adult child under her roof. Maddie was determine to earn her way, but she wasn't sure where or how. She knew that she had a gift for teaching, but wondered if she might find satisfaction using those skills differently.

Her name was still under consideration for the mission field, but they wanted her to have at least two years experience before they sent her to a remote location. She also felt it would be better to stay closer to home, at least for one school year. As she thought about her options, she wondered about her child. Where was he going to end up? Would he be happy? Would she ever have the chance to meet him?

"Maddie?" the secretary called her name and broke her reverie.

She looked up and answered, "Yes, that's me."

"Pastor will see you now."

Maddie got up from her seat, straightened her slacks and top, attempting to keep her stomach hidden from the secretary. She approached the door, took a deep breath and tapped lightly.

"Come." A rich, baritone voice called out.

She entered the office hesitantly, but was warmly welcomed by the minister. He reached out his hand to shake hers and offered her a seat near his desk. She was surprised to see such a handsome man in the pastor's office. *He is tall and lanky, and quite a bit younger than the gentleman that had performed Daddy's service*, she thought. *Maybe I am in the wrong office.*

Sensing her uncertainty he spoke first. "In case you are wondering, I am Pastor Tim Blake, but you can call me either Tim or Pastor Tim. I will be taking over for Pastor Green in just a few weeks, so he asked me to counsel with you... if that is alright with you, that is."

"Well, I don't know... my mother recommended Pastor Green and I just..."

"Let me reassure you that anything you share with me will be held in the strictest confidence. Also, I will work with Pastor Green and ask for his assistance, as needed, so be assured that whatever confidence your mother has in him, you can also have in me."

With that, Maddie relaxed and breathed a deep sigh of relief. It took some courage for her to come in the first place, and would have been harder a second time around.

She looked around the office and saw a bookcase filled with books on counseling and guidance for families, individuals, children, and young adults. It seemed you would find help for any situation in the myriad of literature on those shelves.

"I am in a difficult position," Maddie began. "I am pregnant and wish to find a Christian home to place the child for adoption."

Pastor Tim did not show disgust or surprise at her statement. He leaned back in his chair, his long legs crossed and his arms behind his head and looked at her for a minute. Then he leaned forward with his fingers tented, elbows on the desk, "You do not come across as a promiscuous young lady, so perhaps you would care to tell me the full story…?"

Maddie began as she had when she told Lizzie, and again when she told Mama, with the evening of the rape. Skipping over her depression, she went on to tell him about Lizzie's support, and now her mother's, and how she had been praying about the whole situation. She explained how she became impressed to place the child rather than raise him on her own, and not feeling emotionally ready to look past the circumstance of his birth.

They spoke at length about her pain and fears related to the adoption, how she hoped for an open adoption so she could stay informed of his well-being, and the need to stay in the area for her mother's sake. Maddie found Pastor Tim easy to talk to; he set her at ease with his casual approach. His questions came across as concern rather than meddling or probing. She was surprised when the secretary buzzed to say another parishioner was waiting, and an hour and a half had passed.

"I'm so sorry. I didn't mean to take up so much of your time."

"No problem. I've enjoyed getting to know you. I will talk with Pastor Green about his other placements, and find out if he knows of any potential parents for your child. I'll give you a call in about, let's say, two weeks? By then I should have something for you, OK?"

Maddie nodded her head and got up to leave.

"Before you go, would you mind if I had a word of prayer with you?" Pastor Tim asked.

Maddie nodded, attempting to conceal the tears forming in the corners of her eyes. The kindness and love evident in this church never ceased to amaze her, and she knew that Pastor Tim was going to fit in very well.

With her delicate hands in his large, warm hands, they bowed their heads and he asked God's blessing on both Maddie and the child. He prayed for her family and for the church family to have compassion and understanding. He also prayed for the wisdom to work with all concerned and, finally, Pastor Tim prayed that the solution they were seeking would be accomplished to the honor and glory of the Lord and in His time.

Maddie returned home hopeful that Pastor Tim would be able to find her child a home. And she was more convinced than ever that she should stay in the area. The question was how to approach the interview process, considering her condition. Pastor Tim had suggested she offer her services as a substitute teacher in the area and wait to apply for a full-time position for the following school year, after she had time to adjust, prepare her resume, and go through the interview process when she was no longer pregnant.

Chapter 21

"Are you ready to go?" Suzanne had been ready for well over a half an hour, and Jim was just now combing his hair. Their appointment wasn't for another hour and the doctor's office was only a fifteen minute drive, but Suzanne was more anxious for this than the previous monthly checkups. This one marked her twentieth week and would verify viability of their infant, should he be born early.

"OK, I'm coming, I'm coming," Jim feigned annoyance, but his smile showed her that he was only teasing. "Come along, little mother, we have an important date to keep."

He helped her into the passenger seat, and then he went around to the driver's side. She had not driven since finding out she was pregnant; she was playing it safe in every aspect of her life, from diet and exercise to activities and outings. Her friends totally understood her reluctance to go on lunch dates or other group activities, so sometimes they planned them over at the Buckley home in order to include Suzanne.

Just as he started to pull out of their neighborhood, onto the main road, Jim had to stomp on the brake to avoid being hit by a speeding motorist. The car swerved just in time to miss clipping their front-end. "Are you OK?" he asked Suzanne, checking her seatbelt to ensure it had not tightened up against the baby.

"Oh, aren't you just the protective daddy?" she smiled. "I'm just fine. It jarred me a bit, but no harm, no foul."

They continue on their way, making small talk about their plans after the appointment, even though it was uppermost in both their minds. Arriving at the doctor's office a half an hour early, they decided to stop for a warm drink at the kiosk in the lobby. Suzanne opted for a mild herbal tea and Jim enjoyed his cappuccino, and then they made their way upstairs to the OB/Gyn offices.

After sitting in the waiting room surrounded by other women at various stages of pregnancy, they were finally able to relax when shown to the exam room. Again, they waited for about ten minutes until the doctor came in accompanied by his nurse and a medical student. He spoke to the student as he examined Suzanne, but had little to say to them. It seemed from what he said that all was going according to plan. He instructed the nurse to schedule them for one month out and set up an ultrasound for today.

"There he is..." the ultrasound technician pointed out parts of the baby's body on the monitor. Without her help, Suzanne and Jim would have been guessing at the shadows and white areas. "And, yep, he is definitely a little man!"

Jim held Suzanne's hand as they both gazed at the screen while the technician printed off copies of the ultrasound for the baby book. Once it was in their hands, they couldn't take their eyes off of it. The technician finished wiping the gel off her abdomen and covered her with the sheet. She helped Suzanne to a sitting position and told them they could go once she was dressed. Suzanne pulled on her slacks and Jim helped her put on her shoes and socks, although she was still quite able to help herself; he enjoyed making her feel like a queen.

They walked hand in hand to the car and he again helped her into the passenger side, and then went around and let himself in. They decided to go to lunch at Olive Garden near the hospital and enjoy a quiet afternoon, since Jim was off for the day. Choosing the soup, salad and breadsticks option, Suzanne had the minestrone and Jim, the Suppa Toscano. She only had one serving because it was somewhat salty and she did not want to cause her body to retain fluids.

As they pulled out of the parking lot and headed for the Interstate, Suzanne's cell phone rang, and she looked at the caller ID to see it was a call from her mother. Jim smiled as she opened the flip phone and told her mother about their visit to the doctor, giving her a blow by blow report of the day so far. They continued to chat about various other topics while Jim continued driving toward home. When Suzanne went to put the phone back into her bag, she lost her hold of it and it landed on the floor of the car by her feet.

"I'll get it," Jim said because she could not bend far enough to reach it. He leaned sideways, keeping a hand on the wheel and his eyes toward the road, but just as he looked down to be sure he was touching the phone, they both felt a tremendous blow to their car and it spun around in the road until it faced oncoming traffic. Stunned for a minute, Jim shook his head trying to understand what happened.

Smashed into the passenger side was a blue van, and the door pressed in against Suzanne who was unconscious with a gash on her forehead. *Oh, my God...Suz... wake up.* Jim thought as he leaned over toward her to check her breathing. *Dear God, let her be alright.*

The driver of the other vehicle had not moved, but Jim saw several individuals jump from the rear of the cargo van and run down the embankment and into a wooded area. He wondered, briefly, why they were leaving the scene of an accident, but he did not give it much thought, since his primary concern was for Suzanne. He struggled to get his door open, and once again looked for her cell phone to call 911. He felt like he was in a time warp, like everything was moving in slow motion.

"Sir, are you OK?" "I saw it happen, the guy crossed the median." "How can I help?" Several strangers crowded around Jim as he stood up, dizzy and shaking. He pressed the talk button on the phone, but someone said they already called 911, and the scream of sirens was growing closer. Traffic was at a stand-still and the ambulance was having difficulty passing; it finally cut over onto the shoulder and sped toward them.

Jumping out and running to the Buckley's car, the medics made a quick assessment of the situation. Jim told them that Suzanne was five months into a high risk pregnancy, and asked them to hurry. One medic climbed inside the car to check on Suzanne; he took his pack with him so he could start an IV line, if possible. The other medic rushed back to the vehicle and put in a call for the 'jaws of life'. There was no way to remove Suzanne without taking off the top of the car; the van was inseparable from their car, the impact had been so great.

"Oh, Suz, honey, don't leave me!" Jim groaned. "You have to live, for our little Sammy... please, honey, keep fighting."

The medic struggled to start the IV, but finally he had an open line in case they needed to give her medicines. Suddenly, he looked startled, gazing down at the floor in front of her. Her legs were jammed under the dash, and twisted to the side, but on the floor, he saw a pool of blood rapidly collecting. "We need to get her out of here, NOW!" he yelled, as the fire truck with the 'jaws of life' arrived. "Hurry, we have a bleeder."

Jim did not understand what he meant by bleeder. He'd seen the gash on her forehead bleeding and it didn't seem that bad. Then the realization hit him that she was in danger of losing the baby, and that was the source of the bleeding. His heart sank, not for his own grief, but knowing how compounded this loss would be over all the others. Having seen the ultrasound and having done everything in her power to have a safe pregnancy, was motherhood going to be snatched from Suzanne yet again?

Chapter 22

"I've got the IV wide open; let's get her out, before she crashes!"

The Fire Department, Police and medics combined their efforts and finally, after what seemed like hours to Jim, but was probably no more than fifteen minutes, got Suzanne free, placed on a backboard and strapped down. She still had not regained consciousness, and the bleeding continued.

Her face appeared grey-white against her beautiful brown hair, and Jim could not see the cut on her forehead from his vantage point. She looked beautiful despite her pallor; she did not seem to be in distress. Jim's head hurt, and his eyes blurred, so he blinked and shook his head trying to clear them as they rolled her gurney to the ambulance. He moved to go with her but was stopped by a touch on his arm.

"Sir, we need to take you to the hospital to get checked out, too. You probably have a concussion." The medic steered him by his elbow into the other ambulance.

"I need to go with my wife..."

"You will be at the same facility...you just can't ride in that vehicle... they need all available space to take care of your wife."

Jim acquiesced and climbed into the awaiting van. He sat on a bench-like seat and another medic took the blood pressure cuff and wrapped it around his arm. He didn't care about his vital signs right now; what Jim wanted was to know how Suzanne was; he needed to know if the baby was ok.

It had been too long Jim knew this in his heart. Something was wrong with Suzanne and they weren't telling him. He had signed all the insurance paperwork and consent forms for Suzanne's treatment and his check-up showed only a slight concussion, but not enough to admit him. He was given instructions for closed head injury and told he was free to leave. He wasn't going anywhere, though; instead he was in the waiting room, pacing and waiting for some word on her condition.

"Mr. Buckley?" the nurse approached him with a clip-board in her hand. "The doctor needs to speak to you, and we need your signature on a few more forms." She led him to a private office and invited him to sit to wait for the doctor, but Jim was too antsy to sit down. *Why a private office?* He thought. *It has to be bad news or he would have just come out to tell me.* His imagination started working overtime, thinking the worst.

When the door opened, and a short, elderly man in a long white coat with a stethoscope around his neck walked in, Jim nearly attacked him with his questions.

"What is it? Is my wife…?"

"Please take a seat, Mr. Buckley."

"I don't want to take a seat; I want to know how my wife is. I need to go to her!"

"Mr. Buckley…can I call you Jim?" He raised his eyebrows with the question, and Jim answered with a nod. "Good. Now then, Jim, about your wife… She's had a rough go of it, and we had to take her into surgery to stop the bleeding. Unfortunately, your infant son did not survive the impact of the crash." Jim cried out and buried his face in his hands; the doctor put his hand on Jim's shoulder.

"I'm terribly sorry, but it gets worse,"

Jim looked up with tears in his eyes, "worse? How could it be any worse, unless… "she's not…?"

"No, your wife is fine; at least, she is stable for the time being. She still has not regained consciousness, and that is a concern, but her vital signs are good. However, the other bad news is that we had to do an emergency hysterectomy in order to stop the bleeding. Her uterus was ruptured in the accident, and the tear was too extensive to repair. The placenta tore away from the wall of the womb, also, which is why your son did not survive. There is a short window of viability in situations like this, and I'm afraid the removal from the vehicle and transport took up too much of that window… we just could not save him, even if he were further along…"

Jim hung his head; Suzanne would never have the opportunity to carry and give birth to their child. Tears flowed freely as he grieved for her loss, as well as his own.

The doctor was still talking, but Jim missed most of what was said, until he excused himself to get back to his patients.

"Will we be able to see our son, to hold him?" Jim asked.

"Of course, I will tell the nurses to fix him up and bring him to your wife's room when she awakens."

He told Jim to feel free to stay in the office as long as he needed; he also told him where the OB/Gyn ward's waiting room was, so the nurses could find him when Suzanne returned from the recovery room.

Jim spent some time in prayer, and once he felt in control of his emotions, he made his way to the waiting room. Cell phone use was prohibited, so he asked the nurse if there was a phone he could use and she directed him to the pay phone. He called the church office, trying to reach Pastor Green, but was told about the approaching retirement of their pastor. She offered to put him through to Pastor Tim, and he accepted;

he only wanted to advise them of the situation and ask for activation of the church prayer chain.

"I'll be right there..." Pastor Tim did not hesitate for a moment. Relief fell on Jim like a gentle breeze on a hot summer day. A sense of peace reigned in his heart and he knew the Lord was in control. Needing the presence of another man of faith to encourage him and help telling Suzanne the outcome of the accident, God provided Pastor Tim.

"Pastor Tim, so glad you could come..." Jim reached his hand out and Pastor Tim grasped it firmly with both his, "I'm only to glad to be here with you, Jim. I'm just sorry to meet you and Suzanne under these circumstances."

"Mr. Buckley," a nurse interrupted them, "your wife is awake and asking for you..."

Jim excused himself and followed the nurse through the swinging double doors and down the hallway to the room in which they'd placed Suzanne. One shared look and they both began to cry, Jim rushing to her bedside to hold her in his arms. Not wanting to disturb them midst their shared grief, the nurse closed the door quietly and retreated to the nurse's station.

Chapter 23

"Jim, he was so exquisite!" They gazed down on their tiny infant son's perfect features: his button nose and little rosebud lips, and his peach-fuzz hair on his head-brown like Suzanne's.. The nurses had dressed him in a miniature gown and cap reserved for premies. They'd wrapped him up so only his face showed, but Suzanne had opened the blanket to look at his perfect little fingers and toes; she touched his tiny round head and marveled at how perfect he looked. He only weighed about a pound and neatly fit in her hands at about seven inches long. His skin looked like a poorly fitting pair of long-johns, all loose and baggy. "He was so perfect! They said he was about 23 weeks gestation," she spoke in amazement.

Jim couldn't speak; a lump filled his throat the moment he saw his child, lifeless but beautiful. He wondered at the dreams they'd formed for him and the preparations they had made in their home. What was to become of them? How would they get through this time? This wasn't the usual miscarriage or incomplete implantation; this was their baby that never had a chance at life and involved a funeral and all that went with that.

Suzanne looked up at Jim, tears shimmering in her eyes, but a smile on her face. "You know what Sammy would want for us?" she asked.

Jim shook his head. He had no idea what she was thinking, or how she could even look forward to the future while holding their dead son in her arms.

"He would want us to fill that nursery and the other rooms with children who need to be loved, children that need a good Christian home. We need to look into adoption"

Jim was stunned that she would bring up adoption so soon and on her own without his prodding. Always before, he was the one to present choices, only to have her shoot them down for a variety of reasons. Now, out of the blue, she was the stronger partner, offering a way to mediate their loss.

A knock on the door interrupted their discussion, and Pastor Tim poked his head in when they answered. "Might I come in and have a word of prayer with you?" he inquired. Jim and Suzanne welcomed Pastor Tim's suggestion, because they knew the nurse would return soon to take their Samuel away for transport to the funeral home.

As he prayed for God's grace on the grieving couple and for strength to help them through this time, Jim and Suzanne felt an intense sense of peace. Holding hands, they were touched as Pastor Tim placed a hand on Sammy's forehead; he thanked God for the gift of Samuel's presence these last few months, and asked for a blessing to result from the loss of the child.

Just as he finished his prayer, the nurse came with an isolette in which to take Sammy away. They released him into her care, knowing they would see him again, someday. Then, once he was gone, Suzanne was impressed to speak to Pastor Tim.

"Pastor, we would like to consider adoption. We aren't on any waiting list, yet, but would like to try for a private adoption instead. Would you have any connections within the church that might help us in our quest for an infant?"

He was surprised that she would bring up the subject of adoption so quickly. "Don't you want time to grieve your loss, before you decide on such a permanent…?"

"While I was sleeping, Jesus spoke to me. He told me that Sammy was gone, but assured me that there was another little boy for us, somewhere."

"And you are sure this was from the Lord?"

"It was. I've never been so sure of anything in my life. We have a home ready for a baby and we are ready to love a child."

Pastor Tim nodded and looked thoughtful. "Have you considered an open adoption?" He went on to explain how the open adoption worked, how they would stay in touch with the birth mother and give her progress reports at specified time periods. She could also have visitation and be known to the child as he grew, if agreed upon. Jim and Suzanne agreed to pray about it before deciding if that was the route they wanted to pursue and Pastor Tim agreed to put out feelers and wait for them to contact him with their decision.

"Maddie," Pastor Tim spoke into the phone from his office, "I think I may have a couple for your child. They just experienced the loss of a baby boy they were expecting in about five months, and are open to the idea of adoption. They aren't sure about the open adoption idea, but are praying about it, so I will keep you informed."

Maddie was surprised that a couple had surfaced so quickly. She did not ask any questions about them, reserving that for if or when they made their choice. She told her mother, and the two of them placed it in God's hands.

They decided it was about time to talk to Simon and Samantha about Maddie's situation. Rather than trying to hide it from them, they needed to understand her circumstances and plans. They both took the news better than Maddie anticipated. Simon looked saddened when heard about the attack; Samantha, on the other hand, wondered why she couldn't just keep the baby. "I would help you take care of him," she promised, but Mama put her hand on Samantha's arm to stop her.

"This is hard for Maddie as it is, dear. Let's try to support her, rather than change her mind."

Maddie tried to explain to Samantha the logic of her choice, but Samantha only thought about not seeing her very first nephew and not being a part of his life. When Maddie told her about the plan for an open adoption, Samantha seemed more agreeable. At least she could see pictures, and maybe one day they could all meet him, when he was old enough. They all held hands and prayed for God's help to accept His will, and for Pastor Tim to be His instrument in helping them.

Maddie could hardly wait to hear from Pastor Tim. She was anxious to know if the Lord had already chosen a family for the little fellow. She longed to know if they would agree to the open adoption, and all the details of their home and character. Most of all, she wanted to be sure they were grounded Christians that would treat him well, raise him in the fear and admonition of the Lord, and guide his path to adulthood.

Chapter 24

Teardrops from heaven... that's what Suzanne thought as she and Jim stood under an umbrella in the cemetery. They planned a simple, quiet graveside ceremony for Samuel, rather than a full-fledged funeral. Although they had grown to love him throughout her pregnancy, they realized that others might be uncomfortable at a funeral for a stillborn infant they'd never known. Pastor Tim officiated and a few members of their families joined them, but once prayers were said, and the tiny white casket lowered into the ground, everyone slipped away giving Suzanne and Jim a chance to say a final good-bye.

Jim's comforting arm draped over Suzanne's shoulder while his other arm held the umbrella over her head, protecting her from the elements. "Come, dear. It's time we leave now. We'll be back to plant some flowers and place the headstone..." Jim drew her to him and led her toward the edge of the grass where their car was parked.

Pastor Tim waited off by the parked cars to have a few words with them. He did not want to pressure their decision about the open adoption. Smiling gently as they walked toward him, he hesitated to ask anything of them at this time, but somehow felt impressed by the Lord that Maddie's child was meant for them.

"Jim... Suzanne..." he reached out to shake their hands. "Thought maybe you had made a decision...?"

"We have, actually," Jim started. "We think an open adoption is too much to ask of adoptive parents. We would like to feel we are the family our son needs and not confuse him with those that gave him up for adoption. But we do want you to keep us in mind if you hear of any babies being placed for private adoption."

Through her tears, Suzanne nodded, "When we receive a child into our home, we want to know we are his parents, forever."

"Well, I'm sorry to hear that. I honestly felt that you were well-suited to an open adoption situation."

"Another thing you may need to know is that we may be moving," Jim interjected.

"Oh? Far from here?"

"Well, my job may be moving to the St. Louis area in the fall, so we may be, too." Jim replied. "It all depends on whether the company will relocate us, or if they decide to hire locals from the metro-St. Louis region. You know how it is... cost/benefit ratio and all that has to be considered."

"So sorry to hear that, Jim. We will miss you at church, but maybe a change in scenery will help you two in future months."

Spring passed and with summer in Nebraska, came scorching heat... one of the hottest years on record, according to the weather station. By the Fourth of July, and entering her seventh month, Maddie had expanded in girth and gained about 30 pounds. Her face was round, but not in a disfiguring way; according to some of the ladies of church, 'she glowed'. Through the prayer chain, Maddie's condition and circumstances had become known to the majority of the membership, and because it started with the prayer requests, nobody seemed bent on judging her harshly or questioning her story.

Simon was very protective of his older sister, listening for even the suggestion of gossip about her. Overall, his attitude was supportive but, on occasion, his anger at the man responsible came out in his actions. He often forgot what Daddy taught about '*vengeance is mine, says the Lord*' as he talked about finding him and pressing charges or worse. He hated the thought that the guy was getting off so easily while Maddie suffered the indignities of an unwanted pregnancy, as well as the questions regarding her reputation.

Samantha, on the other hand, still complained about losing her first nephew, despite Maddie's reassurances regarding the open adoption. She longed to take care of the baby, changing his diapers and watching him learn to crawl and walk. "If you change your mind, can you get him back?" she fretted on more than one occasion.

"He isn't a piece of property that you just reclaim," Maddie answered. "He will belong to the adoptive parents, once the initial six month waiting period passes."

"So during that six months you can change…"

"That is why they set that time frame, but I won't change my mind. This is the right decision, Samantha. You have to trust me on this." Maddie felt tired every time they had this discussion. She wondered when Samantha would come to grips with the adoption, if ever. So far, Maddie had not heard from Pastor Tim regarding the potential family for her son; she wondered if they'd reconsidered, not wanting to agree to the open adoption. She did not want to be locked out of the child's life completely, even if she felt unable to raise him on her own.

As she looked toward the end of her pregnancy, Maddie also needed to consider her next career move. She wanted to continue teaching, and still longed for a mission field assignment; however, she wondered how this episode of her life would affect the church's decision on whether to call her for mission work. Then, as if she heard her father's voice, she was reminded of the Bible verse in Jeremiah, '*I know the plans I have for you...they are plans for good, not for evil...*'

She consulted with Pastor Tim and, with his help she put together a resume and letter explaining her dilemma. She asked for them to consider her for a teaching assignment either in an overseas posting, or within the United States, at one of the church schools in need of a teacher. Including a letter of recommendation from Pastor Tim and one from Pastor Green, she sent her packet, and made it a matter of prayer as she had done last year when searching for her first job. She trusted the Lord to move in her life and in the life of her unborn infant.

Feeling the movements of the baby filled her with wonder and joy, knowing that she had been entrusted to bring a new life into the world. At times she even felt tempted to change her mind about placing the baby for adoption. She knew Mama would help her if she chose to raise the child on her own, but she was still unsure of her own emotional baggage. Trusting that the decision she'd made was what the Lord would have her do for the baby, she wondered at what progress the pastor was making toward finding a family.

She heard about a couple at church who was expecting a baby, but it died in an automobile accident, wondering if they might consider adopting, then discounted the idea. She understood that they needed to grieve their loss before they could consider any major decisions like that. Although she did not know them personally, she prayed for them as part of the prayer chain asking that they would find peace and joy in the future.

Chapter 25

"It's from church headquarters!" Maddie held a large manila envelope in her hands as if it would break. "What if they turned me down, again? What will I do?"

"Darling," Mama touched her reassuringly on her shoulder, "remember that God is in control. Either way, it works out according to His plan."

Maddie took a deep breath, let it out and touched her tummy, "Uh-oh!" She laid the envelope on the table and rested heavily on the back of the chair.

"What is it?" Mama looked down at her with worry on her brow.

"I think I'm in labor, Mama. It started earlier this morning, but that was a strong one..."

"Aren't you early? I thought you figured it would be around Labor Day?"

"Well, I guess this guy has other plans! Should I call the doctor or what?"

Mama was already moving in that direction. She left a message with the doctor's answering service. She called to Jason and Jamie, telling them to go next door and tell the neighbor that Maddie had to go to the hospital. She told them to stay there and she would come for them when she got back.

"Is Maddie going to die, like Daddy did?" Jamie asked in her tiny voice. The only time she had gone to the hospital was to watch Daddy die, and Mama and Maddie had not told the twins about Maddie's pregnancy. They figured the twins were unaware or ignoring the changes in Maddie's body, and unless they asked questions, they were better off not knowing.

"No, sweet ones," Mama touched Jamie's and Jason's cheeks, "Maddie just needs to go to the hospital for a couple of days; she will be just fine."

Reassured, they left for the neighbors, again chattering in their twin-speak. Mama hurried into the bedroom to collect Maddie's overnight case that had sat packed for several weeks, just in case. She took it out to the car and put it into the trunk, and then she helped Maddie out to the car. Suddenly, Maddie wasn't moving as easily as she had throughout the pregnancy; she took on the slow, waddling movement so stereotypical of television pregnancy. Holding her abdomen with one hand and the other on her mid-back, she leaned back into the passenger seat and pulled her legs inside. Mama closed the door and headed for the driver's seat.

"Shouldn't you leave a note for Samantha and Simon? They will wonder where everyone is when they get back from swimming."

Rushing into the kitchen, Mama jotted a quick note on the message board, and told them to wait for word from her. Then, Mama grabbed her keys and headed back out to the car. "Now, are we ready?"

"Except for a prayer and a call to Pastor Tim. He needs to know in case that couple has changed their mind." She had been so disappointed when he told them that the couple would not agree to an open adoption. "We need to line up something or the baby will be coming home with us."

Before they started the car, Maddie and Mama bowed their heads, asking for a safe drive and safe delivery of the baby. Then they petitioned the Lord to work on some young couple's heart, so the baby would have a home to go to. Mama started the car and headed toward the hospital, still praying under her breath. Maddie tried to relax between contractions, but her mind kept working on the whole issue of adoption. What would she do if Pastor Tim was unable to come up with a Christian home for the baby? Was this a sign that she should keep this infant? How could she know for sure?

The contents of the envelope were totally forgotten in the middle of all the confusion. When Samantha and Simon returned from swimming and saw Mama's message, Samantha immediately began tidying the house in an effort to stay busy and not worry about Maddie. As she cleaned, she saw the envelope on the table and wondered why it was there. They never placed mail on the kitchen table; it belonged on the desk in the office. She carried the manila package, along with the other bills she found beside Mama's chair, to the office and stacked them on top of all the other unprocessed mail in the in-box.

Pastor Tim received the news of Maddie's premature labor with trepidation. Until now, he had not found another suitable couple to consider for adopting Maddie's baby. He sent out feelers to all the various local churches as well as friends he knew from seminary that also ran churches around the country. He'd heard from many of his pastor friends, but with only friendly replies and negative responses regarding his query.

In his heart, he still felt that the Buckley's were ideally suited in this case. With a breath of prayer, he called Jim at his job. His hope was they would reconsider if they knew the birth was imminent.

"Jim, how are you? How's Suzanne?" The usual questions opened their conversation, with the courteous responses of 'fine, thank you.' Then Pastor Tim jumped right into the reason for his call, telling Jim the story and presenting him, once again, with the possibility of adoption.

"Would you consider changing your minds if the mother modified her request on the open adoption? I truly believe this child is meant for you."

"I would have to talk to Suzanne before I can answer that, Pastor." With a promise from Jim and a plan to talk again in a few days, Pastor Tim drove over to the hospital to sit with Mrs. Galloway and pray for Maddie.

Taking his time getting home, Jim pondered the turn of events. Just when he and Suz had settled in their minds that they would not adopt until they relocated in the fall, Pastor Tim presents this opportunity to them. He hated to think of a baby without a home when they had so much love to give, but would Suzanne be interested? She had slipped back into a depression much like those that followed the miscarriages. He wasn't sure if she would even want to consider adopting until that was under control.

"What if she changes her mind about the open adoption?" Suzanne's immediate refusal surprised him. Despite her bedraggled appearance indicating the depths of her depression, he thought she would at least take a minute to consider the baby.

"Jim, how can you ask that of me? We already decided to put it off; I feel like a yo-yo when we reconsider." The dark circles under her eyes and unkempt brown hair gave her the look of someone much older. He wanted to give her a reason to live again.

"But Pastor Tim said she might change her mind… that was the only reason we gave for not agreeing before…" he felt as though he were pleading with her. *Did he want this child more than he admitted even to himself?* He wondered. "Let's just think about it, OK?"

"If it will make you feel better, I will think about it, but I am not making any promises." She pulled her bathrobe around her as if she was cold, although the summer heat filled their home through the open windows. Jim wondered if he was right to push the adoption issue when she was obviously already having difficulty coping. He decided he would wait for her to bring it up again, rather than pressure her for a quick answer.

Pastor Tim needed patience, too. As if he were the expecting father, he paced in the waiting room, wondering how things were going. Because he was not related, the nurses would only say she was stable, but not give him any details. Mrs. Galloway was in the room with Maddie, holding her hand and wiping her brow. He was amazed at her strength in the absence of her husband; she displayed a fortitude acquired from years in the mission field, he was sure.

"Pastor, the young woman is asking for you to come and pray with them." the nurse called to him from the double swinging doors. "You can't stay long, but we do allow visits as long as delivery is not at hand." And she led him down the sterile smelling hallway to a private room where Mrs. Galloway stood beside Maddie's bed, and Maddie rested against pillows, her hair moist and curly around her flushed face.

Chapter 26

Maddie saw Pastor Tim enter her room and a sense of shame washed over her. No man had ever seen her in bed, except her father, and especially not the pastor. Adding to her discomfort was his handsome appearance. Despite receiving the call and responding so quickly, topped with the long wait in the waiting room, he looked as refreshed as if he just stepped out of a shower and dressed for the day. Not a hint of being put upon showed in his face, and in his eyes she only saw concern.

Then another contraction gripped her, and she looked away, feeling ashamed although he knew the pregnancy was not the result of promiscuousness. Until now, she'd ignored any hints of scorn from people in town who did not know her situation. But in the grips of labor, she seemed unable to draw strength from her faith. Mama tightened her grasp on her hand as if to reassure her and the contraction eased.

"Pastor," Mama left Maddie's side to greet him. "We wanted you to pray for Maddie. The doctors are concerned that the delivery is not progressing, and that she may need a C-section if she doesn't show signs of dilating a bit more. Will you pray with us?"

Pastor Tim was honored at the request and as they all held hands, his left hand holding Maddie's right, and he was shocked to feel the warmth of an electric shock tingle through him when he held her hand. Dismissing it long enough to pray, he asked the Lord to move on her body, and allow the baby to be born without incident. He added to the prayer, that the compromises needed to give the child a good home, would be forthcoming, and that the outcome would be to His honor and glory.

Maddie smiled up at him after he closed with 'Amen' with tears in her eyes. "I have been a bit stubborn about the open adoption, haven't I?" His heart leaped in his chest as he gazed down at her tenderly, wishing he could bear her pain.

"Oh, I wasn't referring to you, Maddie. I was thinking about the couple I told you of. They need to compromise, too..."

"But, Pastor, I realize that I cannot hold this child hostage for my desires to be fulfilled. If I have to relinquish control, I will. I would ask that a picture be sent on his birthday each year, and that I can at least know his whereabouts, even if I am not to know him, or he me."

Pastor Tim realized this was the answer he was seeking for Suzanne and Jim, and hoped they, too, had come to recognize the need to compromise. As much as he wanted to rush out and call them immediately, he held back to give comfort and support to Maddie and Mrs. Galloway. When the nurse came to ask him to leave, he decided he had done as much as he could for the evening, and would go home to await their news.

"We fully understand, Pastor Tim," Mama replied when he approached the subject. "We are only two of your flock; we will let you know as soon as anything develops."

"Jim! Have you discussed the baby with Suzanne?" His high energy caused him to run his words together, and stumble over the question.

"Pastor? It's nine o'clock!"

"Yes, I know, but I had to tell you that the mother is willing to modify her request for an open adoption, and I'd like to share her thoughts with you and Suz…"

"Look, Pastor, I appreciate your help and efforts, but Suzanne is not doing so well these days, and I just don't know about pressing the issue with her."

"I'm sorry, Jim, of course! How inconsiderate of me! Here I thought I was helping, and did not even ask how she was coping. I truly am sorry. Is there anything I can do?"

"We will see you at church, and if Suzanne changes her mind at all, I will call you."

So it was another, 'don't call me. I'll call you' situation, Tim thought. *Guess I need to let it go, and leave it in God's hands.* "Alright, Jim. We will talk another time."

He hung up the phone, discouraged, and turned in after sending up final prayers on behalf of his various members in need, with a special mention on Maddie's behalf.

Around midnight, he received a call from the hospital. "She is being taken into surgery, Pastor. The baby is showing some distress, so they want to do the C-section before…" a sob caught in Mama's throat. "It is so hard to think of my grandchild in distress, and yet he isn't mine, Pastor. I try hard not to think of him that way, because it would only make Maddie's choice harder."

"I think it is unavoidable, since you've watched your daughter's body change during the pregnancy. You couldn't pretend it wasn't a child growing in her."

"Please, Pastor, could you come and sit with me… she will be in the recovery room for a while, and I'd like you there, in case they let me see the baby…"

Pastor Tim was only too glad to return to the hospital and sit with Mrs. Galloway during the dark hours of the morning, awaiting word on both mother and child. When the nurse finally came out, Mrs. Galloway was sleeping in a chair, and the Pastor stood up to hear the news.

"Both mother and child are doing well," she smiled. "Will you and her mother want to see the infant? He will be cleaned up and in the nursery in about fifteen minutes." and she showed him where they could go to get gowned and ready to go in to see the baby.

Chapter 27

The first thing Mrs. Galloway did was place a call to the children. She had already touched bases with Simon and Samantha several times, but wanted them to know their sister was fine, as was the baby. For Jamie, she had called the neighbors house earlier to arrange a sleepover. In the morning they could return home to the care of their siblings, until Mama returned from the hospital; they would be told that Maddie was alright and would be discharged in a day or two.

Once the business of notification was done, Mrs. Galloway and Pastor Tim met at the nursery window. Peeking inside they saw an incubator labeled 'Baby Galloway', but could not see the baby. They went to the door, and a nurse ushered them into a room where they could get ready to go into the spotlessly clean nursery. Fortunately, the baby did not require intensive care and was in the regular newborn nursery.

Pastor Tim followed Mrs. Galloway into the newborn nursery after they donned the requisite paper gowns, washed their hands thoroughly, and received instructions. Although they could see the baby, they could not touch him because he was in an incubator. It was only a precaution because he was about a month earlier than his due date; the doctor confirmed his prematurity by both his development and birth weight, although his APGAR score was very good.

He only weighed five pounds and was a tiny 18.75 inches long. His head was topped with fuzzy brown hair with just a shimmer of red like Maddie's. To look at his face was to look at Maddie; his eyes and mouth reflected hers to perfection, although his button-nose resembled that of most newborns. Because he was a premie, he hadn't had time to fatten up, so his face did not look like Winston Churchill as do so many newborns. The only problem seemed to be a slight yellowing of his skin, neonatal jaundice, which the nurse assured them, would clear in time, although they would check his blood levels to be sure.

Mama looked down at her grandson tenderly trying to hold back the tears forming in the corner of her eyes. She longed to pour love into this her first grandchild, yet she knew she must restrain herself. She reached out as if to touch his fingers when he opened and closed his hand near the side of the plastic isolette. As she admired each of his physical features, she wondered what kind of child he would grow into, and what kind of adult.

Pastor Tim stood a little away from the infant, trying to be there for Mrs. Galloway, avoiding personal attachment to the child that so represented Maddie. He, too, would have enjoyed a chance to shower this child with attention, but also recognized how inappropriate any hint of involvement would be. The best he could offer was to find a home for this child, and he was more certain than ever that this baby was meant for the Buckleys.

When their visit was over, and Maddie had returned from recovery to her room, Mrs. Galloway went in to sit with her. Pastor Tim wanted to stay, as well, but he also had business to attend to. He needed to call Jim Buckley again, just in case there had been a discussion or some change in their stance. He also wanted them to know the terms Maddie was agreeable to and see if they, too, would compromise. Before he placed the call, he made his way to the hospital chapel.

Although he was accustomed to praying anywhere, he often took the opportunity to retreat to the hospital chapel when visiting one of his members. The quiet and solitude of the little sanctuary offered a rare chance to listen to the Lord. Too often he found the noise of life a distraction to hearing God's voice. He could talk out his problems or requests, but it was in the quiet of his 'prayer closet' that he heard or sensed God's answering his plea.

The eastern, early morning sunlight through the stained-glass windows above the pulpit sent rainbows of color throughout the room. Soft instrumental music played from a hidden system, giving the sense of a heavenly orchestra playing before the throne of God. Pastor Tim went into the pew at the rear of the chapel and knelt on the kneeling pad. He poured out his heart, his concerns for both families in this tragedy, and pleaded for wisdom and the right words to convey to Jim and Suzanne what the Lord had impressed on his heart. After he finished talking he spent a long time with his eyes closed, just waiting on the Lord. He did not know how long he remained there, but saw, when he opened his eyes, that the sun had moved beyond the point of illuminating the sanctuary. Feeling refreshed, he rose to his feet, made his way to the parking lot, and drove over to the church office, where he could be assured of privacy for the discussion with the Buckleys.

Arriving at his office, Pastor Tim was surprised to find a message on his desk from Jim and Suzanne. It asked him to come to their home at six that evening, if he could; they needed to talk. He quickly called the number on the note and left a response that he would be at their home as requested. He thanked God for answered prayers, feeling sure this request indicated a change of heart.

Maddie opened her eyes to see Mama dozing in the chair pulled up beside her bed. "Ohhh," she groaned as she felt discomfort in her lower abdomen. The IV in her left hand restricted her arm from moving, but she felt her tummy with her right hand and knew the baby was truly born; it hadn't been a dream. She also realized that she had a C-section, and wondered if the baby was doing alright. "Mama," she whispered, cleared her throat and began again, "Mama," she said, stronger this time.

Mrs. Galloway started awake as she had done through all the years of raising children. She didn't sleep too soundly, always on the alert in case of illness or nightmares. "Yes, dear, I am here," she replied, reaching for Maddie's right hand.

"Is the baby…? Did they do the C-section in time…?"

"Yes, Maddie. The little fella is just fine. He was a bit premature, as you know, so his weight was low, just 5lbs, and he has a bit of jaundice, but otherwise he is just fine."

"Jaundice? Isn't that bad?"

"Only if his bilirubin goes too high, but they will monitor that, so don't worry."

Maddie rested her head back against the pillow in relief. She had more questions, but she was too tired to ask them right now. She could wait… and her eyes closed in a restful sleep. Mama left her sleeping and went home to talk with her other children. She planned to return later that day, after she also got some rest.

Chapter 28

"Pastor, how are you?" Jim greeted Pastor Tim warmly at the door at 6:00pm sharp. They clasped hands in a handshake of brotherhood as Jim pulled Pastor Tim into the entryway of their home. Jim's face was sunny and pleasant and his energy was contagious. Pastor Tim felt encouraged by the warmth and joy emanating from Jim until he saw Suzanne.

Suzanne stood behind Jim, a little ashen with red-rimmed eyes. She did not present as a woman agreeing to adoption, but rather she appeared wrapped in her grief as if it was a cloak she would never shed. However, her clothing was tidy and her hair well-groomed; she even had a touch of make-up on, although the mascara appeared smudged beneath her eyes. *Perhaps it wasn't grief he saw,* thought Pastor Tim. *Maybe it is a combination of regret and anticipation.*

They invited him into the family room and Pastor Tim was struck at the decorations in the home. Everything spoke of a home ready for children. This was not a home with untouchables and breakable bric-a-brac. In fact, it almost looked like a day care, with a high chair in the corner of the kitchen, a playpen planted near the couch and, through the window a swing-set and a molded plastic playhouse stood out in the back yard.

"So, you asked me here for a reason...?" he opened the conversation as he sat onto the plush, gold micro-fiber easy chair near the fireplace.

Jim sat on the couch opposite the pastor, and Suzanne perched on the arm of the couch beside him. "We want to discuss the infant you told us about. We are wondering if the mother is willing to compromise, perhaps not be such an integral part of the child's life, but settle for the occasional progress report."

Pastor Tim smiled. God never failed to thrill him in the ways He answers prayers. Up to this point, Pastor Tim had not had the chance to talk about Maddie's offer of a modified open adoption, and here Jim and Suzanne were, offering nearly the same conditions as Maddie suggested. Before he could answer Jim, Suzanne continued.

"We will still be moving, so frequent contact would probably not be a possibility, anyway. But I would be glad to send a picture, perhaps on his birthday or Mother's Day each year, and a brief letter about his progress. She would know where we are, but would not try to contact us or him until we indicate it would be possible."

"I think this might be just what the young mother needs, to help her agree to you adopting him. I didn't tell you, he has been born, a bit early, but totally healthy. The doctor said he may go home in a day or two, so we need to get your lawyer to draw up the legal papers as soon as possible. I can let her know that it is in the works, so she won't worry as I know she is right now."

Suzanne immediately brightened when she heard that the baby was already born and healthy. She thought she would be following a prolonged pregnancy, worrying whether the baby would survive, or if this chance would also be taken from her. A sigh of relief escaped her lips and a sparkle lit up her eyes. Rosy cheeks replaced the pallor seen earlier, and Suzanne was transformed. Her mind began moving in many directions and her heart raced at the thought of bringing home a newborn son.

Jim looked up at her and saw the change. Saying nothing, he reached up and squeezed the hand she had rested on his shoulder. His heart was full; he couldn't say what was on his mind. He silently praised the Lord for working this miracle for them, and asked for help to strengthen his wife as they went through the adoption process.

"Jim, Suzanne, I would like us to have a word of prayer..." they nodded and all bowed their heads together. Pastor Tim spoke the words they were unable to form, and sent praises to the heavens, glorifying God for His goodness. After they talked for a while longer, he excused himself. He planned to meet Mrs. Galloway when she returned to the hospital this evening, so they could discuss the turn of events, and help Maddie through her own commitment.

Despite her natural longing to hold and love her newborn, Maddie resisted, knowing he was to be placed for adoption. She could not allow herself to even look at his face, lest she change her mind for the wrong reason. Trusting that she had made the right choice, she listened as her mother described the little boy she had brought into the world.

Mrs. Galloway was at Maddie's bedside for about a half an hour when they heard a knock at the door. Pastor Tim poked his head in, asking permission to join them. Maddie was thankful she had had time during the day to shower and make herself presentable. She wasn't wearing the ugly grey gown that opened in the back, but had on a modest flannel pajama with pink flowers scatter all over it. The bed was tidy, thanks to Mama straightening it when she arrived, and Maddie did not have the sense of shame she'd felt the last time Pastor Tim visited.

Her freckles were less prominent than before the pregnancy and the rosy glow of her cheeks hid them even more. Her beautiful green eyes twinkled before she ducked her head to hide her embarrassment. She thought Pastor Tim quite handsome, and he had been so kind to her that she quite admired his character. She knew that he could never be interested in a girl with her history, but all the same, she felt her heart jump when he entered her room.

"I have news for you... I hope you agree that it is good news. The couple I told you about has agreed to your terms for the adoption. They will provide you with photos and reports on the baby's growth and development at regular intervals. There is one glitch, however..."

Mama looked at Maddie and they both looked at the Pastor with concern in their eyes. "It really isn't a problem, at least I don't think so..." he cleared his throat. "It's just that they will be moving within the next few months, so they will not be living in this state. Since you agreed to a modified open adoption, I did not think this was a problem. After all, it is their right to live anywhere; open adoptions don't stipulate residency, as long as they return to this state to finalize the adoption at the six month mark."

He was more winded than after an emotional sermon. He just wanted this to work out for both families. Pastor Tim looked from Mama to Maddie, questioning their response. Did their silence indicate they did not want these terms for the adoption? Should he leave them to discuss it? These thoughts raced through his mind until Maddie looked up and smiled.

"God is good!" that was all she said, but it was enough. Pastor Tim took her hands and blessed her, and then he did what came naturally. He offered to pray with them. Maddie shook her head. "No, pastor, I want to pray, if you don't mind."

Bowing together, holding hands as they had before, Maddie led out in a heartfelt prayer of thanksgiving and joy. She expressed her gratitude for the safe delivery, for the miracle of an adoptive family at just the right time, and for a supportive family and church family, including Pastor Tim, all of whom helped her endure to the end. Then she prayed the prayer of Hannah, releasing her son into God's hands, to be raised by another. She asked that he would grow in strength and stature, and come to know Jesus as his personal Savior and be a servant of God.

Pastor Tim admired the Christian woman who prayed more eloquently than he could, who lived her faith and inspired confidence in those around her. He wondered at the feeling in his heart; he wondered if this was the helpmeet the Lord had in mind for him and his ministry. He left mother and daughter and returned to his lonely abode, thinking about Maddie and her impact on him.

Chapter 29

"Lizzie, I am so glad you could come… what a surprise!" Maddie had been home for several days, and talked to Lizzie both while in hospital, after the birth of the baby, and after she returned home. Lizzie was her best friend and the only one who knew all the struggles she went through in the beginning of this journey. They'd shared tears of sorrow and shared the comfort that only came from a deep and abiding faith. To see her now brought tears of joy to Maddie's eyes; only Lizzie knew how much Maddie needed a friend to talk to.

Lizzie had taken the summer off, rather than teach summer school, and traveled a bit around the mid-western states. Since she really had no family to visit, and with Maddie on her mind, Nebraska seemed like a good place to visit. Not only did she want to spend time with Maddie and help her through this time, she also needed help making a decision about her own life.

She was under contract for one more year in Chicago, which she was prepared to do, but realized that the city was not for her. She longed for the openness she enjoyed as a child in southern Illinois. The noise of traffic and safety concerns when living in a metropolitan area left her with a void; she missed the greenery, the wildlife and peaceful nights where stars sparkled against the blackness. Lizzie wondered what

Maddie had in mind for her future, and whether they would end up working together again at some point.

"Hey, Maddie, have you thought about coming back to good old Chicago, since you're looking at working this year?"

Maddie looked at Lizzie with a puzzled expression in her eyes.

"What is it? Is something wrong?" Lizzie asked, when Maddie didn't reply.

"I just remembered something," Maddie said. "Just before I went to the hospital, I received a packet from the church headquarters… I don't know what happened to it, and I never opened it." She started looking around by the table where she remembered resting it down. A few odd pieces of mail rested in the same spot, but there was no manila envelope. "Mama, do you know what happened to that package?" Maddie called into the kitchen where Mama was preparing lunch for them.

Mama came to the doorway between the kitchen and the living-room wiping her hands on her apron. "No, dear, I don't remember seeing it after that day. I wonder if Samantha moved it… the house was nice and clean when I came home from the hospital. She probably put it in the office with the bills."

Maddie rushed into the office and rummaged through the stack of envelopes laying on the credenza. Sure enough, on the bottom of the stack, under the store advertisements and junk mail, was her manila envelope, still unopened. Taking the letter opener she slit the top and headed back out to the living room where Lizzie sat still somewhat confused.

"You know, I told you about applying to the mission field? Well, this is from the church and…" Maddie looked down at the papers in her hand, "…and they turned me down." Disappointment caused the words to stick in her throat. "They say I can reapply after I have two full years of teaching experience." She continued looking through the papers, and her face brightened. "Hey, they offered me a position in St. Louis, teaching at one of the church schools! I like that idea better than going back to Chicago."

Now it was time for Lizzie to be disappointed. She had so hoped that Maddie would be returning to their school in Cabrini-Green. Now she faced a school year without her best friend and in a secular setting.

Maddie saw her friend's sadness and tried to reassure her. "I still have to interview, so it isn't written in stone..." But Lizzie knew Maddie would get the job since the church headquarters was sending her for the interview. They soon changed the subject, avoiding discussion of the inevitable separation. Maddie told Lizzie of her life in rural Nebraska and Lizzie showed Maddie pictures of her travels along the Mississippi River. By evening they were all caught up, and enjoyed a quiet evening at home.

Maddie was anxious to have Lizzie attend church with her on the coming weekend. The support offered by the church through the loss of her father, and her personal crisis, impressed her so much that she had come to think of the congregation as her extended family. She wanted Lizzie to experience the same welcome and enjoy fellowship with some of her new acquaintances.

"Wow! He's a hunk! Ooops! I don't think I'm supposed to call a man of God a hunk!" Lizzie whispered to Maddie as she saw Pastor Tim take the pulpit.

Maddie had to admit he looked handsome in his suit and tie. But she also thought he was quite striking in his khakis and polo shirts he'd worn when visiting her at the hospital. She wondered at the propriety of admiring a pastor, but nodded to Lizzie, and then she faced forward waiting for the service to start.

As always, Pastor Tim presented a thoughtful and well-prepared sermon. He held the attention of both Maddie and

Lizzie, and each felt the words were directed at her heart alone. He had a way of preaching that left the listener with a challenge to draw them closer to the Lord. He also managed to pick just the right hymns to complement his message. In the closing hymn, Maddie harmonized in alto with Lizzie's soprano and, with the rest of the congregation, made a joyful noise of praise and adoration.

A fellowship luncheon in the annex gave Maddie a chance to introduce Lizzie to many of her new friends. The food was prepared by the ladies in the church, and laid out like a buffet. Each individual portioned out tastes from the entrees and vegetable dishes, helped themselves to salad and beverage, and once all that was eaten, deserts of apple pies and chocolate chip cookies finished the meal. Throughout the meal, Lizzie was welcomed by various members and felt as if she were a part of the family.

"Maddie, I see you brought a friend with you today," the rich baritone that was now familiar to Maddie belonged to Pastor Tim.

"Yes, Pastor, this is Lizzie, my very best friend. She is here from Chicago for a visit."

Pastor Tim clasped Lizzie's outstretched hand in both of his in a warm greeting. "Welcome to our modest group." He looked directly into her eyes. Lizzie felt her heart quiver and her palms dampen as she returned his gaze.

"Uh… thanks. I really enjoyed… uh… your sermon… uh." She never was at a loss for words, but this good-looking minister took her breath away and left her speechless.

Taken into the depths of her eyes, Pastor Tim wondered if the devil was tempting him. First, he had felt shockwaves in his interactions with Maddie… was that just sympathy for her situation or attraction? Now, he found himself equally drawn to her best friend. Perhaps he was more fickle than he thought. He'd kept a lid on his attraction to the opposite sex throughout college and seminary, but suddenly, two women who just happened to be best friends caused him to question his bachelorhood. He subdued his initial response and smiled at Lizzie as he moved away from their table.

"Oh, my, Maddie, he is just wonderful… does he date? Why haven't you told me about him before?"

"Lizzie! I wouldn't know if he dates. And until a week ago, I was a single, pregnant parishioner, not the most attractive prospect for a pastor. Maybe you should hang around town and get to know him." She smiled at Lizzie, but Lizzie just looked thoughtful and gazed after Pastor Tim as he made the rounds in the fellowship hall.

Chapter 30

"Jim, isn't he beautiful?" Suzanne stared at the tiny bundle in her arms as she gently rocked in the glider-rocker. Once Jim contacted their lawyer, the initial paperwork was completed in record time to allow them immediate custody of Maddie's baby. He had stayed in the hospital an extra few days to clear his jaundice but, today they were finally allowed to bring him home.

"Uh, no, he isn't beautiful, he is handsome." Jim replied with a grin. "Boys are never beautiful, you know." He leaned over the rocker and gazed down at the infant; the baby sucked his tongue as if he were nursing. His lashes lay gently on his pink cheeks. Tiny fingers opened and closed as if he were dreaming of grasping at something.

"That's the only regret I have… that I cannot breast-feed him." Suzanne said quietly, but did not dwell on it. The fresh baby powder smell greeter her as she stroked her finger across his cheek, pausing near his pursed lips. She was too happy to be sad. Everything had moved so fast over the last week that it seemed they didn't have time to take a breath.

When the reality of the adoption hit them, they realized they needed to choose a name for their new son. They were determined to have a name before bringing him home, despite the law allowing them more time to file the birth certificate.

It just didn't seem right to take home 'Baby Boy Buckley'. They could not see calling him Samuel, either, because they had already buried little Sammy and it would be too hard to call another child by that name.

"I like the name 'Timothy'," suggested Suzanne. "After all, if not for Pastor Tim, we might not be adopting. And Timothy was a young man who served the Lord, if I remember right."

"I was thinking of naming him after your father and mine," Jim replied, although he already knew her answer. She disliked both their names and preferred something different. She did not want a 'Junior', either, so there would be no 'Little Jimmy'.

"What about one of the lesser known names from the Bible, like Seth or a minor prophet such as Micah?" They mulled over name after name until they were finally in agreement. They would name their son Benjamin Michael Buckley. Benjamin was the much beloved youngest son of Rachel, and Michael, as a middle name, represented Christ's place in the middle of everything.

Soft puffs of baby breath wafted up to Suzanne as she cuddled little Ben. Already she was in love with him and as protective as if she had given birth to him. She felt the peace of the baby's room in its pale green with all the murals she spent so much love and time on. Although the nursery was decorated with Samuel in mind, it was neutral enough to represent almost any Bible story with boy characters. Suzanne knew that this was God's plan for their lives. She was not looking forward to relocating with Jim's job, but decided she could produce a similar result in their new home, perhaps with a different theme.

Jim lovingly built a rocking horse and other wooden toys for the room and painted them to match. Everything he had built, along with the furniture, could go with them to St.

Louis, so that was no problem. He wondered at uprooting Suzanne, knowing how hard it was to change churches, homes, and friends. He considered commuting; he thought about having an apartment in St. Louis for during the week, and returning home on weekends. But when he thought of how much of Bennie's life he would miss, he quickly realized that was not an option.

In the end, they agreed to the move, and prepared to be relocated by Thanksgiving Day. They would use the holiday seasons to get resettled and, by the New Year, be ready to start fresh. Jim's job agreed to work with them on the move, and his hours would be flexible until after the New Year.

The move to St Louis went off without a hitch in mid-November and Suzanne and Jim settled into their new West County home. It was about the same size as their home in Omaha, just configured a bit differently. Suzanne was especially pleased with the yard; it had a huge back yard, although they would need to add the play equipment. It also had a garden shed that looked like a little cottage, and she planned to make good use of that as her art and crafts hideaway. That way she could be close to Bennie when he played in the backyard, but still do her painting and pottery.

The front yard was also quite nice. With the wraparound porch, they could take advantage of sitting outside on summer evenings while the neighborhood was still buzzing with life. Suzanne also looked forward to seasonal decorating; every holiday was a reason to change the look of her home with decorations. Jim was just happy that she settled in so easily. Their little boy was growing bigger, and Suzanne was a wonderful mother. Her depression lifted almost immediately once Benjamin came into their lives, and had not returned, despite the occasional conversation about their loss of Sammy.

Bennie's first Christmas was all they'd hoped for; he was all giggles and wiggles as they opened their presents. He seemed to enjoy hearing the crinkling of the wrapping paper as they opened their gifts. Of course, they had gifts for him, too, but he was too young to do more than smile and reach for the toys as they showed them to him. They took him for a photo with Santa, even though they did not play up his part in Christmas; it was just for the memory of that first year celebration.

With the New Year, life became a peaceful routine of work and church. Bennie chewed on his hand and drooled as he teethed and pushed himself around in an effort to crawl. He could almost sit alone in his high chair and would soon outgrow the rear-facing car seat and be ready for the next stage, facing the front of the car. Already, Suzanne and Jim anticipated his walking on his own, although that was still several months away, and their enjoyment of their son multiplied with each passing day.

Their life continued along a predictable path for the next couple of years as they took pleasure in Bennie's growth and development. In their eyes, he was the smartest, cutest, and, in general, the best child ever. No other child at his play group or at church measured up to little Ben Buckley, and they had high hopes for his future. However, late in his second year, their life took an unexpected turn. Neither Jim nor Suzanne saw it coming and the end result was a tragedy of enormous proportions.

After Lizzie's visit, Maddie made the trip to St. Louis for the scheduled interview with the church school administration. Although they liked her, and she liked the school, a joint agreement was reached that she would be better off taking some time to recuperate and get back on her feet. They promised to reconsider her the following year, if she was still interested, and she accepted this as part of God's plan.

Returning to Nebraska, to her family home, Maddie found her mother needed her more than she let on. Mama found herself grieving the loss of her husband, a process she had avoided in order to be available for Maddie and her needs. Trying to keep up with the four younger Galloway children as well as the home chores became too much for Mama to handle. Just getting out of bed was difficult at times.

Finally, at Maddie's urging, and with the holidays looming in the not too distant future, Mama sought grief counseling. The Christian counselor advised her to see her physician about a short course of antidepressants to help her through her first holidays without her husband. She also joined a support group in their church for newly widowed seniors and found comfort knowing she was not alone.

Maddie helped out as much as she could with keeping the household on track, and found time to volunteer at the local elementary school. She loved the children and missed teaching; she looked forward to getting back into that arena and volunteer work helped.

Lizzie called occasionally during those months following her visit, just to talk and share her experiences back in Cabrini-Green. Since she did not want to seek out her family for holidays, Maddie invited her to their home for school breaks. The arrangement worked well for both young women and solidified their friendship to the point that Lizzie thought about applying in the St. Louis School District if Maddie decided to go there.

Lizzie enjoyed the visits for another reason; she was really taken by Pastor Tim. He even invited both Lizzie and Maddie to dinner with him one evening. Although he did not seem to favor one over the other, it was obvious to most onlookers, that Lizzie had it bad for him. She was totally attentive to his every word, laughed at all his jokes, and watched him out of the corner of her eye, trying to be subtle. Maddie, on the other hand, enjoyed the evening, but was less enthralled by Pastor Tim. She was actually a bit intimidated by his position in the church, feeling inadequate and not quite good enough to see herself as a pastor's date, let alone wife.

Over the Thanksgiving break, Lizzie and Maddie began preparations for children's Christmas program at church. Maddie was in charge after Lizzie left, and it was a joy working with the little ones to present the story of the Christ child. When Lizzie returned for the Christmas vacation, she helped in the final preparations and with the program presented on Christmas Eve. Afterward, Pastor Tim invited them to go Christmas caroling with others from church.

Maddie had a sore throat and did not want to strain her voice, so she decline, but Lizzie enthusiastically agreed. It was nearly midnight when she came in with her cheeks rosy and her eyes glowing. Pastor Tim had asked her out on a real date, for New Year's Eve, and she was thrilled at the prospect; Maddie was happy for her, and prayed for the couple when she turned in that night, asking for their happiness in the New Year.

The New Year came in quietly for the Galloway family. It was the first New Year without Daddy, and his absence was sorely felt. Mama tried to make the best of it, watching the Time Square ball come down at midnight, on TV, with the children. They toasted the celebration with sparkling apple cider and soon turned in for the night.

Just weeks into the New Year, Maddie received a picture of Benjamin Michael Buckley, her first since his newborn photo provided by the hospital. He was held by a department store Santa Claus, and appeared to be laughing at the camera. Her heart was full when she saw how healthy and happy he seemed, and she knew she had made the right choice. Unexpectedly, the Buckleys sent her another picture at Easter, along with a newsy letter about his progress over the past six months. They also assured her of more photos and letters, periodically, in the future, and thanked her for her blessing them with a wonderful son.

Days became weeks, which blended into months and soon the school year ended. Maddie renewed contact with the church school in St. Louis and, as good as they promised, they offered her a position for the next academic calendar, with a contract to span three years, and the possibility of renewal at that time. She accepted the offer, knowing she could leave home once more, trusting the Lord to care for Mama who was coping much better, and getting out with her new friends.

Lizzie, on the other hand, was moving to Nebraska, to a teaching position in Omaha. She had fallen in love with the region, and felt a part of the Galloway clan. In fact, her ties were stronger to Nebraska than they'd ever felt to Southern Illinois.

Both women moved on with their new lives, Maddie in St. Louis and Lizzie in Omaha, but their bond as best friends was as strong as ever, and each time Maddie returned home for a holiday, they had fun together as always. Life was good, moving along without bumps in the road, until one day when everything changed.

Part Two

Chapter 31

Fragrant white dogwood blossoms and the prolific redbud trees midst the many oak, maple and hickory trees of the St. Louis landscape broke through the chill of early spring and announced the soon arrival of warmth and outdoor activities. Maddie was nearing the end of her first year at her new school, and was still familiarizing herself with St. Louis. Through field trips with her class, she experienced the St. Louis Science Center in Forest Park, and the Museum of Westward Expansion buried beneath the awesome Gateway Arch. On her weekends, she often chose to visit one of the many cathedrals and churches open for tourists throughout the city, and once she ventured into Laclede's Landing, a historic, riverfront region with shops, restaurants and the always fun Madame Tussaud's Wax Museum.

Learning the lay of the land and visiting the cultural sites of the city helped her adjustment to the new environment. She missed her family and, although she and Lizzie stayed connected and talked often on the phone, she was lonely. She had hoped to make friends either at work or at church, but had difficulty finding common bonds between herself and other women her age. Her life experiences over the last two years aged her beyond her peers, and left a void in her heart. She was always thrilled when she received the updates on her son from Pastor Tim, knowing she had made the right choice in placing him with his adoptive family. In every photo, she saw his growth and noticed how healthy and happy he appeared; the letters shared stories of his development and reassured her of his adoptive family's commitment to raise him in a Christian home.

Her social life was at a standstill, although she met many young people of her age group at church functions. Trust was a major issue when interacting with groups, and she often isolated herself, especially from the men. Disappointment deepened her sense of loneliness when Lizzie decided to teach in the Omaha School District rather than move to St. Louis. Maddie was certain that Lizzie would join her when her contract in Chicago was up; she had visions of them sharing an apartment or little house, and attending church together. Now she had to adjust her mind-set, realizing she was on her own, far from her family and friends.

Maddie's first-graders were impatient for the end of the school year. Restless, they sat at their desks whispering and giggling until Maddie arrived. They had learned to respect her over the past nine months, and, as usual, quieted down immediately when she walked in. She had promised a special celebration of all they accomplished in the first grade; she also promised them a trip to Forest Park, and their excitement over their last field trip was palpable.

"Class," she smiled at their fresh faces. Everyday was new and wonderful when teaching eager little children, especially in this Christian setting. "Today is the end of your first year of school, but I want you to remember one thing, don't ever stop learning! Learning is a lifelong activity, so what we did this year is just the start. Let's get our things together and head for the bus for our field trip...we have a busy day ahead, and a lot of awards to hand out."

With those instructions, the children grabbed their sack lunches and lined up at the door as they did for every outing. It took a few minutes, but they were quickly ready to file out to their waiting bus. A couple of their mothers were ready to join the group to help Maddie watch them and protect them while out at the park. One mother was hired as a bus driver by the school, so altogether there were four adults to supervise the class.

The drive from their school to the huge park was brief, less than a mile, but long enough for Maddie to glance through her briefcase and box, ensuring the gifts and prizes were all there. She did not plan to leave out a single child; they all deserved recognition, and every child would be promoted to the second grade with their friends. The driver pulled their bus into a parking lot near the World's Fair Pavilion. The children jumped up and down in excitement until Maddie clapped her hands to get their attention.

"Now, children, what did I tell you about today?"

"Stay together!" "Don't wander near the fountain!" "Listen to instructions!" "Don't talk to strangers!" They all seemed to call out together, but were somehow able to recall all her rules. The greatest challenge on any field trip was safety, and today was no different. They needed to stay together, just as if they were in a classroom, and Maddie took a head count to ensure all the children had left the bus, before the driver closed the doors and locked it. Each parent took a group of five and Maddie had four children to keep track of.

The children left the bus, each holding hands with another, following the parent in charge of their group, eager to get out on the grass for their outing. Maddie was pulling a cart loaded with everything for a picnic: large blankets, the sack lunches brought by each child along with additional treats provided by the mothers, and a large plastic drink dispenser which held lemonade enough for the entire group. Trudging along the path while she looked for a spot level enough to lay out the picnic, Maddie contemplated the summer ahead, wondering if she should stay in St. Louis or return to Omaha for the six week gap between one school year and the next. She had so much to get ready for the next term, that she was tempted to just stay in Missouri and relax while getting something accomplished.

"Teacher, Miss Galloway, look... over there by the lake..." little Lisa-Beth pointed just beyond them. A flock of Canadian geese wandered near the water, resting from their usual commute through the St. Louis area. Maddie knew they did not want to have their picnic near the birds, even though the children were excited at the sight; the geese droppings in the grass were known to pass germs to humans, with children even more affected. She acknowledged the wonder of the birds to the children, then steered them to another area, just flat enough, but away from the water fowl and the dangers of the lake.

As the other mothers helped set up the lunch, each gathering the lunch sacks for their group, the children played games nearby. Some played tag, while others watched; some of the students looked longingly back at the geese, but obeyed her instructions to stay close.

They all joined together in prayer, "God is great; God is good; let us thank Him for this food; Amen." Quietly eating their food, Maddie had the opportunity to relax, too. Just as she was about to pull out the awards, something caught her eye. Walking along the path was a mother pushing a stroller. She looked vaguely familiar, but was too far for Maddie to see clearly. Maddie thought it looked like Suzanne Buckley from her church back home, but that couldn't be.

Suzanne and Jim didn't have a child; they were the couple who tragically lost their baby in that accident, Maddie thought. As the woman got closer, however, Maddie realized it was Suzanne. She couldn't go over to talk to her because the children were waiting expectantly for their prizes. Maddie smiled and waved as Suzanne walked by, then turned back to her charges, thinking how happy Suzanne looked.

Could they have adopted so soon after their loss? Maddie wondered as she started handing out the awards: Best Speller, Best Reader, Best in Sports, Best in Teamwork... She'd thought of twenty different 'Bests' that she could award, so every child would get recognition. With each certificate she gave a Dollar Store toy that related to the award, and the children were thrilled to receive them, even though they were modest little gifts.

Could they have adopted her baby boy? She contemplated when she started calling out names for the 'Graduation Diploma she'd made on her computer. Somehow she could not get the site of Suzanne with the baby buggie out of her mind. It didn't make sense, but then, maybe it did. After all, how did Pastor Tim find a family so quickly if it wasn't someone he knew personally? And why did they need the adoption agreement modified to accommodate a move out of the area? *Maybe, just maybe...* Maddie's mind kept spinning thoughts.

It seemed an eternity since she saw Suzanne walk by, when the picnic ended. They packed up all the gear, and the children each held their papers and toys, and they loaded back into the bus. Once back at the school, their parents met them, since it was a half day, and Maddie said goodbye to them for the last time as her class of children. She went into her classroom to cleaning up and head home, still thinking on the day's events.

She began thinking about how she could locate the Buckleys; she could check for a phone listing, but if they were unlisted that would be fruitless. Then she thought about church. What if she could find the church they attended? They probably went to one of the others in town of their denomination. Maddie decided then and there that she would attend every church in the region until she found Jim and Suzanne. She needed to find out if they were the adoptive parents of her little boy, although she didn't know what she would do with the information, if it turned out to be true.

Chapter 32

Lizzie had found a niche in the Galloway family, and enjoyed the church they attended whenever she visited on school holidays. She felt such acceptance from Mrs. Galloway and the other kids, which helped ease the pain of not knowing about her own family. Before she told Maddie of her decision, Liz had already applied to Omaha for a job, and given her notice of resignation to the school in Chicago. Convinced that a town the size of Omaha would have nowhere near the problems she saw in Cabrini-Green, she looked forward to the transition and was ready to send out feelers for apartments or small houses for rent. If the Galloways lived closer to Omaha, she might have considered asking to rent one of their rooms, but that was not a plausible option.

Mrs. Galloway loved Lizzie and truly enjoyed her visits. They lessened her loneliness for Maddie, when distance or weather prevented her return over the school breaks. Her breaks often did not coincide with Lizzie's so, often, Mrs. Galloway had the benefit of double visits from the young women. She found a friendship developing between them and herself on a more adult level than she enjoyed with her teen-agers and children. The loneliness of widowhood frequently hit hard during holiday seasons that year and, if not for her volunteer work with the church Ladies Society, she might have been overcome with depression. However, she saw the helpless and needy as she gave of her time, and realized how truly blessed she was to have a loving bunch of kids.

Lizzie finished off her year at Cabrini-Green and packed up her few possessions from her desk and locker. Because she'd been preparing for this move for several months, she had very little to collect, and soon had her car loaded and heading for her apartment. Even her apartment was fairly empty considering how much she once had it furnished with. The furniture belonged to the landlord, and Lizzie had only added those items she needed to live comfortably, like dishes and pans, decorations and knick-knacks, but even the addition of those items had filled it up giving it the feeling of home.

To clear out her apartment in preparation for the move, she either gave away or sold various items so she would not have to rent a U-haul. With no sentimental value attached, it wasn't hard for her to part with most of the stuff. She weeded it down to some boxes that she had already taken to the Galloways, and the remainder that she would add to the load in her car. She planned to spend the summer with the Galloway family and use the time getting familiar with Omaha as well as finding a place to live.

Lizzie arrived in Nebraska in early June to the news that Maddie had decided to stay in St. Louis for the summer break. She could not believe that Maddie wasn't coming home for even a few weeks, and wondered at her friend's choice to isolate herself from family and friends. *Had she met someone and not told me?* Lizzie wondered. When she talked with Mrs. Galloway that evening, though, no mention of a boyfriend was even hinted at in Maddie's letters home.

Was she suffering with depression again? Lizzie mused. Then she realized how little she knew of Maddie's life in Missouri. She hadn't even visited Maddie there before choosing to teach in Omaha; she had not even explored St. Louis as a possibility, and she knew why. Although she wouldn't admit it to anyone else, she was fascinated by Pastor Tim. From the moment she met him, he had captured her attention. Now she just wished she could catch his eye.

Suddenly, she decided she would go to St. Louis for the Fourth of July and spend a week with Maddie. At least that way, she couldn't say Lizzie had neglected to check out Missouri. After telling Mrs. Galloway of her plans, and receiving a warm endorsement from her, Lizzie called Maddie to solidify the arrangement. Maddie seemed thrilled with Lizzie's idea, and they talked long into the night.

The next day Lizzie got on-line and booked her flight from Omaha to Lambert International Airport in St. Louis, and sent a copy to Maddie's email address so Maddie could make plans to pick her up on the first of July. That left just three weekends at the Galloways; just three weekends to see Pastor Tim at church, and Lizzie wanted to make the most of her time there. The church had a number of activities planned for the weekends in the summer months for the young people of the church, which included those in their twenties, like Lizzie. Pastor Tim always came along and, although Liz did not know exactly how old he was, she was glad he did.

They went roller skating one Saturday evening, and Pastor Tim partnered with her several times, although she saw him skate with several other young women, too. Unless he asked her on a date, she didn't place much stock in the attention she received. She figured he was just being nice by skating with each of the girls in turn.

On another occasion, they all went out bowling. Lizzie wasn't much good at rolling the ball down the lane without it heading for the gutter. Then Pastor Tim came over to give her some hints to help her get it down to the pins. She flushed at his interest in her game and her nerves sizzled when his hand touched hers as he showed her how to position herself for a strike. She did start picking up a couple of pins each time after using his pointers. It seemed strange to have a man show any interest in her, and she didn't know how to flirt like some women did, so she just enjoyed the game and socialization.

The last Sunday before she was to head to St. Louis, someone arranged for an old-fashioned hay-ride on Sunday after potluck, and Lizzie was delighted when Pastor Tim asked her to sit beside him. He helped her up onto the back of the wagon, and climbed up next to her. As the horses pulled off, the wagon jerked, and Pastor Tim reached his arm around Lizzie's waist to stabilize her. He didn't move it once they were on their way, though, choosing to just keep her close to him, which left Lizzie speechless and blushing.

"Lizzie, I was wondering if we could go out on a date sometime," he asked suddenly, so softly she wondered if she had imagined him speaking. She looked up at him and he raised his eyebrows as if expecting an answer.

"Sure…I mean… I'd love to, but I am leaving town this week…"

"You are? Where are you going, if you don't mind my asking, that is?"

"I am going to spend some time with Maddie, in St. Louis," Lizzie replied, surprised at finding her voice.

"How nice!" he said the words, but his voice echoed disappointment.

"But I will be back in just a week…"

Pastor Tim brightened up and smiled at her. "Oh, that is wonderful! Give Maddie my regards when you go there, will you?"

Lizzie nodded, wondering if he perked up because of mention of Maddie, or because her visit was only a week long. She hoped it was the latter, because she still felt a little envious of his initial interest in Maddie; she wanted him to like her, to be interested in dating her, not as a second choice, but because he liked her. *Anyway*, Lizzie thought, *at least he asked me out.*

"So, I'll give you a call when you get back in town, if that's alright, that is..."

Tim was still praying that God would help him in his social life. He longed for a wife, for children to complete his picture of happiness on earth, but he wanted to be sure it was done according to God's plan for his life, not his own desires. In his mind's eye, he could see himself with Lizzie, but he wanted to hear affirmation from the Lord before he got too serious with her. He would spend the time while she was away praying more seriously than ever, and listening for God's answer to his pleas.

Chapter 33

Suzanne and Jim adapted well to life in St. Louis. As little Ben grew and began to walk, the challenges of parenting him and keeping him occupied increased, but Suzanne counted it all joy. She could not imagine life without their little boy, though on the occasion of the birth of Sammy, she did wonder what he might have been like, if he had lived. With Ben's birthday so close to Sammy's it was easy to imagine the two of them playing together, until reality hit. She remembered that they probably would not have adopted little Ben if Sammy had lived. It was at times like this that Suzanne found diversion in outdoor activities welcoming.

Suzanne often used Forest Park as a place of reflection at other times, taking Bennie for a walk by herself during the week. She remembered the time she saw that class having a picnic, back in late May, and the teacher waved to her. She looked familiar, but Suzanne did not recall where they'd ever met. Perhaps it was just in passing somewhere, but that teacher seemed pretty sure of their acquaintance, so maybe they ran into each other at church or in connection with Jim's job. Finally, she let the matter drop; she didn't figure she would ever run into that teacher again.

Suzanne looked forward to their family walks in Forest Park; they often used the visits to Forest Park as a chance to renew their relationship although, on some occasions, Jim would actually jog through the park as Suzanne and Bennie followed with her pushing his stroller. But, at other times, they would let Bennie run ahead, playing on the grass or chasing pigeons, as they strolled together like a courting couple.

Spring melded into summer and with the Fourth of July looming, so was anticipation of Bennie's second birthday. They had had the usual celebration for his first birthday, with the cake that he demolished and other children from the church playing games and having more fun than Ben. He ended up taking a nap shortly after taking a bath to wash off all the frosting and cake, while the rest of the party continued without him.

Suzanne was determined to include him more in the celebration of his second birthday, and spent a great deal of time finding games that he could play along with the other preschoolers from church. She took pictures for his baby book, and enjoyed watching her toddler as he tried to keep up with the bigger kids. Children and parents alike enjoyed the party setting in the Buckley's backyard, and the social benefit was wonderful. Suzanne was exhausted by the end of the day, but enjoyed a sense of accomplishment with all the participation in her 'Give a Gift' project. Rather than bringing gifts for Ben, church families were asked to bring gifts suitable for any age group, wrapped and labeled for boys or girls.

Suzanne had made arrangements for all gifts to be left wrapped and to be donated to a local shelter for children of women running from abuse. She was actively involved with the local program, helping women adjust to a life away from the abusive spouse or boyfriend. Occasionally, she monitored the 24-hour help line that women called for information; she felt good knowing she was making a difference, but experienced a desire to do more, to learn more about counseling and helping families in need.

She considered going back to school, but did not want to leave Ben with a sitter. Perhaps when he was school-aged, she might consider it. She didn't think life could be much better, and decided that school could wait. Her priorities were set in stone…Jesus, others, including her beloved family, and then herself. Suzanne delighted in motherhood and all that entailed; she also loved keeping a wonderful home for Jim and Ben.

Jim's new job was going well; he advanced to a senior position within six months of their arrival in St. Louis, and future promotions were nearly guaranteed. His joy with fatherhood overflowed to his dealings with his subordinates and co-workers, and he was well-liked by all. The daily commute from West County to Clayton was long and arduous, but well worth it when he considered the beautiful home and surroundings in which they were raising Bennie. Seeing how happy his little boy was, and the joy Suzanne had in decorating their home and caring for little Ben made any sacrifice worthwhile.

Jim really liked the fact that he could provide for his family well enough that Suzanne did not have to work, that she could spend time with Bennie and with her various church groups. His only concern was her health. She seemed more fragile than he liked; she had lost weight since they moved, although she chalked it up to the stress of the move. She also seemed more fatigued, but she denied this, claiming to be a typical mom with a toddler to chase after.

He wasn't convinced, however, and his concern grew as he watched her for several months. She became even more fragile until finally, she agreed to see the doctor for some tests. Bennie had a well-baby check scheduled just after his second birthday, and they went together to hear the pediatrician praise their parenting skills. Bennie was on target for growth and development for his age; he was even advanced in his language skills for his age, able to count to ten and sing his ABC's with only a few misses. After that appointment, in the same building, Suzanne had her scheduled check-up.

After taking her history and a cursory examination, the doctor asked Suzanne to put on a gown for the remainder of the physical. She was due her well-woman exam, anyway, so Jim took Bennie to the waiting room to allow her the privacy needed for the exam. Bennie kept himself busy with some toys they brought along, but Jim worried as he watched the happy, little fellow. What if something was wrong with Suzanne? His heart told him she was sick; he just didn't know what it could be, and he was totally unprepared for the results of this visit.

"Honey, what's wrong?" Suzanne's face was pale, ashen, her eyes bloodshot as if she'd been crying. Her shirt was buttoned crookedly and her hair was messy, like she hadn't bothered to run a comb through it when she dressed in the exam room. It frightened Jim to see her so disheveled. Suzanne was always so put together…except when she went through her depression during their attempt at having a baby. "Suz…? Say something, hon. Bennie is getting scared."

Bennie stood at her feet, raising his pudgy arms to Suzanne, "Mommy, you ok?" His big brown eyes looked even bigger as he gazed adoringly at his mommy. He looked like a miniature farmer in his blue-jean overall and striped T-shirt. One of Jim's old baseball caps covered his auburn hair and sat with the brim hanging down his back as he looked up at Suzanne. The wrinkles in his smooth forehead touched her heart.

"Suzanne, what did Dr. Campbell say? Does he know what is wrong with you?"

"He is concerned about something he found during my exam," she answered quietly in a monotone voice. "He doesn't want to say for sure until he does more tests." She reached down and picked Bennie up; she cuddled his face close to hers and he reached up a tiny hand to rub her cheek gently.

"Mommy, you ok?" he asked again as he patted her back with his other hand, and her eyes filled with tears as she pressed her cheek to his head.

With his hand in the small of her back, Jim led Suzanne to chairs along the wall in the waiting room. The buzz of voices and hum of elevator music faded into the background as he focused on her and her needs. Sitting with his knees near hers, and holding her hands in his, he tried again to get Suzanne to talk about what the doctor said that had her so upset.

"Ok, honey, what did he say? Did you tell him all your symptoms?"

"Yes, Jim. I told him about my low back pain, the bloating, and my weight loss. As a matter of fact, he asked me if I had anorexia because of my weight loss...that was before I could tell him the other symptoms." Jim nodded to encourage her. "So then he did the physical exam. Everything was alright until he did the pelvic...even though I had the hysterectomy he needed to check my ovaries that they left in." Suzanne paused, hesitating for a moment before continuing.

"He said he felt a lump, a mass he called it...he had me go down the hall to the ultrasound room, and the technician did an ultrasound right away. It showed the mass by my right ovary, and it doesn't look like a cyst, so then Dr. Campbell ordered an abdominal CAT scan, which is scheduled for the day after tomorrow. He also had the nurse draw some blood, but I don't know what he is looking for."

Jim was taken back by this news. He thought Suzanne had something simple like irritable bowel syndrome or something, but a mass? *Did this mean cancer? Or was it just a benign tumor?* He needed to talk to the doctor, but didn't want Suzanne to think he was panicking. He tried to reassure her and maintain a sense of calm as they got ready to go to the car. "I'll be there in a second, Suz," he guided her to the door, and as she went out, he returned to the receptionist desk. "Could you leave a message for Dr. Campbell to call me?" he asked, and the receptionist took his contact information and promised to leave the note for the doctor.

Later that afternoon, while Suzanne took a rest and Bennie was down for his nap, the phone rang; it was Dr. Campbell.

"Jim, sorry I didn't get back to you sooner," he began, but Jim interrupted him.

"Doc, what's going on with Suzanne? She didn't seem to understand what you are looking for…"

"Jim, I think she understood. She just doesn't want to face what I told her. I am concerned about the mass near her right ovary. Now, it may be benign, just like I told her, but there is the risk that it could be a malignancy, too, so I am ordering a battery of tests. Depending on what we find, I may refer her to a specialist that deals with gynecological cancers."

"Whoa! Cancer? What makes you go in that direction so fast? Aren't you over-reacting to a little bump in her tummy? I mean, you haven't even gotten the test results yet, and already you are talking 'cancer'?" Jim's heart beat rapidly; he felt like he was suffocating.

"Jim, we look at the whole picture, and Suzanne presents with what we in medicine call textbook constitutional symptoms: the bloating, the back pain and, what concerns me the most, the weight loss. Sudden, unexplained weight loss is, until proven otherwise, a red flag for cancer. I don't mean to scare you unnecessarily, but I also have to be honest, and I have a bad feeling about this."

Jim sat staring at the phone... "Jim, are you there?" He heard Dr. Campbell's voice in the distance and realized he'd dropped the handset from his ear. "Yes, I'm here. Sorry. I just need time to absorb this. Guess, once the tests are done, we'll have a better idea of what we're dealing with."

Jim didn't want to hear anymore from Dr. Campbell; he heard little Ben stirring in the bedroom which gave him an excuse to get off the phone. Dr. Campbell promised to keep him informed as the test results came in, and reluctantly let him go. Just seeing Bennie standing in his crib warmed Jim's heart, but also made him want to cry. He knew how much Suzanne longed to be a mother, and how much joy she felt with every new thing Bennie learned. *What would happen to her dreams if she did have cancer?* He also felt guilty, wondering if the fertility medicines had had something to do with the development of this mass.

"Jim, why are you just standing there looking at Bennie?" Suzanne walked up behind him, touching his shoulder. "What's wrong?"

Jim turned to her and took her in his arms; he snuggled his face into her warm hair, smelling the scent of shampoo, and enjoying how she fit so perfectly in his embrace. Bennie seemed to enjoy seeing his parents hug because he began to gurgle and giggle, reaching over the side of the crib toward them. They both smiled as they saw his cherubic smile and heard his adoring, "Mommy...Daddy..." as he reached out to them.

Suzanne looked at Jim knowingly. "We'll talk later." And Jim just nodded. An unspoken agreement to not show worries in front of Bennie gave them strength to move on with their evening plans. They were going to Forest Park for a walk to enjoy the sunny late summer day with their son, and nothing was going to get in the way of those plans. They would talk more later, after Bennie was down for the night, and Suzanne knew their talk would be mixed with tears, because just thinking about it brought sorrow to her heart.

Chapter 34

Pastor Tim made every effort to include Mrs. Galloway and others with bereavement issues in his visitation ministry. Knowing that loss often isolates a member, causing them to avoid church attendance and other activities, he made concerted efforts to encourage and build relationships with each one, and to encourage fellowship between them for a support system of sorts. Through his visits to the Galloway home, he often saw Lizzie's presence, and sensed the importance of her friendship to Mrs. Galloway.

Her gentleness with Mrs. Galloway and the love she gave to the Galloway children spoke to her loving nature, and Pastor Tim appreciated that aspect of her character. She was living out the verse from James 1:27 that said, "Pure religion and undefiled before God and the Father is this, To visit the fatherless and widows in their affliction, and to keep himself unspotted from the world." In Tim's mind, there was no character trait more important that this in a pastor's wife.

He watched Lizzie from a distance for some time, although he felt a certain attraction to her. Not only was she pleasing to look at, and she did not seem to know it, but her interactions with others were never flirtatious or frivolous, as some other women were. He also enjoyed the time they shared during the various outings with the young people. Group dates always seemed safer when beginning a relationship, and even at his age, he thought it more proper, especially in his position as pastor. The last thing he wanted was to come across as forward or impetuous in relationships, and he certainly did not want to give gossips fodder for their activity. He continued asking for God's guidance as he prayed for a helpmeet to aid his ministry and with whom he could enjoy companionship and parenthood.

At thirty, Pastor Tim was feeling pressure to marry; congregations didn't always trust a minister without a family. They often felt he could not understand the pressures of marriage and family life and, therefore, could not counsel them on those issues. Despite all the education he had in counseling, theology, and sociology, without a family to solidify his position, he would soon receive less interest from other churches in need of a pastor. It wasn't just his ministry that concerned him, however.

He was experiencing a sense of angst whenever he saw a father with his son; he yearned to fill that roll with a son of his own. Women called this feeling their 'biological clock'. Perhaps it was the same for men, he didn't know. All he knew was that he felt he was missing a vital part toward completion. Paul counseled the Corinthians to remain unmarried like him, if possible, but then he added that it was better to marry than to burn.

In other words, Tim thought, *if the desire to have a wife filled your heart, don't let that desire overtake you, but through prayer, make your desire known to God, and if it is His will, you would know. How long should I continue asking, Lord? When will I know for sure?* The more time he spent with Lizzie, the more certain he was that she might be God's answer to his longing. So, after her return from St. Louis, he approached her to ask her out on a private date.

"Lizzie, would you have dinner with me Saturday evening," he took her aside at the potluck to ask her privately, just in case she turned him down.

Lizzie's eyes glowed brightly as her smile traveled from her lips to encompass her entire face. Her cheeks flushed ever so slightly, giving her a most appealing warmth that made Pastor' Tim's heart twitter in a way he hadn't experienced before. It took his breath away, and felt like a butterfly flitting between his heart and his stomach.

"I'd love to, Pastor," she replied as she lowered her eyes shyly.

"Hey, I think if we are going on a date, we need to move past that pastor thing… think you could just call me Tim?"

Again she flushed, this time deeper from her neck upwards. "Of course." She replied, and between them they set the time for him to pick her up from the Buckley home. Tim left the potluck feeling like he was floating, and Lizzie's excitement was visible to all the Galloway family.

"Lizzie's got a boyfriend!" exclaimed the twins from the back seat of the family sedan.

"Jason! Jamie! Shame on you! Don't give our Lizzie a hard time, now." Mama reprimanded them, but her eyes smiled as she looked into the rearview mirror. She was just as happy as they were to see that Lizzie was going out on a date, and with the Pastor at that!

Samantha scowled beside the twins. She wanted Pastor Tim for her sister, and felt that Lizzie had taken advantage of Maddie's absence. She didn't share in the celebratory teasing, but held her peace. Since Daddy died, everything seemed wrong; she could not find joy in anything, and everyone else seemed to have just moved on without a thought for Daddy. Even Mommy was going to her meetings and getting involved at church again. It wasn't fair, and she wasn't going to pretend it was!

Simon sat on the other side of the twins, quietly looking out the window. He would soon graduate high school, and was exploring options for college. Before long he would move on into adulthood, and he didn't have time to worry about Lizzie's social life, or the twins teasing her. He was focused, determined to make his parents proud, and nothing would deter him from that road.

Lizzie called Maddie that evening to tell her the news. She also wanted to be sure that Maddie wasn't interested in Pastor Tim. After all, she had seen him first. And Lizzie thought some sparks had flown between Pastor Tim and Maddie in the beginning. She was happy to hear Maddie's unreserved approval of her going on a date with Tim (*It seemed strange to think of him without his title*.)

"Oh, Liz, I think that is wonderful! Do you know where he is taking you? What are you going to wear?" Maddie had a dozen questions, and she and Lizzie talked for hours. At the end of the conversation, Lizzie tried again to find out why Maddie seemed so quiet of late, but again she had no success. Maddie staunchly denied that anything was up; all she wanted was time to prepare for the next school year, without a trip back home to interrupt, or so she said. Lizzie let it go, too excited to dwell too long on Maddie's secretiveness.

Saturday night came, and Lizzie was ready by 6:30pm, although Tim wouldn't be over until 7:00pm. She had on an emerald green gown of soft velvet with braided straps of gold and green. The effect of the green against her pale skin was remarkable, and her eyes looked green with the reflected beauty of the color. Over her shoulders she wore a lightweight bolero-style jacket in gold lamé fabric. The silkiness of the bolero with the softness of the velvet yielded a pleasing result, and Lizzie felt like a princess waiting for her prince charming. She even wore matching mules with three inch heels... a bit hard to walk in, but again the end product was one of height and elegance.

Tim dressed up for the dinner with Lizzie. He had reservations at a restaurant in the Old Market district in Omaha. He had heard that some of the best restaurants in the city were found in that historic region, and he wanted to impress Lizzie on their evening out. His newly cleaned and pressed dark grey suit with a solid gold tie provided him with a different image than the one she saw weekly on the pulpit, conservatively dressed to please even the oldest church member. He had been anticipating this date for days, and now that it was time to pick Lizzie up from the Galloway home, he had a case of nerves. He took one deep breath and went out the door to his car; he was on his way.

As he drove to the Galloways, he let his mind wander from his date to the news he had received earlier that day from Jim Buckley. Pastor Tim had maintained contact with the Buckley family in order to ensure a connection between them and Maddie. He received their updates and photos and promptly forwarded them on to Maddie in a new envelope to prevent her knowledge of their place of residence, as agreed upon in the adoption papers. He often wished he could let her know just how close she was to her son, but the wisdom of her not knowing guided his actions, and he resisted that temptation.

This time the contact was not about their little boy; Jim Buckley had called with concerns about Suzanne. Pastor Tim heard it in Jim's voice before he spoke the dreaded word, cancer. Although it was not a foregone conclusion (they were still waiting for test results) it was enough of a worry to warrant a call to initiate the prayer chain. Tim called his most stalwart prayer warriors to set the process in motion, and immediately knelt in prayer for the young family before he prepared for this date. Despite not wanting his concerns to impact his date with Lizzie, he wondered how much he should share with her. It would be difficult to just enjoy being with her. After all, if he was considering her as a serious contender in his search for a wife, perhaps he needed to test the waters, perhaps sharing concerns with her would reveal just how she might respond if she was a pastor's wife.

Chapter 35

Suzanne and Jim, together, faced the tests Dr. Campbell needed in order to give an accurate diagnosis. The first step was the CAT scan; the blood-work had yet to come back, and hopefully both the lab and the radiologist would get their results to Dr. Campbell before the next follow-up visit. The stress of not knowing was almost worse than the possibilities they faced in the event of a bad diagnosis. At least, once they knew, they could plan a course of action, look at treatment options, and know what was ahead.

Jim had called Pastor Tim to give him a heads-up on what was going on. They needed all the prayers they could rally, so Jim enlisted both of his parents and Suzanne's, as well as those faithful prayer warriors in their church back in Nebraska. From past experiences, he knew the mighty power of prayer, and in many ways this was so much worse than what happened in the past. He was afraid he might lose his precious Suzanne. Now they had to get the results of tests that might confirm that fear, and he felt sick to his stomach.

"Jim, Suzanne, come on in," Dr. Campbell shook their hands and motioned to the two chairs in front of his desk. "As you know, we have more information now, with the results of both the lab work and the CT scan in."

"OK, Doc, give it to us straight," Jim sat forward in his seat, while Suzanne seemed to disappear into the cushy chair. "What are we dealing with, and how can we beat it?"

"As you know, we drew blood for one specific test – the CA -125 levels in Suzanne's blood. Although not diagnostic, it helps us understand if we are dealing with the possibility of cancer, because it is often elevated with ovarian cancer. The problem is, there can be false positives, too."

"Well, why draw it then?" Jim asked impatiently, "I mean... if it is known to give ambiguous results, why bother?"

"Like I said, it adds to the other information." Dr. Campbell was a very patient man. He looked at Suzanne to ensure she was in on the conversation. In the past, doctors would talk with family and not explain things to patients for fear of adverse psychological effects, but he was of the generation that believed in full disclosure. "We also did a CBC where we look at the blood to see what types of cells are there; a differential counts the varieties of white cells, specifically, to make sure you have the right proportions of each. As I expected, you are severely anemic." Jim started to interrupt, but Dr. Campbell stopped him with a raised hand, " I anticipated this after Suzanne shared how fatigued she'd been, and after noticing the remarkable weight loss."

"Doc, please. Can we skip all these details, and just get down to the diagnosis? Does Suzanne have ovarian cancer or not?" Jim really was getting impatient with the flow of the conversation.

"Jim, I feel I need to go over all the tests so you will both have a better understanding of what we are dealing with. If I just stood up and gave you a diagnosis, you would want to know how I arrived at that conclusion. I prefer to lay the groundwork, then talk diagnosis and, if necessary or possible, treatment."

Suzanne nodded ever so slightly, indicating her agreement with Dr. Campbell's approach, so Jim sat back in his seat as if preparing for a college lecture. He also nodded for Dr. Campbell to continue, and promised himself that he would stay quiet for now.

"We also did a Chem-24, which yielded very little in the way of specific information, aside from the fact that your electrolytes are somewhat off. Now, here is the big part, the CAT scan. The CT showed us that we are indeed dealing with ovarian cancer. Cancer cells appear to have spread to tissues outside the pelvis and to the regional lymph nodes. Small cluster of cancer cells were also found on the outside of the liver. There is also a fluid collection in pelvic area which may be contributing to the sensation of fullness you experience." He paused for a minute seemingly deep in thought. "We need to do a laparoscopy to be sure, but it seems we are dealing with Stage III Ovarian Cancer. It comes in stages 0 – IV, although Stage III has three divisions. The laparoscopy will determine for sure, what division Suzanne falls into, then we can plan treatment accordingly."

Jim had no more questions, at least none that the doctor could answer. Right now, his questions were for God. *How could God let this happen, knowing what trials we have already endured?* He wondered at the injustice of it all. He wanted to shout at God; he wanted to ask why? He held back his tears, trying to be strong for Suzanne.

Suzanne seemed to be taking the news in stride. Jim thought she would fall apart with this diagnosis, but evidently she had gone through the shock and disbelief already and was accepting the news well. She did not perk up, but neither did she break down.

"I need to get home to Bennie," she said quietly.

"We need to schedule the surgery..." Dr. Campbell began.

"No," she shook her head and moved toward the door, "Right now, I just need to be with my son; he needs me." And without another word, she exited his office and headed toward the car.

Jim shook his head in disbelief to Dr. Campbell, and told him they would call in a day or so to schedule the surgery. Then he hurried after Suzanne, let her into the car, and they silently drove home to relieve the sitter, a neighbor who was kind enough to watch Bennie during his nap.

Chapter 36

Everywhere she went in St. Louis, Maddie found herself looking into the faces of two year old boys, searching for the auburn hair and big brown eyes of her son. She watched adults, too, trying to find Jim and Suzanne Buckley. She spent time visiting the favorite sites in town for parents with toddlers: the St. Louis Zoo and the Botanical Gardens were two choices that she preferred. She never did sight a child or family even resembling the Buckleys, but she didn't give up easily.

She began to wonder if she had really seen Suzanne or if it was just her wishful thinking. Even if she had seen her, maybe they didn't live here… maybe they were just visiting from Omaha… people did visit St. Louis on vacations. But then she thought of how casual Suzanne looked, and the fact that Jim was not with her. If they were on a vacation, they would be together sightseeing. No, they must live in St. Louis, and Maddie was determined to find them. She needed to know if they were the adoptive parents of her little boy.

She did take a short recess from her search when Lizzie came to visit. Maddie enjoyed her visit with Lizzie over the Fourth of July; they went to the VP Fair and watched the fireworks over the Mississippi River from a spot on the steps at the waterfront. Altogether it was an enjoyable time, but Maddie could not get her mind off Suzanne and the stroller.

She had visited several churches in St. Louis of the same denomination, but had yet to see either of the Buckleys. Lizzie's visit put a temporary stop to those efforts, because Maddie did not want to tell her what she was doing. It was too personal, and Maddie had a hard time understanding her own motivation. After all, she had given the baby up for adoption; just what would she accomplish from knowing if the Buckleys were indeed the adoptive parents?

She just couldn't let it go, though, and she started looking through local phone books trying to see if James Buckley or Suzanne Buckley was listed. When that yielded nothing, she thought to widen her search. Maddie had come to realize that when people said they were from St. Louis, or lived in St. Louis, they might actually live in one of the suburbs as far south as Fenton, as far west as Wentzville, or even in what was known as Metro-east – Southern Illinois as far as thirty miles into the state. It was impossible to find all the telephone directories for all the hamlets in between these corners of the St. Louis metropolitan area, so Maddie launched an Internet search.

Why hadn't I thought of this earlier? She wondered. *There is so much information on the Net… I'm sure to find them this time.*

Despite all her efforts, Maddie was unable to locate Jim and Suzanne Buckley. Each time she found a James or Jim Buckley on the Internet, it turned out to be someone other than the couple she knew from Nebraska. She felt like she was at a dead end. The only one who really knew where Jim and Suzanne lived was Pastor Tim, and he wouldn't break their confidence, even if she asked. Maddie realized she had become somewhat obsessed with the whole idea of finding them and her son, and for what?

She spent more time searching for them than she did with the Lord these days, and her spiritual life was suffering as a result. Although she attended church looking for them, she totally missed the messages because she was too focused on looking around the sanctuary, looking for her son. She realized she had not really released him when she gave him up for adoption. A part of her still thought she might be able to see him, maybe even get to know him, like she originally planned when the open adoption was suggested, but the modified plan put an end to that, and she needed to accept it.

Late one evening, shortly before the start of the new school year, she could hear the cicadas in the trees and in the clear sky she saw the multitude of stars winking at her as she walked around her neighborhood. The crisp air announced the soon arrival of autumn and she knew she needed to clear her mind in preparation for teaching the new group of children. The stars seemed to talk to her; just as God had promised Abram of old that his children would number like the stars, she felt the Lord telling her that she, too, would have more children, other children. She needed to let her son go, and be at peace and when she got home, the first thing she did was kneel down in prayer.

"Oh, Lord, I am sorry for letting something take the place of You in my heart. I placed my son ahead of my relationship with You and I need Your forgiveness and help. Help me to release him to the adoptive parents, whoever they are. And if Jim and Suzanne are his parents, bless them Lord, and help them to raise him to know You, as I would have done. "

She talked to God for a long time, praising the way He had helped her forget the man who forced her, who fathered the baby, enough so she could feel love in her heart for her child. She talked to the Lord about her yearnings, her lack of trust, her loneliness. She laid everything before Him and, by the time she was finished, she was exhausted, but at peace. She fell into her bed safe in the assurance that she could move on with her life.

Early the next morning, she placed a call home, to Lizzie. "I'm coming there for Labor Day weekend," she announced, "I need to see everyone... I've been so lonely."

Lizzie was amazed at the change in Maddie's voice, but she too had news for Maddie. Her dates with Pastor Tim had increased in frequency, and she hadn't told Maddie a thing about them. They talked about nothing in particular, making plans to get together, and then Liz handed the phone to Mrs. Galloway who was thrilled to hear that Maddie was coming home. She, too, wondered at Maddie's absence and infrequent contact. She worried about her eldest, concerned that she had had to grow up too quickly and too far from them, and was now unable to be with the family like before. However, she was glad that Lizzie was there for Maddie. Labor Day promised to be just like old times where they could sit and laugh, talk and share, and renew their friendship once again.

Chapter 37

Lizzie had been glad to return to Omaha after the Fourth of July, and back to the place she had begun to think of as home, the Galloway's home. Maddie had seemed so distant, so quiet, during her visit, that Lizzie did not enjoy the time as she thought she would. She could not tell if it was truly depression affecting Maddie, or if something else was on her mind. It was the first time since their friendship started that Lizzie was unable to read Maddie. And it was the first time Maddie chose not to share her thoughts and concerns with Lizzie, leaving Lizzie feeling isolated and unneeded.

Now, with Maddie coming there for the Labor Day weekend, Lizzie was all in a twitter. She couldn't believe her friend was back to normal, or at least closer to it than she'd been in a long time. Lizzie had so much to tell her; her summer had proven to be very eventful, and up until now Lizzie had not even told Mrs. Galloway everything that transpired on her dates with Pastor Tim.

Her first 'real' date with him was magical; they went to the Market District in Omaha and ate at a wonderful steak restaurant with private booths and dim lighting. They appeared to be just another couple when they drove up and allowed the valet service park their car. He was striking in his suit, and without realizing it, he had chosen a tie that matched her outfit to perfection. Lizzie wondered at the glances they got from other patrons. Was it how they looked, like a prince with his princess? Or did they know he was a pastor out on a date?

Whatever the reason for the stares, it was romantic, and something Lizzie was unprepared for. She knew he was taking her to dinner, but did not know that romance was in the works. After all, even though she'd been acquainted with Tim for more than a year, they never talked about feelings or emotions. It had been superficial, more like good friends at least that was how Lizzie thought Pastor Tim saw it.

She definitely had feelings for Tim. Each time his hand touched her, even brushing lightly without intention, it sent electric shockwaves through her. Her heart beat so rapidly whenever he came into a room that she thought it would leap out of her chest. Yes, she had feelings for Tim like she'd never had for a man before. She avoided the dating game in high school… too much drama in her life already without complicating it with boys. Then, in college, she was more intent on her education and less interested in the complexities of dating, so she only dated sporadically and usually as a double date or in a group.

Once she was out in the world, so to speak, and teaching, she thought about the type of man she would be interested in, but there never seemed to be one that met her standards. She wanted a Christian young man, first and foremost, and it seemed most of them found their spouses while still in college. There were very few available in her age group, at least not at her church. That was until now. Pastor Tim was everything she wanted in a husband.

Lizzie loved his sense of humor, the laughter lit up his eyes before escaping his lips. She enjoyed discussion of literature and music with him, as well as the occasional debate on politics. Most of all, she admired his sensitivity in dealing with his church members. He was always at their disposal, never turned away a prayer request, and when he saw a need he could meet he would. If he didn't know how to help, he would find someone who could. He often put the needs of others ahead of his own, which she noticed on occasions when he lacked enough sleep or missed meals because he had errands to run.

During their dinner date, initially, Tim made small talk, but soon the conversation turned serious. She remembered how tears filled his eyes as he shared the difficulties of the Buckley family. He mentioned that they had adopted a little boy about two years before after the tragedy of their car accident, and how happy they were. Now they were facing an even greater challenge and needed the prayers of the congregation. Tim asked Lizzie if she would pray with him, and she nodded.

Right there, in the middle of a luxurious, romantic restaurant, he took Lizzie's hands in his and bowed his head. She was surprised at first; she thought he meant for her to pray for the Buckley's in a collective way – with him and the congregation in their personal prayers, but he meant right then and there! Lizzie dipped her head and listened as he pleaded with the Lord for the health of Suzanne Buckley and for the family in general. His prayer was so heart-felt that even Lizzie had tears in her eyes when he said "Amen".

Although there was nothing remarkable about the rest of the evening – both Lizzie and Tim ate in silence – the shared prayer experience seemed to bond them in a way that was unexpected. Tim realized that Lizzie was truly someone with whom he could see himself making a lifetime commitment, and Lizzie accepted for the first time that, not only was she attracted to Tim, she was truly in love with him.

Their subsequent dates were even more intense, if that was possible. Tim shared his hopes and dreams for the future, including his desire for a family, with Lizzie, opening up a little more with each date. He was never inappropriate with Lizzie, only touching her hand during a conversation, or giving her a kiss good-night. Always, before they separated for the evening, he took her hands and asked the Lord's blessing on Lizzie and on their relationship.

It meant the world to Lizzie to hear him pray in such a personal way about the two of them. Although he had yet to speak words of love, his actions told her of his intentions, and her heart begged her to tell him of her love. But she held back, not out of some old-fashioned belief about the roles of men and women, but because she did not want to move ahead of God. She did not want to rush His plan for her life, after all. In her heart she recalled the verse in Psalm 37, "Delight yourself in the Lord and He will give you the desires of your heart" and knew that she had to be patient.

As the summer waned the time they spent together grew; either they met for lunch or had an evening date, or they would spend long spells on the phone, talking, discussing, getting to know each other better and better. Tim had even begun to talk about what marriage for them might be like. Lizzie still waited to hear the three words that would seal it for her, but in the meantime she enjoyed the dream.

Chapter 38

When Jim and Suzanne got home from the doctor's office, Suzanne headed upstairs to the nursery without a word. Silent tears had streamed down her cheeks on the drive home, but she wouldn't speak to Jim. No effort at conversation on his part could get her to respond, and finally he gave up, just the long drive in silence. Jim settled with the neighbor who had been sitting with Bennie, then climbed the stairs, feeling like he had weights on his legs, and went down the hallway to the lovingly decorated children's room. Suzanne was sitting in the rocker in the corner, watching Bennie as he slept, two little hands under his cheek and his puffy baby lips moving ever so slightly as if talking in his dream.

"Suz…?"

No answer.

"Suzie, you can't make it go away by not talking about it."

She still didn't answer him; she turned to look out the window at the backyard ready, waiting for children with its swing-set and playhouse. *Would this house ever be filled with children like we hoped?* She wondered, sensing Jim's impatience with her.

"Honey, I know you are scared… who wouldn't be? But we need to do what the doctor said and get that surgery scheduled. Then we can get you treated so you can get better…"

Suzanne scoffed quietly, and then she looked him directly in the eyes.

"Do you really believe that? Do you really think I am going to get better? Well, I don't! And I don't feel like pretending!"

At the doctor's office she had seemed so accepting of the diagnosis that Jim thought they would just follow the plan and see her through this. Now, he realized that it wasn't acceptance of the diagnosis; it was resignation, the idea of giving up without even trying, and that made him angry. He understood when she grieved the loss of pregnancies and their stillborn son. He understood when she suffered depression and lack of motivation. But giving up without a fight? That was something he could not, would not, understand.

He looked at her with an expression void of recognition. *Who was this woman he married? Had he ever really known her? He thought she had faith. Didn't faith say 'with God* ***all*** *things are possible"? How could she abandon the battle before it even began?* He looked away, trying not to show the disgust he felt in his gut, and then he walked away, downstairs to his den, where he could pray and think in peace and quiet. *What did God want from him? How much more could they bear?*

When Jim left the doorway of the nursery, Bennie began stirring. He woke up in typical baby fashion, stretching and yawning, and then he saw Suzanne and his eyes lit up with love only a baby shows for their mommy. "Mommy" His sleepy voice raspy and her name dragged long as he stretched yet again. Then he stood by the railing of his crib and reached his arms to Suzanne.

Her heart hurt; her eyes were dried of their tears, but they hurt, too, as did her head. She smiled at Bennie and stood to go to him, but dizziness seized her and the room darkened as she collapsed to the floor.

Jim heard the crash and thump on the ceiling above him where the nursery was located. He heard Bennie start wailing and thought perhaps he had fallen from his crib. But that didn't make sense, because Suzanne was there; she would have stopped him from falling. Then he realized that the loudness of the noise could only come from an adult falling, and he ran up the stairs two at a time to the nursery.

"Suz! Suz!" He cried as he knelt beside her and lifted her head. "Darling, what happened?"

Suzanne struggled to open her eyes; Jim's face was blurry, then it gradually cleared and she saw the worry wrinkle in his brow. "I... I don't..."

"Don't try to talk, honey, I am calling the ambulance." Suzanne tried to argue, tried to tell him she was alright, but couldn't get the words out before he was on the landing dialing 911. He hurried back to put a pillow under her head and cover her with one of her hand-crocheted baby afghans. "I have to go down to open the door. Just stay still." He instructed her, quietly, and she willingly complied as she closed her eyes and let her head sink into the pillow.

"We are admitting you, Suzanne." Dr. Campbell had met them in the Emergency Department of Missouri Baptist Hospital. "We need to go ahead with the laparoscopy and get going on your treatment. I will be assisting the Gyn-Oncologist with the lap, but she will be in charge of your treatments once we have the disease staged and your care plan laid out."

Jim nodded in agreement and Suzanne didn't argue. She had no fight left in her. She would go along with the program, if only for the peace and quiet it would afford her.

"We need to discuss treatment options, Suzanne...Jim." Dr. Campbell ran through the various scenarios, the chemotherapy and radiation, the side effects of each and any alternative therapy she could use to supplement traditional treatments. If nothing else, she might get stronger using herbal complementary medicine. He also encouraged her to consider nontraditional methods, such as yoga or reflexology; he even gave her leaflets describing acupuncture, acupressure and massage therapy as alternatives if and when pain became an issue.

"But, Dr. Campbell," Suzanne finally found her voice, frail and shaky as it was, "like Jim said in your office, you don't know how bad it is...."

"I'm sorry if I mislead you, Suzanne. I tried to state it honestly, without causing you undue stress... by the CT we already can assume it is about Stage III, which means it has left the pelvic region, which we saw on the liver, and may have metastasized even further. We need the laparotomy to confirm this, especially in regard to the lymph nodes, and to remove, or debulk, as much of the mass as we can, to slow things down."

"I see." And this time Jim believed she really did. Her face showed understanding, but as she looked up at Bennie, asleep on his shoulder, she seemed to find her resolve. "So let's get on with this...," and she closed her eyes for a second. "I know you all think I am too fragile to think for myself, but after seeing Bennie in his room, I realized I could not just give up. I have to fight this thing!"

Dr. Campbell looked at Jim, raised his thick grey eyebrows and nodded. Jim returned his nod and the two of them smiled at Suzanne. They were pleased she had come to the realization on her own, without their prodding. That showed progress, and a better chance at success in her treatment. Dr. Campbell left to contact the Gyn-Oncologist, Dr. Pai, to make the arrangements for her surgery as soon as possible, and left Jim and Suzanne to work through their concerns together.

Chapter 39

Maddie arrived home on the Friday before Labor Day, thinking she and Lizzie would have all weekend to visit. She was a bit disappointed when she found out about Lizzie's dinner date. She pushed aside her own feelings of letdown to help Lizzie get ready for her evening out.

"What do you think of this dress?" Lizzie was getting ready for another date with Tim, but this time she had Maddie there to advise her on what to wear. They wore the same size, although Lizzie was conscious of differences in some of the most important places. Somehow, when Maddie put a dress on, it looked like it was made for her, but Lizzie always felt as though the same dress pulled wrong in one spot, or hung too much in another. She just hadn't found the same level of comfort with her body that Maddie had. Then she remembered a line from a poster she had in her room in college called the Desiderata. She couldn't remember it verbatim, but it was something like, 'don't compare yourself with others, because there will always be those better and others worse off than yourself'.

"I love that color with your eyes," Maddie proclaimed. Lizzie appreciated the positive spin Maddie put on her comments. She had a way of making Lizzie feel better, without even saying the words. Just her acceptance of Lizzie and all her silly insecurities helped Lizzie's confidence level. "Now, where did you say he was taking you?"

Lizzie blushed. Tim expressly told her to dress up for the dinner date. He said it promised to be their best yet! She didn't see how that was possible considering how much she enjoyed just being with him, even if it was only sitting on the porch together. Her love for him was growing stronger by the day, and she believed that the Lord had brought them together. She just couldn't rush Tim. She'd seen so many friends plot and plan to get a boyfriend to propose, only to see them divorced a year after the wedding. Tim needed time and the space to hear the voice of God, to convict him as it had Lizzie.

"I really don't know. He just said it would be special, and to dress up. It's a puzzle, because he usually tells me… it's not like this date has any special significance for us, either!"

"Maybe he's going to propose?" Maddie teased as she worked on Lizzie's hair; she looked over Lizzie's shoulder into the mirror and smiled. "You do look like a blushing bride!"

"Maddie! Now quit it! Your teasing is what is causing me to blush!" But in her heart, Lizzie hoped Maddie was right. She so longed to hear those words from Tim's lips. Just then the doorbell rang, and Samantha called to them to say Tim had arrived.

"How do I look? Is my hair OK? Oh no, my dress is wrinkled!" She smoothed the front of the dress, which really wasn't wrinkled. Then they walked together to the front room where Tim stood waiting, dressed in the same neatly pressed suit he had worn on their first dinner date.

His broad smile showed straight white teeth against his tan from being outdoors so much over the last few months. His hair was neatly groomed (obviously just clipped, because his tan line was exposed) with just one lock escaping from the product-stiffened style and fell over his forehead on the right side. He seemed uncomfortable, despite having been in the Galloway home on many occasions, wringing his hands, putting them first into his pockets, then pulling them out and rubbing them on his slacks.

"Er...Hi, Maddie. How are you? We haven't seen you in a long time!"

Maddie grinned at his awkwardness. "I'm just fine... are you?" She emphasized her question to him by looking directly at his nervous hands.

"Oh... um... yeah... that is... uh... Lizzie, are you ready?" and he reached for her wrap, placing it over her shoulders as he guided her to the door, obviously anxious to get out the door without further embarrassment. Lizzie allowed herself to be guided, and he took her hand and led her to the car where he opened the door for her. Once she was settled into the seat, he gently closed the door and hurried to the other side, started the ignition and backed out of the driveway.

"Wow!" exclaimed Maddie to Simon and Samantha, and then they burst into laughter. They finally regained control when Mama came out of the kitchen to investigate the commotion. "If you don't quiet down, you'll cause the neighbors to call in a noise complaint," she joked with them. Then Maddie told her about Tim's obvious nervousness. "It was something you'd have to see to appreciate," she said when Mama did not catch the humor of the situation.

They settled down for an evening in front of the DVD player, watching one of their old favorites, munching on popcorn and chatting like the old days. Maddie wondered why she'd put off coming home for such a long time. Suddenly, she felt that this was where she belonged; however, she still had a contractual obligation with the school in St. Louis, so she had to be careful not to allow discontent to enter her heart. *It was too easy to give in to selfish desires and not allow God to guide my path,* Maddie thought, as she leaned against the arm of the couch with her feet curled up under her. Mama sat in her easy chair, crocheting a baby blanket for another young woman in the church expecting her first child. The kids sat on the floor, or sprawled as was the case with Simon, and became totally engrossed in the beloved Disney story.

Lizzie and Tim drove into Omaha again, and once again they went into the Market District, but this time Tim took them to a lovely French Café styled restaurant. The setting was quite lovely with photos of Paris on the walls and a maître d' taking them to a secluded table, placing their napkins in their laps and presenting them with large menus in French. Tim was obviously prepared for all this since he had made the required reservation, but Lizzie was still in awe.

Tim ordered for them, although Lizzie did not know French; she had no idea what he ordered and was curious at his command of the language of romance. Without any communication between Tim and the waiter, a bottle of chilled champagne was brought out, wrapped and sitting in ice on a stand beside his chair. *This was a special night!* Lizzie thought. *He'd never ordered champagne or any alcoholic beverage for them before!* She wasn't even sure she would like the taste of it, but was prepared to try a little sip, at least.

Dinner progressed smoothly; a violinist came to the table (obviously a special request, since he hadn't played for anyone else), and favored them with some gentle but beautiful music. Lizzie closed her eyes and listened, imagining she was somewhere in Europe, a place she'd never even visited. If she thought their first date magical, she had no words to describe this. It was beyond her dreams, until they were finishing their desert, and Tim rose from his chair.

He came to her side, knelt down on one knee, and took her left hand in his.

Lizzie gasped! *Surely he wouldn't propose before he even spoke words of love to her?* But, yes, that was exactly what he was about to do. He reached into his chest pocket and brought out a blue velvet box...

A loud crash and a mess of food fell on top of his head as a waiter tripped on his out-stretched foot. The large platter filled with several dinners landed on Tim and in Lizzie's lap, and suddenly the restaurant was in an uproar as the maître d', waiter, and a variety of kitchen workers descended on them trying to make amends, trying to pick up the stray dishes and food, and repair damages, but the mood was broken, and Lizzie's dress soiled. She needed to excuse herself to the ladies room to clean up, and Tim, likewise, needed to try to remove the gravy and juices of meats from his shirt and jacket.

Lizzie stood in the bathroom, looking at herself in the mirror, totally demolished from the avalanche of food. She broke into tears and sobs, and the ladies room attendant came to her assistance, trying to calm her, helping her to sit on one of the long benches in the outer room. She tried to tidy Lizzie as best as she could, and when nothing more could be done, Lizzie went out to find Tim waiting for her.

"Maybe we need to head home?"

Lizzie nodded sadly, and followed him to the waiting car the valet had brought around. She knew they couldn't continue their date smelling like meat and gravy, but she longed to turn the clock back. Tim drove in silence, a clenching of his jaw the only sign of his frustration with the outcome of the evening. *Perhaps another time,* he thought. *Maybe tonight wasn't in God's plan. Maybe I was too nervous. Maybe I did something that made the waiter drop his tray...*

They arrive at the Galloway house and all the lights were still on; they were still watching their show, and Lizzie wished she could just slip past without their notice, but she knew that wasn't possible, so once Tim walked her to the door, gave her a quick peck and said good-night, she took a deep breath and opened the door to hear all the questions, exclamations, and concern (***that*** came from Mrs. Galloway). She tried to answer as quickly as she could and hurried off to shower and clean-up. She did not even want to have a midnight chat with Maddie. She just wanted to sleep, and cry!

Chapter 40

Lizzie did not hear from Tim for the entire weekend while Maddie was home, and she ran out of ideas to distract Lizzie from her sadness. Even she wondered why Tim hadn't called; it seemed so unlike the Pastor Tim she knew. When the weekend was over, and Maddie headed back to St. Louis, she left behind a gloomy Lizzie half-heartedly preparing her teaching plan for the next week.

Maddie arrived back in St. Louis ready to throw herself into teaching her new bunch of children. She loved to see the bright eyes and joyful enthusiasm of the five and six year olds assigned to her each year. They were like sponges just waiting to absorb all the new ideas she could give them. And there were always a couple needing extra hugs and attention which fed into Maddie's nurturing nature.

Summer melted into a spectacular red-golden autumn in the St. Louis area which brought with it the scarecrows and pumpkins of Halloween. The children enjoyed the festivities, although the church discouraged participation in Trick-or-Treat and ghoulish costumes. Instead, the Halloween celebration was held in the school gymnasium with old-fashioned Bobbing for Apples, Water Tank Dunking target, and a costume contest of Biblical characters – the contest was to guess which character was depicted by the costume and a brief charade. The whole group, nearly a hundred children and teachers, joined in Musical Chairs with the loudest laughs from the kids when a teacher landed on the floor.

Halloween decorations soon gave way to the usual Thanksgiving pilgrims and cornucopia, and Maddie was in her element. She loved telling the Thanksgiving story and letting the children put on a skit complete with a cardboard Mayflower, Plymouth Rock (made out of a beanbag) and the festive table. They made food and a huge turkey out of construction paper and glue, and a few of the rowdier boys volunteered to dress up as Indians. The little girls in the class brought in their dolls to use as babies and borrowed aprons from their mothers and grandmas for their pilgrim dresses. Topping off their costumes were the paper hats – black hats with buckles for the boys, and large white bonnets for the girls.

The Thanksgiving program was the highlight of the day on the last Friday before Thanksgiving. They had the whole week off for Thanksgiving providing time for travel for both staff and children alike. Maddie went home to enjoy the time with her family. She was surprised to hear that Lizzie and Tim were still not engaged.

"So, you're telling me, he didn't propose after the fiasco?"

Lizzie looked down, avoiding eye contact, "Nope… not even a hint."

"Well, have you guys gone out in the past couple of months?"

"Only on group outings with the young people…skating, bowling, you know."

"Has he said anything, anything at all?"

"Just that he needed time to think and pray on our relationship. I think he is afraid of commitment." Lizzie seemed resigned, not depressed or angry, just resigned to the whole situation.

"Lizzie, I am so sorry it hasn't worked out. I will keep you in my prayers, though. I think you two are great together. Maybe he does just need time. After all, you said he never used the 'L' word; maybe he is afraid. Maybe he wonders if he should follow Paul's advice to remain unmarried..."

Lizzie gasped, and tears filled her eyes.

"Oh, Liz, I am sorry. I didn't mean... I mean... Oh, shut up Maddie!' Maddie was frustrated with herself, frustrated she couldn't say the right thing. She changed the subject to a more neutral topic – their classes and activities. She and Lizzie loved bouncing ideas for teaching off each other, and this weekend was the perfect chance to share ideas for the next holiday activities.

Tim was miserable. He was so embarrassed by the attempt to propose gone wrong. He had wanted everything to go perfectly for Lizzie's sake and, when it didn't, he had second thoughts. He wondered if the upset evening was a message from God telling him to slow down. They had only dated for the summer. He was rethinking the proposal, wondering if Lizzie would consider just dating a while longer. But he was afraid to ask her, afraid she would say no. Then what would he do? He couldn't see himself without her, either. *Sooner or later I'll have to break down and talk to her. It could not go on this way indefinitely*, he thought.

Thanksgiving in the Galloway home was a magnificent enterprise. Every year, even when they lived in the mission field, Mama prepare a wonderful feast and they invited church members who had nowhere to go, those without families, or widows and widowers. When they were overseas, Mama often substituted a native dish for one of the long-established American fares, but this year was fully traditional from the green-bean casserole and sweet potatoes swimming in brown sugar to the largest turkey she could fit in their oven and half a dozen pies – pumpkin, apple, and Nonesuch mincemeat.

It was hard for even Lizzie to stay sad with so much joy and celebration all around. One of the families invited to the

Galloway's home, had recently lost their home and all their belongings in a fire. How could she be grim or feel sorry for herself when others suffered so much? Before they began eating, each person shared their blessings from the past year, they gave thanks for one major event in their life, and by the time everyone around the huge table had their say, Lizzie was smiling and realizing that life goes on beyond a failed relationship.

They ate and chattered and gradually as they had their fill, some moved to other areas in the house to visit. The women joined in clearing the table and doing the dishes. Maddie and Lizzie volunteered for drying the dishes, and had just picked up their towels when the doorbell rang.

"Busy Lizzie!!!" Jason loved to tease Lizzie. "You have a visitor!" He and Jamie jumped around singing out, "Lizzie has a visitor, Lizzie has a boyfriend!" until Mama shooed them out to where the other children were playing board games.

Lizzie walked out of the kitchen tentatively and saw Tim standing sheepishly at the front door.

"Can I come in? Or am I persona non grata?" He smiled feebly and reached for her hand. "I am so sorry! Lizzie, I have missed you so much! I love you and want us to start again, if you are willing?"

Lizzie looked up at him with her misty eyes clouding her view of his face. But she didn't need to see him clearly; she knew his face, his smile. She knew him by heart, and her heart said yes before her lips could reply.

He tilted her chin with his index finger, "Well? What do you think?"

Lizzie nodded her head and Tim lowered his lips to hers ever so gently. Suddenly, all around them they heard cheering and laughter and they looked up to see the family and all the guests, most of whom were members of Pastor Tim's church, smiling at them in approval, and he put his arm around her waist and they smiled in return. Then he took her jacket out of the coat closet by the door, put it over her shoulders, and the two of them went out into the crisp air to walk and talk and make up for lost time.

Chapter 41

For Maddie, returning to St. Louis after Thanksgiving was harder than usual. She was so happy for Lizzie, yet felt so alone and empty. The events three years before, in Chicago, continued to plague her mind during this time of year, and she wondered just how much that interfered with her ability to date and find someone special as Lizzie had done.

She even suffered a little remorse for not encouraging Pastor Tim when she had the chance, but quickly pushed those thoughts from her mind. *All things work together for good for them that love the Lord and are called according to His purpose…* She heard the verse in her mind as clearly as if someone had spoken to her. *Even an unplanned pregnancy and releasing a baby for adoption?* She wondered. Then answered the question herself, *Yes, Lord, I trust you to work it out. Take these doubts from my mind and replace them with hope and joy.*

The classroom, as in other years, was a great escape for Maddie. The Christmas season was so much more fun when teaching at a Christian school. Rather than tiptoeing around being politically correct, she could help her children understand the reason for the season, and encourage them to celebrate unselfishly by reaching out to those in need.

One activity in which the entire school participated, was putting on a Christmas play for each of the local churches.

Each class would prepare a part of the program, and the grand finale was presentation of the story of the birth of Christ in a skit. The first graders usually played the role of angels or farm animals because those required less memorization of lines. The older students played the speaking parts: Mary, Joseph, the three wise men and the shepherds. Since the school only had a total of 48 students for the six grades, there were enough parts for all to be involved. Those that didn't feel good on stage could help behind the curtains with props and cues.

Excitement grew as each class practiced their parts, and Maddie's students were no exception. With the help of the classroom moms, animal costumes of sheep, camels and donkeys made their appearance and, before long, Maddie's classroom looked like a zoo. "Children! Children!" Maddie clapped her hands trying to gain their attention as they admired all the animal costumes lined up near the cloakrooms. "Come on now, we have lessons to learn. We will practice our parts later; right now it's time for us to work."

"Tea...teacher... my mommy made me wings!" little Dawn Smith showed Maddie her angel costume. "I...Is it OK?" Her nervous stammer was more noticeable than usual.

Dawn's face shone with pleasure when Maddie replied, "Yes, sweetie, it is beautiful!" "Now, class, don't make me repeat myself!" She clapped again.

The kids all moaned and groaned as they made their way to their desks. They had a hard time concentrating when there was a fun activity in the works. With only one week left before they started doing the program for the various churches, they had only one focus – the play. Grudgingly, they sat down and got quieter. They folded their hands and prepared for the opening prayer, after which they would say the Pledge of Allegiance and sing 'God Bless America'.

"Jason, would you say our prayer this morning?" Maddie tried to rotate through the group so each child would learn to pray publicly by the time they graduated first grade.

"Dear Jesus, thank you for this day. Thank you for being a baby at Christmas so we can have Christmas. Help us be good for Miss Galloway and not bad like yesterday, amen."

Maddie smiled before she opened her eyes. The children looked up at her expectantly and she asked little Summer White to lead them in the Pledge of Allegiance. It was amusing to hear how they heard the words and repeated them each day. In the beginning of the school year the words sounded nothing like the Pledge, but now most of the students had most of the words right. The same was true when they sang "God Bless America', which was led by the tallest boy in the class, George Christiansen, a sturdy seven-year-old who started school later than the others. He also was more advanced in his language skills, not making the cute mistakes of some of his classmates.

Like Art Linkletter used to say, "kids say the darnedest things!" Maddie knew this was true from her teaching experiences. The early education training she had in college prepared her for the funny twists children put on phrases, from 'ellem yellow' in the alphabet to 'marching up the walls' in Onward Christian Soldiers instead of 'marching off to war'. Children hear things differently, and Maddie got a kick out of some of the phrases they came up with.

Once they got through the preliminaries, Maddie got the class to settle into their lessons on reading and numbers. They always looked forward to art right after lunch recess, where they were still energetic from their food, and restless from recess. Art was a relaxed time and the kids never balked at pulling out the finger paints or crayons.

Each afternoon, for this week, the whole school gathered in the auditorium to practice the program for an hour before school let out. They had five churches to go to for the programs: one on Friday evening, one Saturday evening, and three on Sunday – one for the morning service, one for afternoon, and one for the evening service. When they finished, they had a social at the last church where the children played games and worked off excess energy.

Practices went well and, by Friday, everyone was ready to do the programs and go on break for the Christmas holiday until the New Year. Using the two school-owned buses, two of the father's with the right driver's licenses, drove the bulk of the students to each of the churches. Some of the larger families chose to drive their children in their own vans, and they all met at a prearranged spot at each of the churches.

The programs went off without a problem and Maddie was happy to see her little angels and animals play their parts. She always stood off in the wings to make sure any costume glitches were taken care of before the student made it a crisis. At the last church, she stood in her usual position and looked out over the audience. The fellowship hall was crowded; it seemed every church member was there to see the program. This church, The Central St. Louis Christian Church, always had full participation since they also hosted the after program social.

Suddenly, Maddie's knees went weak and her heart thumped wildly in her chest. Sitting off to the left, she saw Suzanne and Jim Buckley, and he was holding a child on his lap. She couldn't see the little one, but she clearly recognized the Buckleys. Maddie felt like she couldn't breathe. *What should I do?* She thought. *What do I do? Lord, help me!*

She hardly noticed the scene changes, and although she fixed several costumes, she didn't recall whose or why. She moved on remote control, as if the Lord Himself had control of her body, because she felt paralyzed. On one hand, she longed to rush over and look at the child to see if it was her son; Benjamin was the name given him by the adoptive family. On the other hand, she had agreed not to interfere, not to be in contact with the adoptive family. But, she didn't know if the Buckleys *had* adopted her son. She would just be talking to them from their acquaintance back home. Her heart pounded loudly in her ears; it felt like those around her should be able to hear it too.

The children all went out to receive the appreciation of the audience as they stood and clapped for the presentation of the Christmas story. Then parents came to claim their children and help them change into their play clothes for the church festivities. The church members congregated in the gymnasium and women went into the kitchen to prepare refreshments to set out on the tables. Since Maddie had neither children of her own nor food to prepare, she headed for the groups of members chatting alongside the wall of the gym.

She quickly saw Jim Buckley standing nearly a head taller than those around him, with his arm on Suzanne's shoulder. Holding the child, she had its head laying on her shoulder as it lay relaxed and asleep against her. Others stood around talking to them and Maddie was self-conscious about walking up to them, but as the group dispersed and Jim and Suzanne looked like they were heading toward the door to leave, Maddie got up her courage and walked toward them.

"Mr. and Mrs. Buckley?"

They turned toward her, puzzled as if they did not know her. Then, although they hadn't formally met at their church in Nebraska, they did recognize Maddie by sight. They both smiled a greeting and stopped to speak.

"I just saw you here… do you go to this church?" Maddie asked, a little breathless from hurrying over. She noticed Suzanne's gaunt appearance and the sunken look of her eyes which were also ringed with dark circles beneath them.

"Yes, we do…and you?" Jim replied.

"No, actually, I am a schoolteacher at the St. Louis Christian Elementary School. I teach the first grade."

"How wonderful! It must be fun to spend your days with children." Suzanne remarked, a little pink showing on her cheeks and a sparkle in her eyes as she talked of children.

"I do enjoy it, although kids can test your patience," Maddie smiled. "I see you have a little one, too?"

"Oh, yes, this is our little Ben..." Maddie's heart skipped a beat at the name, "we adopted him nearly two and a half years ago now." Suzanne seemed proud of her son as she rubbed his back gently.

"Maybe I can baby-sit sometime for you...?" *Where did that come from?* Maddie wondered at her own boldness.

Jim looked at Suzanne and she looked at him, and together they quickly agreed, much to Maddie's surprise. "You see, Suzanne is sick," *that explains the circles under her eyes,* Maddie thought, "and needs to go to the doctor quite often for treatment, so the more sitters we can line up, the better!" Jim seemed to choke up as he talked of her doctor's visit. They exchanged contact information, and promised to be in touch. Suzanne and Jim immediately left, while Maddie made her way back to her students and the church social, trying to put the auburn hair on that little boy named Ben out of her mind.

Chapter 42

When the results of Suzanne's pathology report, following her surgery, showed Stage III Ovarian Cancer as Dr. Campbell expected, he brought in Dr. Pai, a specialist in treating cancers in the female reproductive organs. Dr. Pai advised Jim and Suzanne that, after looking at the pathology report, she felt Suzanne's best chances for survival would mean a course of intraperitoneal chemotherapy. They would put the chemicals directly into her abdomen using a needle and tube similar to IV fluid administration. She would need six treatments each given at about three week intervals.

"Doctor, what kind of side effects are we talking about?" Jim asked, "I mean, we have heard of all sorts of bad things with cancer treatment, especially the hair loss thing and nausea."

"You're right about the nausea. This particular type of treatment is often accompanied by nausea along with abdominal pain, bloating, fatigue, and infection. Sometimes these can be so bad that the patient doesn't finish the six treatments, but we need to try to aim for completion, because that improves Suzanne's chances."

"Do I need to stay away from my little boy? I don't want to contaminate him or make him sick...?"

"No, Suzanne, you don't need to isolate yourself from anyone. Enjoy your son and your husband. Just know that you may not feel very good, and may want someone to help with him when you feel your worst."

"Also, let me tell you that we are trying some combination meds that help prevent some of the worst side effects, especially the possible anemia which contributes to the fatigue I mentioned. The hair loss is individual, but be assured that it is a temporary condition. Once the treatments are done, and the cells regenerate, hair growth returns."

The first treatment was scheduled for the next week, and Suzanne tolerated it well, at first, but by the time she got home she was sick - nausea and vomiting for several hours until she finally dozed off, exhausted, with her quilt wrapped around her in an effort to warm her skinny, weak body. Each treatment was worse than the one before, the bloating and abdominal pain almost unbearable, but Suzanne persisted, determined to beat the cancer.

By the Christmas program, Suzanne had received all of the treatments and was ready to start feeling better. Dr. Pai was right about the side effects, but Suzanne stuck it out for all six of the required treatments; she wanted to be sure to get all of the cancer on the first go around. Jim had been great in helping with little Ben, and some of the ladies from church helped him. She hoped they would not need to take advantage of Maddie's offer; she hoped she would not have to get any further treatments. Suzanne wanted to believe that it was all behind her, that she was on the road to remission.

Christmas in the Buckley home was always a special time of year but, this year, Suzanne wanted to make it extra special for Bennie. Although she tried to think positively, she wanted to make this the best Christmas ever, just in case... Mr. and Mrs. Buckley (Jim's folks) had agreed to come for Christmas morning, and Suzanne's parents had said they would think about it.

Despite her fatigue and continuous sense of nausea, Suzanne pulled out the decorations and, bit by bit, put up greenery on the stair banister and across the mantel along with a collection of David Winter cottages and candles all over the living room. Beside the huge tree in the front room, she placed at least one little artificial tree in each room of the house, decked out with all the trimmings, and she exchanged all the towels in each of the bathrooms for red and green linens with gold stars or snowflakes embroidered on them. She even took time to change out kitchen décor to more seasonal ornamentation. All in all, she was pleased with her efforts to bring in the spirit of Christmas. One thing was missing, but she needed Jim to bring that in; the nativity scene he made out of wood for her for their first Christmas as a married couple.

Jim brought in the big box with the nativity scene, and set it up in the corner near the fireplace on a rag rug Suzanne had made out of beige and green rags to replicate grass and sand of the Holy Land. It was too large to set on a table, and they were concerned that Bennie wouldn't leave it alone. To try to discourage him, Jim rigged a low wooden fence, just enough of a barrier to deter him, but not too distracting from the scene.

When Suzanne thought the decorating was finished, Jim surprised her with a huge box… it was exactly what they needed to finish off the Christmas tree. Jim put it together, the track in a large circle, around the tree. It was an electric train, and he set it up so the power could turn on by a wall switch. Puffing as it went, the miniature engine pulled several cars and the caboose around in the circle, whistling every so often. *Perfect*, thought Suzanne. *Now Bennie won't get to the gifts under the tree.*

Maddie went home on her Christmas break with trepidation in her heart. *What if the Buckleys called over the holidays needing a sitter? What if she missed her chance to see Ben again?* But she knew she could not put her life on hold based on a chance, just a possibility. Anyway, she was expected home for the holidays, and she couldn't wait to hear how Tim and Lizzie were doing since Thanksgiving.

By the time Maddie arrived home, Lizzie was already settling into her room. Maddie quickly unloaded her car and changed into something more comfortable, and then she and Lizzie curled up on the easy chairs in the living-room, laughing and chattering away. Lizzie happily shared her news about the dates she and Tim had been on, both group dates and alone. She absolutely radiated love as she talked about Tim. Maddie tried not to show her gloom; she wanted to be happy for Lizzie, but felt left out. Despite her pleading with the Lord, she hadn't had a date in a long time, let alone someone she could love, and she had difficulty hiding her woe.

"I'm sorry, Maddie, you should have stopped me. Listen to how I just keep running my mouth!"

Maddie smiled, although it didn't quite reach her eyes, "It's ok, Liz. I can't ask you to not be happy… and when you are happy, you talk, I know that!" Then the smile covered her face, including her eyes. "Pray for me, OK? I need to learn patience. After all, I am only 25 years old. Lots of women are a lot older that that when they meet Mr. Right."

They talked a bit more until Mama called them for dinner. Simon was at an away game for the basketball team, and Samantha was at her friend's house for the weekend, which left only Mama, Jason and Jamie. Dinner was peaceful in the Galloway home, and on Fridays it was a chance for the kids to talk about the week's events at school. Jason and Jamie didn't stop, except to take bites of food; when one wasn't talking the other was, so Maddie and Lizzie just ate and listened, smiling at their childish enthusiasm and joy.

Lizzie didn't have a date that evening so she and Maddie spent an evening with Mama and the kids, playing board games – Scrabble and Monopoly. After Jamie and Jason turned in for the night, Lizzie popped some popcorn for them and she, Maddie and Mama all sat down to watch an old movie on TV. It was comforting to Maddie to be home and doing normal things with her family, but every now and then, Maddie's mind wandered back to St. Louis and the Buckleys.

Lizzie noticed how distracted Maddie seemed, but didn't say anything around Mrs. Galloway. She didn't want to worry Maddie's mother, or embarrass Maddie, in case it was something serious. When Mrs. Galloway decided she'd had enough TV for the night and turned in, Lizzie saw her chance to get Maddie talking.

"Maddie, you seem miles away tonight," she started.

"Oh, Liz, I thought we'd never be alone so I could talk to you. I feel like I'm about to burst!" Maddie turned to Lizzie and looked her straight in the eye. "I found him!"

"You found who? Mr. Right? What are you talking about? You didn't tell me you were looking for anyone."

"No, I wasn't looking… it was like God dropped him in my lap! Not Mr. Right! My son!"

"Your what?" Lizzie screeched in a shrill whisper. "Your what? Oh my goodness, do you know what this could do to him, to his family? What are you thinking? You signed off on his adoption… you have no claim to him now!"

"I know, I know, I know! I mean, intellectually I know, but my heart doesn't accept that. I offered to babysit him…"

"Oh, Maddie, you are playing with fire! Babysit? Are you kidding? Do the parents know who you are?"

"I don't think so. I just said hi for a minute and offered to help, because the adoptive mother is sick. But I don't think they made any connection between me and Ben."

"Ben! Ben? Ben. You even know his name?"

"Well they wrote his name on the photos Pastor Tim gave me from them."

"Oh, I see. So you think because your child was named Ben, and this child is also Ben, that they are one and the same? Come on, Maddie. Be real! How likely is it that you would run into your child in St. Louis? Who would Tim know there…?"

"They were members here. He's the right age. They lost a pregnancy around the time I gave up my baby. Don't you see? It all fits."

Lizzie was speechless. She couldn't believe Maddie would go so far to reclaim her child. She didn't even know what Maddie planned beyond this point. Her heart was racing because she knew the damage that could be done, not only to the adoptive family, but also to Maddie if it didn't work out the way she pictured it. She had to get her to see things realistically, and she only had ten days to do it before Maddie headed back to St. Louis.

Chapter 43

January rolled into February and Lizzie and Tim went out each week, and talked for hours on the phone during the week. Once Lizzie heard Tim say, I love you, it made it easier for her to share her feelings with him. Sometimes, when they walked down the street, others would comment on the love just emanating from them; they glowed! Once again, Tim planned the perfect evening. He decided to take Lizzie back to the first restaurant where they had dinner together. He couldn't face the French restaurant, although he thought it more romantic. The recollections of that fiasco were too much, and he wanted this evening to be full of joy and happiness, not ghosts of bad memories.

Lizzie bought a new dress for their Valentine Day dinner. Although Tim hadn't hinted at his plans, in her heart she felt this was the night he would propose. After all, they had dated for nearly a year (minus the time apart after that 'almost proposal'), and he had finally admitted his love for her, and she had told him how much she loved him. The time was right, and she wanted to be ready. She avoided the cliché red dress so many chose for this occasion, in favor of a chaste-appearing white.

The winter white satin dress had folds across the bodice extending up to the shoulder seams, looking like a modified cowl neckline. It had an empire waistline that neatly accentuated her figure as it hugged her curves down to just below her knee. She chose a pair of gold Nine West dress that mimicked the shoes with the style of the straps and, with their 3 1/2" heels, she could stand taller next to Tim's striking height. Her wrap was a simply draped matching white satin scarf. She loved the effect once she added her gold accents of dangling earrings and a delicate gold chain necklace with simple cross pendent.

Tim decided he would go all out, and rented a tuxedo for this special evening. Lizzie had enjoyed the gold tie he chose before, so this time he selected a gold lame cummerbund and a gold bowtie to match. He even decided on a jacket with tails to finish off the effect. He looked in the full-length mirror, pleased with the end product. He picked up the corsage box off the table in the entryway where he'd set it, grabbed his keys and headed out the door. Then he returned, realizing he'd forgotten to pick up the ring box. He snatched it and put it in the inside jacket pocket, and headed out once again.

Tim arrived at the Galloway home fifteen minutes early. He wondered if he should wait, or go to the door; he hesitated just a minute, then strode up the walk and rang the doorbell.

"Pastor Tim, how nice to see you again," Mrs. Galloway opened the door wide and invited him into the living room. "Lizzie will be ready in just a minute. Have a seat."

Tim stood just inside the door. "I'll stand, if you don't mind, ma'am."

"Ma'am? Why so formal? Are you nervous?" she smiled at him, recognizing the signs of an anxious young man about to pop an important question. "You look very handsome in that tux!"

Tim flushed and looked down to avoid eye contact with this member of his church. *Guess I don't come off like much of a pastor in this tux,* He thought. *Sure hope Lizzie accepts...Lord, You know the desires of my heart! Thank You for working it out so far, just help me do it right this time, please."*

His chest tightened and he couldn't catch his breath when he saw his beautiful Lizzie come out of the hallway, a vision in her white dress. She already looked like a bride, now if she would only agree to be *his* bride. He walked to her, staring into her eyes that glistened and sparkled. She smiled as he took out the corsage and attempted to pin it on her, and then Mrs. Galloway took over, with a laugh at his clumsiness. He couldn't take his eyes off Lizzie. After she put her wrap over her shoulders, he led her to the car with his hand on the small of her back. He graciously opened the door for her, helped her get in, and closed it quietly. Only then did he take a cleansing breath, and realize how shallow he had been breathing. *I'm like a school kid*, he thought. He got in and double started the motor because he was so nervous.

They drove in silence to the steak restaurant in the Market District of Omaha. The setting was just as Lizzie remembered from their first dinner there. She wasn't very hungry, but ordered a large spinach salad with bleu cheese dressing, and Tim asked for an 8 oz. steak, baked sweet potato with brown sugar and butter, and a house salad. It seemed to take forever for the food to come out, and there was an uncomfortable silence between Lizzie and Tim.

He got up from his chair, knelt beside her chair and took out the same box she remembered from his first attempt to propose. He took her left hand in his right and rubbed his thumb on the back of her hand.

"Lizzie, my blessing. You know how much I love you. You know how I've prayed about this, and how I long to join my life with yours. Now I need to ask you, will you join your life with mine? Will you be my bride, my wife, my helpmeet in serving the Lord? Will you marry me?"

Lizzie was watching his thumb mark a circle on her hand and listening to his voice, gentle, soothing, and she felt relaxed and peaceful until she heard the final question. Then her heart leapt in her chest and she looked up at him with all the love her heart contained. "Oh, Tim. I prayed that God would send me someone I could trust, someone with whom I could be myself, someone that wanted to serve the Lord. When I met you, I could hardly believe He had answered my prayer in such a wonderful way, with such a wonderful man. Yes, Tim. I will marry you. I will join my life to yours."

Just as they sealed their promise with a kiss, they heard someone clear their throat. It was the waiter with their food. Tim laughed, and got up carefully, getting out of the way so the waiter could set up his serving tray. He did not want a repeat of the tumbling serving tray episode. He sat down and replaced his napkin in his lap, then he looked at Lizzie and the two of them burst into laughter. Their joy and exuberance filled the section of the restaurant where their table was, and congratulations sounded from every corner. They enjoyed the rest of the dinner, and afterwards Tim drove them to a secluded park where they could look at the stars and share quiet conversation in a private setting.

They discussed when they wanted the wedding; of course, Tim wanted it as soon as possible, but Lizzie wanted time to plan a nice, albeit simple, wedding, so they agreed on a June wedding. Lizzie already knew that Maddie would be her Maid of Honor, and Tim wanted his brother James to be his best man. Before long they had many of the basics decided on. Since Lizzie had been out of touch with her father, she knew he would not help with the cost of a wedding. She had put aside a modest sum to use for this purpose, and Tim promised to help with the expenses if she allowed him.

It was nearly midnight when Tim drove her back to the Galloways. Normally, Lizzie was home much earlier, both for the sake of appearances for her reputation, and for his reputation as a pastor, but tonight was a special circumstance, which they knew would be overlooked.

Tim kissed her at the door with the usual good-night kiss, and then he took her firmly by the shoulders and planted a firm, more passionate kiss on her lips that left her weak and dizzy as she unlocked the door and slipped inside.

"Liz, tell me all about it," Maddie was sitting in the dark waiting for Lizzie.

Lizzie jumped, surprised to hear a voice in the dark, especially Maddie's voice. Then she remembered that this was a long weekend for Maddie, too, with President's Day celebration on Monday. Rather than hang around St. Louis, Maddie had decided to fly to Omaha and spend a couple of days with her family. *She couldn't have had more perfect timing,* thought Lizzie. *Just when I need to talk to her, she shows up!* Then she kicked off her shoes and curled her feet under her as she sat down on the couch next to Maddie to share her joy.

"This is all about it!" Lizzie showed Maddie the delicate ring with a central round diamond surrounded by tiny yellow sapphires. The effect was like a flower, set on a delicately filigreed band.

Lizzie's face radiated the afterglow of her special evening as she shared the evening with Maddie. She and Maddie talked long into the morning hours about the proposal, plans and the future for Lizzie and Tim. Maddie was happy for them; she'd spent time in prayer, asking God to take away any envy from her heart, and He'd answered in a big way. All she felt for Lizzie and Tim was enthusiasm and excitement at the idea of planning their wedding.

Chapter 44

With Christmas celebrations over Suzanne looked forward to the New Year, hoping for a better year for Jim, Bennie and, especially, herself. She felt better by the day throughout the month of January and her visits to the doctor were encouraging. According to Dr. Pai, they had removed nearly all the original mass, but a small amount remained. As long as that mass did not grow during her chemotherapy, the outlook was pretty good. She also talked about Suzanne's CA-125 levels, which neither she nor Jim really understood too much about, but they figured it was like most other things, smaller is better.

Suzanne had no noticeable growth in the tumor for the first two months after surgery, and her CA-125 levels were stable. When she went in for her tests in February, however, things changed. Her levels had risen for reasons unknown, until they did another CT scan and realized that the mass had increased in size. Dr. Pai was obviously concerned at the change of events, as was Jim; Suzanne was devastated.

"We need to start a second course of chemotherapy…" Dr. Pai started to discuss treatment options with Jim and Suzanne.

Jim interrupted, "What about another surgery to remove some more of that mass?"

Dr. Pai was accustomed to patients and family members trying to suggest alternatives to chemotherapy. After all, it wasn't easy to watch a loved one waste away because of nausea and vomiting, or lose hair, or many of the other side effects they endure for the sake of killing the cancer. "We don't usually recommend a second debulking procedure, mainly because we know cells are throughout the abdominal cavity, as well as the pelvis, so removing parts of one tumor won't fix the problem. And I think I know what is next in your questions…"

"Radiation?" Jim asked, hopefully.

"Again, because we are dealing with a large area, not just a single tumor mass, it would be hard to focus the radiation energy to kill all the escaped cells that are also developing into tumors. Radiation is something we aim in as small an area as possible, that's why we mark the skin, so the beam goes straight to the same spot each time,. It's ok for a single tumor where there is no metastasis…"

"There must be some other way," Suzanne's weak voice interjected into the dialogue between Jim and Dr. Pai. "I can't bear the thought…" and she broke into deep, heart-wrenching sobs and buried her face in her hands.

Her tears and her slender frame shaking in grief moved Dr. Pai with compassion; she got out some tissues for Suzanne. Jim went to her and held her closed until she was cried out and able to resume the meeting with Dr. Pai. They talked about starting chemo again, but Suzanne asked for a couple of weeks before the first dose. She just needed time to get used to the idea.

It was the middle of the month when they started her treatment regimen. It was modified from the first chemicals; Suzanne didn't pay attention to all the names, she just wanted it to work this time. She experienced the same symptoms as before, with the nausea and vomiting she couldn't keep down any food. Just before she was scheduled for her second dose, in March, she woke one night to find her nose bleeding.

Jim quickly got a huge towel for her to hold to her nose, and called 911, but before they got there the towel was saturated and the bed linens had splatters of blood. Suzanne was weak; she laid back onto her pillow waiting for the ambulance and, before they arrived, she had fainted. Jim was panic-stricken. Once again he was looking at the possibility of losing his precious Suzanne, and he couldn't bear the thought. He called the neighbor who offered to watch Bennie, and she was glad to help once again.

"Jim, Suzanne has lost a lot of blood. We had to give her platelets, packed red cells and a couple of units of blood, already, and she may need still more. The chemotherapy triggered a drop in the parts of the blood that make it clot, the platelets. Once we get her over this, she will be good to come home, but we need to keep a close eye on her blood count."

They talked for a while, Jim asking questions and Dr. Pai doing her best to answer them. Suzanne was resting quietly so Jim went to the cafeteria for a bite to eat. On the way back, he stopped by the chapel, just for a moment, to say a prayer. He also needed to call and check on Bennie and make sure everything was alright at home. He hated that so much time was spent without Ben while Suzanne got her first round of chemo, and he wondered how they would make it through another course. Suddenly, he recalled the phone number he had in his wallet; that young woman from Nebraska, Maddie Galloway, had offered to help. Maybe now was the time to call her. *No,* he thought, *I better wait and talk to Suzanne. She's kinda funny about who watches little Ben.*

After making sure Ben would be alright (the neighbor, Linda Stone, promised to take him to her house for the day)

Jim returned to Suzanne's room. The grayish pallor of her face accentuated the deeply sunken eyes and long lashes on her cheekbones. Even in this condition, anyone could see what a beauty she was before she lost so much weight. Now her skin looked taught over her cheekbones and jaw, and her cheeks were hollow. The sparse, short, feathery hair on her head had only just started returning, and now she would lose it again. Suzanne was not one to wear wigs; she opted, instead, to wear stylish hats to match her outfits when she went out of the house, or turbans lovingly made by some ladies at church when she was at home.

"Jim?" Suzanne reached her hand out, searching for his. It seemed to take too much energy to use the muscles needed to open her eyes, so they remained closed. Her lips were cracked and dry, so Jim lifted her glass of water and guided the straw to her mouth.

"Here, Darling, drink a little," as hard as he tried, tears still welled up in his eyes.

Suzanne took a small sip, choked a little as if swallowing also took too much effort. Then she sipped again, this time without incident. "I'm so glad you are here. We need to talk about Bennie."

"What about Bennie? Linda is watching him just fine."

"I mean, if I should die, we need to have a plan…"

"Don't talk like that!" Jim was angry that she would talk about dying because of one set-back. "You aren't going to die! This was just a… a… well, anyway, you aren't dying. Dr. Pai says you can come home once your blood count is stable."

"Jim, I need to say this. If I die, I need you to promise you will look for another wife. Bennie will need a mommy, and you will need someone, too. Please, promise me?"

"I can't talk about this! This isn't happening! Stop this, Suz! I need *you* , not some other woman. And Bennie needs you, too! You're the only mommy he knows, and you can't talk about leaving us!"

"I know it hurts to talk about it. It hurts me, too, but I need to know you both will be ok when I ..."

Jim got so angry, he placed the glass on her over-the-bed table hard and it slopped a bit onto the table. "I am going home now to check on Bennie. You sleep and we will talk later, OK?" He kissed her on the lips, harder than he needed to, but the fury in his heart was boiling to the surface, and he couldn't contain it. He left a few minutes later with no further conversation between them. Suzanne cried softly as she heard the door close, and then she did fall back to sleep.

Chapter 45

Maddie was taken by surprise one windy March Saturday morning, when she received a phone call from Jim Buckley. Her heart jumped into her throat for a moment, before she reminded herself that the Buckleys didn't know who she was, other than a former member from their church in Nebraska.

"Uh...Maddie? Maddie Galloway?" Jim hesitated. "This is Jim Buckley... from the Christmas program... from church in Omaha." Suzanne did not want him to bother Maddie, but Linda was out of town, and their other friends from church were busy with their own children. The only person he could think to call was this stranger, this first-grade teacher, who had offered her assistance so casually at the Christmas program.

"Yes, this is Maddie Galloway. May I help you?" She knew already in her heart why he was calling. She also knew what her answer would be. Without hesitation she would agree to watch Ben anytime, anyplace. She could not turn down an opportunity like this despite what Lizzie had said when she was home in February. Lizzie had strong opinions about Maddie keeping her distance from the Buckleys, but Maddie hadn't chased them down. Jim Buckley was calling her for help without any prodding from her.

"I... we were wondering if you could watch Bennie for us on Tuesday coming up? Suzanne has another treatment that day, and..."

"Yes, Mr. Buckley, I'd be glad to help, although I am teaching that day."

"Well, I thought I could drop him at the Christian Day Care there at your church..."

"Yes, I am familiar with the nursery run by the women at our church. It's just across the parking lot from our school where I teach."

"That's why I thought of it. It is also near the hospital where I take Suzie. Anyway, if I drop him there in the morning, could you watch him after school until prayer meeting that evening... I think that it starts at 7:00pm? Then I could pick him up on our way home, if that is alright for you?"

"That sounds wonderful, I mean, fine. I can get him from the Day Care and take him home until time to come back to church. He and I can have fun together."

"You don't know how much this means to me...uh, us. Thank you so much."

They talked for a bit about the details and then, when Maddie got off the phone, she squealed, "Yeeeah!" and jumped in the air, until she remembered her neighbor in the apartment below her. Her heart took flight at the thought of spending a couple of hours with her little boy, and she began rushing around tidying up her house and thinking of things she needed to get to keep him occupied.

Later that evening she called Lizzie to tell her about the plans for Tuesday. Lizzie wasn't happy with Maddie's decision; she felt Maddie should have turned Jim Buckley down, although she understood Maddie's conflict. She was worried that Maddie would let herself get hurt again.

They also discussed some of Lizzie's wedding plans. Mama promised to make the wedding cake – she had a knack for decorating cakes although she hadn't done one in several years. They would be married by Pastor Greene, the pastor who had the church prior to Pastor Tim, and they planned it for the sanctuary of their own church, since they planned to keep the number of invitations down.

The ladies at church had already assured her that they would provide everything for the reception. All that left was the decorations, the ribbons, flowers, candles and guest books. Lizzie was going to enlist the help of several teen girls at church, one to write down gifts and names of the giver, so Lizzie could send out thank you cards. She also needed a young lady to stand by the guest book to encourage everyone to sign. The others could help set up the tables in the fellowship hall and show people to their tables.

"Lizzie, it sounds so wonderful! I am so happy for you!" and this time Maddie truly meant it. Her own life had taken a positive turn, which made it easier to be thrilled for Lizzie without the green-eyed monster of envy intruding into her thoughts. They were all talked out when Maddie realized it was time to go to bed. She needed to be at church on time in the morning; she was attending the Central Church for a change, on the off chance that she would see the Buckleys and make acquaintance with Ben. Jim had suggested this, but it was one idea left unsettled, so Maddie thought she would take advantage of the opportunity.

Maddie fussed in front of the mirror; she had changed her dress three times, trying to look just right for church. She knew it was really all about Ben that she was so flustered. Finally, she felt put together enough, and headed out to church in time for the Divine Worship Service. She arrived shortly before it started and asked the usher to seat her near the rear of the church. She slipped into the back pew and looked around trying to locate the head of Jim Buckley which was usually above most others.

Then she saw him come in the same doors through which she had just entered the sanctuary. He had little Ben in his arms; Ben was playing with his daddy's collar in the back as he held on. The usher showed them to the same pew in which Maddie had been seated, and she slid over to make room. She smiled and Jim acknowledged her smile, then recognized her face and his smile broadened.

"I'm glad you could make it," he leaned over and whispered to her. "Bennie can get to know you a bit today, maybe during potluck, so he won't be scared on Tuesday."

She nodded in agreement, trying to appear calm, but her pulse was anything but calm. It was racing, her heart thumping so hard, she was surprised others didn't hear it. She reached out a hand to touch Ben's tiny fingers. He pulled away, just a little, looked up with his big brown eyes, and a big grin showed his tiny pearly teeth. He reached out to her with both arms and Jim looked surprised, but released him into Maddie's arms. Bennie sat on her lap playing with her necklace, then her watch, then near the middle of the service, he climbed up and lay his head on her shoulder and promptly fell asleep, his gentle snores blowing past her ear, ruffling her hair.

Maddie's happy smile didn't leave her face for the rest of the service. She remained seated during the final hymn, and reluctantly gave Ben to his daddy after the benediction. Bennie didn't waken. He just curled into his daddy's arms and went on snoring.

"He is such a sweet child,: Maddie said reverently.

"We are certainly blessed," Jim replied. "We just need to get through this patch, so we can be a family again."

"What exactly is wrong with your wife, if I can be so bold…?"

"No, I don't mind you asking… she has cancer, yup, the big C. It's pretty bad, and now she has had a relapse, so we have to do a second round of therapy."

Maddie expressed her condolences, and wondered what kind of life Ben was having if his mommy spent so much time in hospital. She couldn't allow herself to go down that road in her mind, or she would begin to second guess her decision. She had to believe it was the right choice, to give him up for adoption. She just still had that maternal desire to protect her child from the sorrows of life.

Jim was pleased with the compassion Miss Galloway showed toward both his son and their family. She seemed ideal to watch him, once in a while, and meeting her today took away any doubts he might have had. He stayed long enough for potluck, woke and fed Ben who wanted to play more than eat. Maddie took him to the children's room so he could play with other toddlers while the parents ate. Once Jim finished his dinner and spoke to a few of his prayer partners about his concerns for Suzanne, he went to reclaim Bennie, and was pleased to see him responding well to Maddie. *Yes, she will work out well as a helper for little Bennie*, he thought as they drove away and headed to the hospital to see Suzanne.

Chapter 46

Tuesday could not arrive fast enough for Maddie. She was so thrilled at the idea of having a couple of hours alone with her baby. She had not talked to her mother about her plans, but she was sure Lizzie would, and Mama hadn't called to voice her opinion. Maddie was sure that Mama would call if she was against the idea. Perhaps, being a mother, she understood Maddie's thoughts on the matter. She knew what it was like to be away from a child, since Maddie was so young when she came to the states to go to boarding school for high school. Surely Mama understood how it felt for Maddie to be apart from her baby, and her desire to spend time with him.

Then again, maybe Mama just decided to let Maddie make her own mistakes. Would she let Maddie head into peril without trying to give her guidance? Suddenly, Maddie felt the urge to call Mama, just to hear her reassurance that Maddie was doing the right thing.

"Mama?" Maddie spoke tentatively.

"Why, Maddie, I didn't expect to hear from you this evening. Lizzie said you had plans for tomorrow, and I thought we wouldn't hear from you until afterward."

"So you know about Ben?"

"Yes, dear. Lizzie told me that you found your little Ben, and that tomorrow you would be baby-sitting."

"Well, what do you think, Mama?"

"I think you are a wonderful young woman, with a bright mind, who will always ask for the Lord's guidance and not press forward without his affirmation."

"Mama, would you pray with me right now? I just feel like I need your prayers on this matter, too. I am excited, but scared at the same time. What if I love him too much?"

"Can a mother ever love her child too much? Come now, let's pray together."

Nobody prayed like Mama in Maddie's mind. She spoke with Jesus as if talking to a friend on the telephone. She had no trouble finding the right words or organizing her thoughts. She just laid out the situation to the Lord and asked him to help Maddie make the right decision. *It was that easy,* Maddie thought. *What took me so long to call home? The enemy always gets into my brain with doubts and fears, when all I have to do is lean on Jesus like Mama does.*

"Thanks, mommy," Maddie reverted to her childhood name for her mother whenever she was really stressed, so Mama knew this was a hard path for Maddie to walk.

"Remember, my dear, the old saying, ***Courage is just Fear faced with Prayer!*** As long as you put the Lord first, you can't go wrong!"

They talked on for a while, Maddie telling Mama about her time at church with Ben, describing him down to his little hands and fingers. She asked Mama to pray for the Buckleys, not aware that the church Prayer Warriors were already activated in behalf of the Buckley family.

Maddie was able to sleep soundly that night, and woke refreshed and ready for school the next morning. She stayed busy with the children to keep her mind off of Ben, until nearing the end of the school day, she could no longer pretend he wasn't on her mind. She had the children playing games in the classroom for the last half an hour, to burn off energy, and to save her from trying to teach when her mind wouldn't cooperate.

"Oh, Miss Galloway, how nice of you to visit our day care!" Exclaimed one of the mothers as Maddie entered the day care, her hand on the shoulder of one of her students whose mother volunteered her time watching the little ones.

"I am here to pick up little Ben Buckley," Maddie felt shy, although she had every right to pick him up.

"Oh, yes, Jim Buckley said you would be getting Bennie today. So nice of you to help them out during this trying time..."

The mother went into one of the rooms down the hallway and came out with Ben, his jacket in her hand. He looked like he'd only just woke from a nap, his hair slightly mussed. "Here you go, Miss Galloway..."

"Maddie, please!"

"OK, Maddie, here is little Bennie Buckley. " she turned to help Bennie put on his jacket and zip it up. "Now you be real good for Miss Galloway, y'hear?" and she gave him a light swat on his backside as he headed into Maddie's arms.

"OK, Ben, what shall we do first?" she was really talking to herself as she took him to the car carrying his car seat in one hand and holding him in the other arm.

"Cookies!" Bennie clapped his hands.

"Oh, do you get cookies when you get home?"

He nodded his little head and his long auburn hair shook into his eyes. He giggled and pushed it out of his eyes, then put his hands on either side of Maddie's face, as she put the car seat down beside her car. He held her face in his and gazed into her eyes as if reading her soul.

"Home!" he said and began bobbing up and down as she tried, with difficulty, to set him into his seat.

"Settle down, honey, Maddie needs to fasten you into the seat." Ben quieted down, and looked down at his hands with curiosity, then he touched Maddie's hair as she fastened the clasps on his seat.

"Hair, Maddie."

"Yes, that is Maddie's hair." She smiled, wondering if he noticed the similarities between her hair and his, although hers was a bit brighter red. She went around to the driver's seat once she was satisfied that he was safely fastened in. She drove even more cautiously than usual, knowing she was carrying precious cargo. They got to her apartment, and she left the car seat in place, lifting Ben out and to the ground. She held his little hand and they walked to the stairs, and then she picked him up and carried him up the stairs to her apartment door.

He stood near her leg as she unlocked the door, her hand resting on his head. Once the door was open, Ben had no problem rushing in and exploring as if it was his home. He climbed up into a chair in the kitchen, and promptly said again, "Cookie!" Then just as firmly, he cried out, Milk!"

Maddie realized who ran the show in his house. She went to the fridge and pulled out the half-gallon of 2% milk and poured each of them a small glass (his in a plastic glass she kept especially for visitors like Ben). Then she went to the big cookie jar on her counter that looked like a Pillsbury Doughboy, and took out two peanut butter cookies, one for him and one for herself. She had already cleared with Jim whether Ben had any allergies, and was thankful he had none.

She sat in a chair near his, and together, in silence they ate their cookie and drank the milk. When he was done, Maddie washed his hands and face with a damp paper towel, and he rushed to the corner of the living room where he had spotted a box of toys. Before long he was totally engrossed, and Maddie had Sesame Street on TV for good measure, just in case he got bored.

She figured they would have macaroni and cheese for dinner, then head back to the church in time for the prayer meeting. Her plans changed abruptly when the phone rang.

"Maddie? I'm sorry to ask you this, but could you bring Ben to the hospital? Suzanne had a situation today with her chemo, and she isn't doing well… I'm afraid to leave her for more than a few minutes… it's touch and go…. She had an anaphylactic reaction to the chemicals!"

"Yeah, sure, I can do that. Is there anything you need? Anything else I can do?"

"No, I just need Bennie here in case she wakes up, so she can see him. Her love for him keeps her fighting, and right now, I need her to fight!"

Maddie got off the phone and immediately bundled Ben up for the evening drive to the hospital. As they drove, she prayed for Suzanne, for the Buckleys and most of all for little Ben, that his mommy would be safe and well.

Chapter 47

Maddie arrived at the hospital with Bennie and, after asking at information, found Suzanne's room. Although children were not normally allowed in certain areas of the hospital, an exception was made in Bennie's case once Dr. Pai intervened. When it was in the interest of the patient's recovery, the occasional waiver was given. Jim stood outside her room, leaning against the wall, his arms crossed and his chin down on his chest; he almost appeared to be sleeping on his feet. Maddie's heart went out to this husband and father, suffering so much alongside his wife. She admired his devotion to Suzanne and his love for Bennie. When Bennie saw him and called, "Daddy", she saw Jim's eyes light up with love for his son; Maddie released Ben's hand and he ran into his daddy's arms.

Jim lifted him up in an embrace reciprocated by the tiny arms wrapping around his neck. Jim buried his face in Ben's neck and sobbed, suddenly releasing the sorrow and tension he'd held back all day. Ben patted his back and said, "It's ok, daddy, it's ok," as he'd heard his mommy say so many times when he was sad or hurt.

Maddie stood at a distance, not wanting to intrude on this private moment. When his tears subsided, Jim gave her a look of gratitude.

"Thank you so much! I'm sorry to impose on you this way..."

Maddie interrupted his apology, "Don't even think about it. I am glad to do whatever I can to help. Don't think twice about it!"

Jim smiled weakly. Bennie was still clinging around his neck; his father's tears had him worried. In his child's world, daddies weren't supposed to cry or show weakness. He continued to pat his daddy's back once in a while just to be sure daddy was ok.

"Well, it was hard enough asking you, a virtual stranger, to baby-sit, and then to have you change plans like this... I just want you to know I appreciate it."

Maddie tipped her head in acknowledgement. She usually tried to stay in the background, remain anonymous, whenever she did a kind deed for someone at church. She wasn't comfortable with compliments or thank yous and decided not to reply, rather than dispute her merit of the gratitude. To bring them back to the reason for her being there, she asked about Suzanne's condition.

"Oh, she is doing much better. They got her through the crisis; next time, they say there is some drug they can use to prevent the allergic reaction, so we will see in a few weeks."

"How often does she need chemotherapy?"

Jim went on to explain the proposed course of treatment to Maddie. "Of course, it all depends on how she tolerates it, whether she can complete the full course. I am praying this is the last time she has to go through this." He told Maddie how long they had been fighting the cancer, and how he understood Suzanne's prognosis. He also shared information about this set-back.

Maddie was saddened to hear how hard things had been for them; she had envisioned a happy, carefree home for her son. Then she was reminded of her father's cancer fight. They, too, had been a 'normal' family up to that point; no one was immune to the ills of the world. As Christians they knew there was no guarantee of an easy life, just strength through Christ to endure the trials presented to each believer.

"Do you want me to stay? Do you need me to take Bennie home with me so you can stay the night with your wife?" Maddie offered.

"Oh, no, I don't think that will be necessary. Suzanne is stable for the night. I just want her to see little Ben, to lift her spirits, and then I'll be taking him home. I was wondering, though, if you could do a repeat performance tomorrow. I need to see to her discharge tomorrow, and I want to get her settled at home."

"Of course! I don't mind at all!" Maddie agreed to pick Ben up at the day care tomorrow afternoon and to keep him occupied until Jim called for her to bring him home. Jim gave her directions to their home in West County, which she realized was quite a distance from her apartment in the city, but she was willing to do anything for another chance to spend time with Ben.

The next few weeks passed with Maddie watching Bennie in the afternoons several times a week. Suzanne had stabilized and things in the Buckley home were returning to a more normal routine except for the two days Jim took him to day care to give Suzanne a rest. On those days, Maddie picked him up until Jim got off work in the evening, then he would come by her apartment to get him.

Maddie almost regretted agreeing to go home for Spring break; it would mean missing a couple of days with Bennie. She needed to return to Nebraska for the ten days, though, because Lizzie needed more help with her wedding plans. There were invitations to send out, and Lizzie was counting on her. She also had a bridal shower to plan for Lizzie, and that was difficult to accomplish long distance.

As soon as Maddie got home, Lizzie met her at the door. She seemed anxious, worried, and Maddie was concerned that something was wrong at home. Then Lizzie started chattering away about wedding plans and gowns and reception plans and honeymoon details, and Maddie couldn't get a word in.

"Maddie, time is moving so fast toward my wedding date!" Lizzie was flustered, but in a happy way. She looked forward to putting all the planning behind her, and moving on with her life with Tim.

"Liz, it's only mid-April, you still have plenty of time..."

The wedding is scheduled for the first weekend in June, which leaves about seven weeks, and there really was a lot to get done, thought Maddie. *How can I help when I am all the way in St. Louis?* Then she realized that her school year ended before the Omaha school district's term, and that she would have nearly two weeks before the wedding to finish up her duties as Maid of Honor. She wanted to schedule the bridal shower for a week before the wedding, then there was the rehearsal dinner to plan, and final fittings on gowns and... her mind was whirling thinking about everything still needing to get done.

Lizzie wanted Maddie to meet the best man and had set up a 'date' for Maddie and James. Maddie hated blind dates, and since she hadn't dated in a long time, she felt rusty at the whole process. She didn't know what to wear, didn't have a clue where they were going on this so-called date, and what would they talk about. She wondered if they would have anything in common, and did it even matter. After all, this was just part of the preparations for the wedding, not a set up for marriage.

Maddie decided to dress casually in a pair of slacks and button-down shirt with a knit v-necked pullover, leaving the tails and folded back cuffs exposed. She liked what she saw when she looked in the mirror. *Green was definitely my best color*, she thought, as she admired her loosely curled red hair hanging on her shoulders against the sweater. Thankfully Lizzie had chosen a pale green for her Maid of Honor dress; the bridesmaids would wear pastel floral colors: yellow and dusty rose.

As she mused in front of the full-length mirror, the doorbell rang and startled her from her revere. Samantha called her name loudly down the hall and she met up with Lizzie as she stepped into the hallway. "Oh, good, I was hoping you would introduce us," Maddie said to Lizzie.

Lizzie grinned impishly. "I don't know how I can introduce someone I haven't met!"

"What!" Maddie whispered and grabbed Lizzie's arm before they got to the living room. "You mean you fixed me up, sight unseen?"

"Oh, come on! How bad can he be? I mean look who his brother is, and how handsome he is!"

Maddie didn't have time to argue the point, but she promised to talk to Lizzie when she got back home. Together they entered the front room, and standing by the door was a younger version of Pastor Tim. James looked so much like Pastor Tim, that Maddie did a double take. The main difference was height; James stood about 5'10", a little shorter than Pastor Tim, which was fine for her. She didn't care to be looking up too high at her date, it made her neck hurt.

James stepped forward, unsure of which young lady was his date. He held out a bouquet of spring flowers, and Maddie saved him from embarrassment by reaching out for them. "Thank you, James, I guess?" and he nodded. "I'll get these into a vase..."

"Let me do that for you," Lizzie offered. "Hi, James, I'm Lizzie, Tim's fiancé."

She shook his hand, and they made small talk, then she took the flowers from Maddie and encouraged them to be on their way as she went to the kitchen to get the vase.

James and Maddie went out to his waiting car, a white convertible, and she wished she had put her hair into a ponytail, but before they left, James put the top up out of consideration for her. "I know how women are. They don't like their hair all tangled by the wind." He smiled as he said this, obviously not bothered in the least. Maddie liked his soft-spoken, casual demeanor and enjoyed the light conversation they engaged in on their way to dinner. He took her to the local Olive Garden, once he made sure she liked Italian food.

The evening was nice. Maddie saw what she had been missing by not dating. But she wondered how often men like James came along. He was polite, well-mannered and had a wonderful sense of humor. They even had the opportunity to discuss their faith, and Maddie was pleased to hear that he was following in his brother's footsteps, studying at the seminary to be a minister.

The evening ended too soon for Maddie's liking, but James asked if they could go out one more time while she was in town, and she consented. *What could a second date hurt?* She thought, *it's nothing serious, just a second date.* But her hands shook slightly as she struggled to get her key into the front door to open it. Lizzie had waited up and wanted all the details of the date, so they stayed up talking until well after midnight.

Chapter 48

Spring break turned out to be more fun than Maddie anticipated. The second date with James went well, and he promised to stay in touch with her; he had both her phone number and email address, so they could discuss any issues that might come up related to the wedding, or anything else they chose to talk about. As James put it, he wasn't ready for a serious relationship, but a friend of the opposite sex often came in handy. Their views on different subjects are valuable when trying to grow spiritually. His studies and future as a pastor took priority in his life right now, and Maddie was only too glad to keep the contact platonic without complication or commitment from either side.

She went back to St. Louis to finish out the school year, and found out that Jim felt Suzanne was able to cope with Bennie, now, and that he wasn't going to day care anymore. She felt the disappointment deeper than she should have, knowing the child belonged with his adoptive family. Deep in her gut, she felt torn and saddened at the thought of only seeing him at church, and then only if she attended the Buckley's church. Making it a matter of prayer, she asked God to give her the strength needed to relinquish Ben, to not yearn for him and to be able to go back to the role she had before her life became so intimately involved with the Buckley family.

The children in her class were antsy those last couple of weeks, and since they had covered all required material for the year, Maddie decided to let the class explore their creative sides with arts and crafts taking up the bulk of the time at school. She also scheduled more outings to the St. Louis Science Center, to the St. Louis Zoo (which the children adored because they could run and play with little restriction, as long as they stayed within view), and to the Botanical Gardens, another favorite of the kids. The last three weeks passed quickly and Maddie was once again driving back to Omaha, this time for Lizzie's wedding.

The bridal shower went off without a hitch; fellow teachers from her school as well as other young women from church joined in wishing Lizzie happiness. The same evening, James took care of providing a bachelor party for Tim. Unlike the typical raunchy party with women and alcohol, this party was more like a spirit-filled prayer meeting with the young men of the church and some of the elders joining to give advice to the soon-to-be husband. They enjoyed refreshments, but no alcohol was served and everything was kept on a high note.

On the first Saturday in June, the church was tastefully decorated with white organza loosely draped from one pew to the next along the center aisle and fastened with a bouquet of calla lilies. In the front were two large floral displays of fresh spring flowers in every variety and color and on the altar table sat three candles, two tapers for the young couple to use to light the unity candle, the large center candle. The fellowship hall was also decorated with white disposable tablecloths and a candle in the center of each round table surrounded by flowers.

Mama did a beautiful job with the four-tiered wedding cake with two side cakes connected using decorative plastic columns. She used the theme of spring flowers to surround the cake with delicately created sugar-frosting flowers of many types. She also placed flowers strategically around the sides and used frosting to replicate the organza draping around each tier. On the top stood the traditional bride and groom under an archway covered with tiny artificial flowers, the only inedible items on the cake.

At three o'clock Sunday afternoon the church was crowded with well-wishers, family and friends. In the front stood the two Blake brothers, Tim, the groom, and James, the Best Man. Beside them were two other groomsmen, friends of Tim from college days. Pastor Green stood one step up from floor level, and they all looked down the center aisle as the organist began the wedding march.

Maddie walked in first, her lovely mint green gown had a short train trailing from her shoulders to the floor. With her hair pinned up in a French twist with just a few loose strands curling near her face, she looked like a Greek goddess carrying a simple single calla lily in her hands. Behind her followed the two bridesmaids, also college friends, but this time they were from Lizzie's school days. They lined up on the opposite side of the groomsmen in the front of the chapel.

Then quiet laughter traveled through the sanctuary as the requisite ring bearer and flower girl made their way down the aisle. They were two children of church friends of Lizzie. The little boy was just three years old and he took his job very seriously as he helped the little two year old flower girl stay focused and walking up the aisle all the while balancing his pillow with the rings tied to it. Dressed in a child-sized tuxedo, and she in a full-skirted frilly dress, they looked like a miniature bride and groom.

With the chimes preceding the bridal march, the congregation stood in unison and faced the center rear of the church. Lizzie was radiant in her old-fashioned wedding dress with a traditional veil over her face. Her gown had a full skirt gathered to the tiny waist above which was a beaded and embroidered bodice with a heart-shaped neckline. The gown was modestly designed to cover her shoulders and back without appearing prudish, and the train was also a modest length. Her bouquet reflected the arrangements in the front of the church; it was a tinier arrangement of spring flowers with multi-colored pastel ribbons trailing down, nearly to the floor. Nothing about her said 'overdone'; everything was in good taste and modest.

Tim had eyes for only Lizzie as she came up the aisle alone. Without her father, and with no elderly friend to accompany her, she chose to take the walk alone. As she passed, the congregants sat down and faced the front of the church and once she reached the front, Tim reached out his hand to her and guided her into place beside him before Pastor Greene.

Maddie observed the entire processional and turned to the front to hear the sermonette aimed at anyone thinking of marriage, not just the young couple. She took Lizzie's bouquet so they could exchange vows and rings, and then, too quickly, it was over, and the recessional played as Mr. and Mrs. Timothy Blake joyfully exited the sanctuary followed by their attendants. Everyone made their way to the fellowship hall where they formed the receiving line and greeted those attending the reception.

The reception lasted into the evening, and was as beautiful as the wedding itself. Altogether it was the most joyful wedding Maddie had attended. The love emanating from the young couple along with the love of the congregation for their pastor and his new wife made it a very special occasion right up to the end where Lizzie and Tim left to change into traveling clothes for their honeymoon. They were showered with birdseed rather than rice as they ran out to find their car decked out with crepe paper ribbons and tin cans. 'Just Married' was scrawled across the rear window and hearts decorated the side windows. They laughed at the monkey business and left the reception heading for the airport in Omaha.

Lizzie and Tim were taking just a brief honeymoon to Dustin, Florida which was on the panhandle and had lovely beaches. They kept the cost down by staying at a modest hotel, despite the congregation's desire to present them with a more extravagant hotel package. Pastor Tim declined saying the money could be put to better use elsewhere in the ministry, and Lizzie fully agreed with him.

The reception gradually fizzled out with the guests of honor disappearing, and soon all that remained was the clean-up crew. Maddie and her family went home where they got out of their fancy clothes and relaxed together in the front room. After weeks of planning, Maddie felt a bit of a let down now that it was all over. She still needed to organize the wedding gifts in Tim's house so they would be ready when Lizzie and Tim returned, but otherwise her job as Maid of Honor was done. Overall, she was pleased with the results of her labor of love, and hoped Lizzie had been pleased, too.

Chapter 49

Lizzie and Tim returned from their honeymoon looking tan and happy, every bit the newlywed couple. After they had a few days to settle in, Maddie and Lizzie got together for lunch and a chat. Lizzie seemed to have matured overnight; her discussion topics no longer frivolous and girlish. Instead she talked about the plans she and Tim had for his ministry, both here and in the future. She spoke with compassion of several church members in need of prayer, without revealing private information, and she shared with Maddie her dreams of motherhood, something she never discussed previously.

"Oh, Maddie, I'm sorry. I shouldn't have brought up that topic with you. I didn't mean to make you sad… are you ok?"

Maddie wasn't at all bothered talking about Lizzie's dreams for motherhood, after all, she had her hopes for the future, too. She reassured Lizzie, and then told her about the time she had spent with Bennie, and the serious condition of his mother. Although Lizzie was aware that Maddie babysat Ben, she didn't know how often or to what extent Maddie was involved with the Buckleys. Before the wedding, she hadn't had the time to tell Lizzie anything about her time in St. Louis, and it felt good to talk about her emotions regarding taking care of Bennie.

Their lunch was over too quickly for Maddie, but Lizzie had some women's meeting to plan and other obligations as the wife of their pastor, so her leisure time was more limited now. Maddie returned home somewhat glum. She realized that their friendship was at a turning point. As with other friends from school and college who had married, the terms of the relationship changed when one of them married. The focus changed because they now had husbands to look after and with whom they did things, instead of just outings with the girls.

Lizzie was putting her teaching career on hold now that she was a pastor's wife, which also gave them less to talk about. Maddie, on the other hand, needed to use the summer break to prepare for the upcoming school year once again. She thought, *It's the same cycle every year. Teach nine months, plan during the summer. No social life, no outside activities. I have become boring. No wonder I have no dates or possibilities.*

She felt herself slipping into depression, and knew that she needed to nip that in the bud or it would grow. She had seen too many suffering with depression, and prayed that the Lord would help her deal with her disappointments in life. The counselor she saw after the rape helped her see the warning signs of depression, and gave her hints on how Christians can mediate melancholy. She also explained that sometimes medicine is needed to help one over a particularly rough spell.

But Maddie did not feel this was that serious. It was a matter of adjusting her mind, and seeking other outlets. She needed to get involved with people her age, a social life, where she could meet others and make new friends with common interests. She decided she would return to St. Louis early for that very purpose, since that was where her life and career was focused. She would spend a couple of weeks with Mama and the family, but then she planned to go back to her apartment and check out the local churches for group activities for the twenty-something generation.

On return to St. Louis, just after the Fourth of July, Maddie was shocked to find a message on her phone from Jim Buckley.

"Maddie, this is Jim Buckley. I know you are out of town, but when you get back, could you give me a call. If possible, we need your help with Ben again. Suzanne has had another set-back, she isn't doing well at all, and I need a stable caretaker for Bennie. If you can help, please give me a call. Thanks. You know our number."

After listening to the message, Maddie was convinced that the Lord had led her to return early to St. Louis. It couldn't be a coincidence that she returned just when she was needed again. Maddie couldn't call that evening; it was too late to call anyone. But she promised herself she would call first thing in the morning to see what was up. She had no idea when Jim had called or if the situation had improved since, but she would put everything else aside for the few weeks until school started, for the sake of caring for Ben.

"Jim? Hi, this is Maddie…"

"Oh, Maddie, I am so glad you called. Say, could you watch Ben today? I know it's short notice, but I am in a bad spot this morning."

"Sure, Jim, be glad to help. How is Suzanne doing?"

"Not good. Not good at all. She's failing fast and the doctor's don't have much hope… the cancer has metastasized to her lungs, her liver is severely affected, her organs are failing." Jim's voice choked, he cleared his throat, then in a strained voice continued, "She just wants to hang on until Ben's third birthday which is later this month, then I don't know…"

"I'm so sorry, Jim. I'll be happy to keep Ben as much as necessary."

They made the arrangements for Maddie to meet Jim to get Ben, and got off the phone. Maddie rushed her morning routine and hurried out the door to meet Jim as planned, and on time.

Bennie was happy to see Maddie, he reached out to have her take him from his car seat, and she gladly unbuckled him and lifted him into her arms. He wrapped his arms around her neck and said, "Maddie," as he smoothed her hair with his tiny hand. He looked at Jim and said, "Daddy, me go with Maddie?" Jim nodded as tears crept into the corners of his eyes.

"Yes, son, you go with Maddie. I'll see you later today, kiddo." And with that, he kissed Ben's cheek and told Maddie he would call later with an update.

For several days, this routine repeated itself. Maddie took Bennie to the zoo and spent time in Forest Park allowing him to chase pigeons and watch the fish in the lake. They played on the playground at the Christian School where Maddie worked, and on days when the weather was bad, she spent time indoors teaching Bennie his ABCs and 1,2,3s. She began to wonder why she had decided to give him up for adoption. *This mothering thing doesn't seem so hard,* she thought, but quickly caught herself and prayed, *Lord, help me to not covet this child. I gave him to You when I signed him over for adoption and I need help to trust You. Please, Lord. I believe, help my unbelief.*

Bennie's birthday was just around the corner, and Suzanne was scheduled to be released from the hospital the day before his birthday. Hospice would be involved with her home care because the doctors considered her terminal with less than six months to live. Maddie was watching Ben at their home that day, so he would be able to greet his mommy when she arrived. Jim hoped that being at home and seeing Bennie would put the fight back into her, but when Maddie saw her get out of the car it was like seeing a walking skeleton.

Suzanne had lost so much weight that she was skin and bones; her clothes hung on her like a sack, and she wore a turban on her head to hide the baldness from chemotherapy. They were still administering the chemicals in hopes of slowing down the process to give her more time; no longer was their goal to cure her. Jim had his arm around her waist helping her along, nearly carrying her because her legs were so weak. She wanted to appear ok for Bennie's sake, so she would not let Jim carry her, or he would have lifted her into his arms as easily as if he were carrying a child.

"Bennie." Her weakened voice cracked. "My little boy, come to mommy."

Bennie held back, holding onto Maddie's leg. He didn't recognize his mommy in this woman with the sunken eyes, dark circles around them, grayish skin and unkempt appearance. His mommy had always looked nice, not with clothes hanging on her like this lady. Maddie tried to encourage him to go to his mommy, but he held back, clinging to her.

"No, Her not mommy," he said. "Daddy, me want mommy." He looked up into his daddy's face. Jim looked back with tears on his cheeks.

"I'm sorry, sport. This is mommy. She's just sick. Give mommy a hug to make her feel better." Then Bennie slowly went to Suzanne and reached his arms up to her to hug her around her neck. She leaned down just enough to hug him, but she was too weak to pick him up, so Jim lifted him up for her, and held him close to Suzanne.

As they went into their home, Maddie touched Jim's arm, "I'll leave now. Call if you need anything." Then she went back to her empty apartment and prayed for the little family she'd just left. Her heart was breaking for her little Ben, but also for Jim and Suzanne and the sorrow that lay ahead. She remembered her mother's grief when her father died and she could tell by Suzanne's emaciated appearance that it would not be long before Jim would be saying his good-byes to his beloved Suzanne.

Chapter 50

Bennie's third birthday passed more quietly that the past two celebrations. Suzanne had neither the strength nor inclination to plan a party, and she could not have entertained even if someone else had taken over the planning of the party. Jim bought an ice cream cake from Dairy Queen with colorful little cars decorating a race track on top, and a big number three candle off in the corner. He had purchased some gifts that Suzanne suggested while she was in hospital, and had the gifts wrapped in childish wrapping paper and lots of ribbons.

The morning started off with a call from Maddie to check on Suzanne and to wish Bennie 'Happy Birthday'.

"How did you know this was his birthday?" Jim asked, not recalling if he had told her or not.

Maddie couldn't remember if he had told her either, so she had to think quickly. "Didn't you say they were discharging Suzanne the day before his birthday? Anyway, I figured it was sometime soon…" her voice faded. She wondered if he believed her.

"Well, thanks for calling. Suzanne is doing ok, no change really. We plan to spend a quiet day with Bennie."

"I bought him a gift. Do you mind my bringing it by… or should I bring it some other time," secretly Maddie hoped she could see Bennie on his birthday.

"Maybe some other time; I think today will be just us. I hope you understand."

Saddened, Maddie accepted his decision without further question. She got off the phone and wondered what she could do to get her mind off little Ben, and then the ringing of the telephone broke into her thoughts. She hurried to answer thinking perhaps Jim had changed his mind, or Suzanne had suggested inviting her over, but was let down when she heard Lizzie's voice on the other end.

"Maddie, I called to say hello, and to see how you are doing today."

Once Maddie got over her initial disappointment, she realized Lizzie's voice was the best thing she could hear right then. Lizzie knew what she would be feeling on this the third birthday of her adopted out child. Lizzie knew that every year it was the same, sadness, worry, regret, wondering if she had made the right choice. And this year was even worse, knowing what the Buckley family was going through.

They talked for over an hour, and when the call was nearly ended, Lizzie offered to pray with Maddie. *The words of a true friend on my behalf seem to help more than when I pray on my own*, Maddie thought. She appreciated Lizzie so much right then; she cherished the bond they had forged over the last four years. Then she realized that that was the same length of her friendship with her college friends whom she had lost contact with. *I can never let that happen between Lizzie and me, she mused. I need to work harder to keep friendships alive. Maybe that's why I am so lonely lately, because I don't put out enough effort to build and keep relationships.* Lizzie wished her a wonderful day, and they got off the phone with Maddie feeling encouraged and hopeful for her future.

For the next couple of weeks Maddie continued to watch Bennie on alternate days to ease the burden on the Buckley household. Suzanne's mother was there to care for her, along with the hospice nurses and staff who made frequent visits, but a busy three-year-old took too much energy with so much care needed for Suzanne. Her health steadily declined after Ben's birthday; it was as if that was the last thing she needed to take care of.

To save Maddie the long trip to West County, Jim continued to bring Ben to Maddie's apartment on his way to work. They chatted each evening that he came by to pick Ben up. He shared tidbits about how Suzanne was doing, and Maddie told him some of the cute, funny things Ben did that day. Jim would take those stories home to Suzanne to keep her up on their son's activities and development. He seemed to change daily, and was learning well from Maddie, getting ready for the pre-school he would attend starting in the fall.

Suzanne loved hearing how good Bennie was doing learning his alphabet and numbers. She longed to be the one working with him, but she couldn't even get out of bed most days. One evening, about two weeks after Ben's birthday, she tried to talk to Jim; her heart was full, and she had so much on her mind, so many things left undone.

"Jim, we need to talk."

"Sure, honey, what do you want to talk about," Jim was sitting up in bed beside her reading a book.

"Please, Jim, put down your book. I need to talk to you about something serious..." her voice was weak, but insistent.

Jim turned to her to hear what she had to say. Whenever she got serious, she wanted to talk about when she was to die, and Jim tried to avoid that topic.

"Jim, remember when I asked you to promise...?"

"Now, Suzanne," he interrupted. "If you are going to ask me to promise to remarry, forget it! I love you; I don't want to lose you and I don't want to talk about you dying!"

"But I need to talk about it, Jim. I need to know that you and Bennie will be ok when I'm gone. I am going to die, and you have to accept that. Please, Jim..."

Tears flowed freely from Jim's eyes as he took her hands. He was too choked up to talk and all he could do was to pull her boney frame into his arms. He was afraid to hold her too snugly, afraid she might break; she seemed so fragile. She whispered into his ear, pleading with him to promise her and she was sobbing, too.

"Shhhh, ok, ok. If it will make you feel better, if it will make you stop crying, I'll promise. I can't say how soon, but I will try to find someone who can love Bennie like you do. But I can't promise to love them like I love you. I love you so much; I could never find another love like ours."

"No two loves are ever the same, Jim, but promise you will try to love again, not just for Bennie, but for you, too. You need love; I know this and so do you. I love you so much, my dear."

They held each other, grieving for their lost future together, as they fell asleep that evening. They never again spoke of Jim's promise, but Suzanne seemed at peace after that conversation. No longer was she intent on wrapping up undone tasks. It was as though she had accomplished her last, most important job, and was ready whenever her time came.

One muggy August day, less than a month after Ben's third birthday, Maddie received a call in the early morning hours.

"Maddie, it's Jim Buckley." A tired, grief-weary voice spoke quietly.

"Jim, is everything...?" she could hear in his voice that everything was not alright.

"She's gone. My Suzie passed during the night." Maddie could hear weeping, a cough, and then he spoke again, "at least she didn't suffer. She died in her sleep."

"Jim, I am so sorry! Is there anything I can do? Do you need anything? What about Ben, is he doing ok?"

"Family is coming in, so I'll be running to the airport, but Suzie's mom will take care of Bennie. We'll be fine, as fine as we can be considering…" and he broke down again. "I need to go…"

Off the phone, Maddie shared his grief from a different perspective. She grieved as a girl who'd lost her father too young, and now saw her son lose his mother at such a tender age. She wept, her heart breaking for the Buckley family, for Suzanne's family, for all their friends and family impacted by the loss of such a beautiful young woman. When her tears abated, she picked up the phone and called home. She needed to hear her mother's voice; she also needed to talk to Lizzie, but that would come a bit later.

The church rallied around the Buckley's bringing the usual baked goods and casseroles and volunteering to help keep track of cards and gifts so Jim could respond to the well-wishers at a later date. They offered to do chores, run errands, anything they could to ease Jim's burden. The pastor came to accompany him to the funeral parlor and he seemed to be sleep-walking through the preparations. He did not recall providing her favorite dress to the undertaker, or choosing the white casket with silver handles. He wondered who had chosen the spray of spring flowers to place on the casket from the family, and how they picked the date for the funeral. All the activities seemed surreal to him; he felt like an onlooker watching a movie.

The funeral itself took place in the church and the speakers and songs were chosen by a group of friends who planned those details for Jim. The graveside service was the only thing Jim recalled later when he tried to remember that day.

Rain drenched the green awning in the cemetery covering the spot where dirt lay under another tarp, having been dug out of her grave. Straps across the opening supported the beautiful casket that contrasted so sharply with the muddy soil. The pastor spoke once again, as Jim and Bennie sat in chairs beside the grave. Bennie was restless, "Me want mommy," he whined to his daddy, and Jim lifted him into his arms and cried into his hair, "I know, son, I know… me, too!" Onlookers were touched by the tender scene, and those not already crying, felt moisture in their eyes.

Maddie stood a ways off. She wanted to give the family and close friends a chance to say their good-byes; she was just there to give her respect. Suzanne and she had not become close friends or anything. She was just Bennie's babysitter, a mother's helper, but she had to be there all the same.

Jim took time off from work to grieve and to take care of his personal affairs relating to Suzanne's death and, by the time he returned to work, Maddie was also back at work, teaching her children at the Christian School. She often wondered how Ben was doing, but when she called to check on him, she found out that Suzanne's mother had taken him to her home for an undetermined length of time, just to help Jim out.

The school year moved along as usual, with the same subjects and the same celebrations to plan. Although Maddie tried to keep it new and interesting each year, to stay up on new teaching plans, this year was different. She lacked the enthusiasm she usually felt with a new group of kids. She performed by memory, rather than feeling excited to present new information to eager little students. Despite her prayers, she felt desolate, empty. Without Ben to watch and love, she felt hollow, empty-armed, and wondered at the strength it took for Hannah to leave her little boy at the temple with an elderly priest.

She began to have second thoughts about her career choice. Then she wondered if a change of venue might make the difference. Perhaps if she wasn't so close to Ben, she would find that spark she was missing. With her contract extending through the end of this school term, she had no choice but to make the best of it, but she was determined that, beginning in the New Year, she would send out resumes to see what opportunities were available, maybe even something nearer to Mama and her family.

Chapter 51

Months passed after Suzanne's death, and Maddie was still struggling to function well in her classroom. She missed Bennie so much that it was affecting her job, her spiritual life, and her personal life. In spite of her resolution to start seeking out young people activities, she still had no social life, no dates, and no possibilities.

She spent long periods in prayer, pleading for the Lord to take away her yearnings for her child, and she had enlisted the prayers of her home Prayer Warrior group to pray about an unspoken request for her. Lizzie knew all about her situation, although Maddie was thankful she never said 'I told you so' to her. She had every right after giving Maddie so many warnings about involvement with the Buckleys.

Lizzie had said she would only be hurt, but Maddie kept thinking she could remain detached, that she was only babysitting. It didn't work out that way. She fell in love with her little boy, and now she didn't know what to do with that emotion. She hadn't seen Jim Buckley in church, but she hadn't been to his church, either, since Suzanne's funeral. On occasion she was tempted to drive to his church, but she recognized the temptation as coming from the enemy. Her Lord would not lead her into temptation, and she claimed that promise. So she was left wondering about Ben.

One day followed another at school, and one week followed the previous week, until months had passed and it was time to prepare for Christmas. The children were again putting on the Christmas program for the various churches, but Lizzie had little enthusiasm for the preparations. Her class's excitement and joy over their costumes and learning their parts did little to lift her spirits. She tried to force a smile and keep up the pretense, but as the weekend of the performance approached, she felt more dread than enjoyment.

Every presentation of the program went smoothly, and Maddie's anxiety lifted slightly as they approached the final program. The Central Christian Church was again hosting the finale and the reception social following the program. They arrived at the church on Sunday evening as planned, and as they were unloading the costumes and props, Maddie heard a voice behind her.

"Maddie!" It was a tiny voice, so familiar, yet older than she remembered.

She turned around and reached out for the little boy who had stolen her heart, "Oh, Bennie," she said as she held him close in her arms. She cried as she pressed her face into his neck, "Oh, Bennie, I missed you!"

"Me miss Maddie, too." He pulled back and smiled into her face. His hand reached up to her face and wiped a tear from her cheek. "Maddie OK?"

"Yes, darling, Maddie is more than ok, now!"

Jim stood watching the interaction of his son with his former sitter, and his heart melted to see how attached Bennie still seemed to Maddie. He was also amazed at the amount of love he saw in Maddie's face; he wanted to find out what was behind that love. Surely it didn't come from the few times she baby-sat for them. It was so deep and heart-felt, almost as strong as what he felt for his son.

"Hello, Maddie," he said once they finished their greetings.

"Oh, I'm sorry, Jim. I was so taken with little Ben, I didn't speak to you! How are you doing these days? I see Bennie is back from his grandma's house..."

"Yeah, I wasn't doing so well without him around after Suzanne died," he coughed and cleared his throat, "anyway, we are managing. It's day by day, you know."

"Yes, I do know. I lost my father a few years ago, and I know that kind of grief."

"So, you're presenting the program again this year?"

That question brought Maddie back to the reason she was there, and she realized she was needed inside to help set up. She quickly excused herself, promising to talk more during the social, and hurried into the fellowship hall. This program also went off without any major glitches. There were the usual cute mistakes children tend to make, but overall the message of the reason for the season came through in the skit and songs.

Afterward, once the props and costumes were returned to the vehicles, and space was opened up for the social, the children played the games and participated in various traditional church activities. Maddie went over to the tables and sat in a chair to watch all the fun. Emotionally, she was wiped out and, as a result, her energy level was also way down. She sipped on her glass of punch and munched on a few of the nuts from the bowl in the center of the table. Then she saw Jim Buckley coming toward her and her heart fluttered.

Now why would my heart do that when I see him? she thought. *That's really strange. We have no history, after all. No future either, for that matter. Hmmm.*

Jim joined her at the table; Bennie was running and playing with the other smaller children and having a blast. "So, how are *you* doing?" Jim asked her pointedly. "You seemed really down when we saw you by your car."

Maddie wasn't sure he really wanted to hear about her depression, and she felt certain he wouldn't want to know the reason, so she treated it like a rhetorical question, "Oh, I'm just fine." She answered a little too cheerfully.

"You know I know you better than that. After all the chats we had when I was picking up Bennie, I feel like we became friends during one of the hardest times of my life." Again he choked, looked down, cleared his throat and then looked back up at her.

Maddie didn't know how to take that comment. She had never thought about Jim Buckley as anything other than Ben's adoptive father. She never took time to think about a friendship with him. She had been so focused on Bennie, and the impact of Suzanne's illness on that family that there hadn't been time to think of that type of familiarity. But she looked at him and realized he was a nice looking man. He had been such a loving husband to Suzanne, too. Suddenly her heart flip-flopped again and her cheeks flushed brightly.

"What do you say? Bennie misses you. Maybe we could be friends and take him on outings occasionally, if you didn't mind, that is?"

"Oh, you know any chance to be with Bennie is a joy for me," She smiled, this time her smile reached her eyes and they sparkled.

He gave a deep sigh, as if he had been holding his breath. Since Suzanne's death, he hadn't sat and talked to another woman, and he felt out of practice, but with Maddie it felt natural. "How about going to Union Station with us this week? It's all decked out for the Christmas season, and I have some last minute shopping to do that you could help me with...for Bennie, you know."

At first, Maddie hesitated. Should she talk to Lizzie first, ask her advice? Or should she go with her first reaction. How could she know if it was the Lord or if this was another temptation meant to lead her astray? "Can I call you tomorrow, and let you know?"

"Sure, that's fine. I was thinking about going on Wednesday or Thursday, so give me a call...same number, ok?"

She agreed to call either way, and then she got up to leave. Her knees felt shaky and she wanted to get home and think. She couldn't get her mind straight with the noise of the children playing. She needed to think and pray.

On Wednesday, Maddie met up with Jim and Bennie at Union Station down on Market Street in St. Louis. It was a converted train station and had a wonderful history. St. Louis Union Station was a mixture of clothing stores, novelty shops, candy stores and vendor carts and Bennie was especially fascinated by the singing at the Fudgery. They even got to taste some freshly made peanut butter fudge which made Ben happy. For lunch they went to Houlihan's and had burgers and fries, and by the end of the day, Bennie had fallen asleep in his umbrella stroller Jim brought along 'just in case'.

When preparing to leave, Jim thanked Maddie for making the day easier for him. He explained that he had only gone there with Suzanne and the idea of going without her made it difficult. Bennie had begged for some time, remembering their previous visits. Maddie's agreeing to go along really helped, according to Jim. Then, just before she started toward her car, he asked if she would consider going somewhere with them again sometime.

Maddie was glad to agree this time. She believed they could have a friendship for the sake of Bennie, and if it was the Lord's will for something to develop between them, it would, otherwise she would be happy with a platonic relationship allowing her to spend time with Ben.

Chapter 52

Maddie and Jim met about once a month for a prearranged outing with Bennie. Many of the places they took him were venues where Maddie had taken her students, and she was well acquainted with them. When the weather was warm enough, they went to outdoor places like the Botanical Gardens or the Zoo, but if the weather didn't permit an outdoor outing, they went to the Gateway Arch and walked through the museum underground at the base of the arch or they would go to one of the many other museums in town. The Science Center was always a favorite for children and Grant's Farm provided a chance for Bennie to pet animals and ride on rides.

Springtime arrived rainy and windy as usual for St. Louis, and the Mississippi River was near cresting when it finally stopped pouring down rain. Easter weekend Maddie had decided to stay in St. Louis instead of taking her spring break with her family and it was sunny and warm. Jim invited her to take a drive along the River Road to Pere Marquet State Park where there was supposed to be a great restaurant at which they could eat. The drive was both relaxing and beautiful. Bennie loved seeing speed boats and barges on the water and was oohing and ahing whenever another went by.

They decided to ride the Brussels Ferry across the river and back just so Bennie could experience that, then continued north on the Great River Road until they reached the state park. They enjoyed their late lunch, and as they headed south again, Bennie fell asleep in his car seat allowing them to enjoy some adult conversation. They chatted about many subjects before Jim brought up the one subject Maddie did not want to discuss.

"Maddie, I need to ask you something. Did you have some experience with a child that causes you to love Bennie so much? I mean, it just seems that you are very attached to him, and I was wondering if you lost a sibling or student or something that made you sensitive to my little boy?"

Oh, Lord, is this the time to tell him the truth? Maddie prayed silently, looking out the window toward the water.

"If it's too hard to talk about, I understand. I was just wondering..." he noticed the prolonged pause.

"I don't know if I can share it with you, Jim. I think we have become good friends, but I am concerned it might change our relationship and that you won't let me be around Ben anymore." She looked over at him expectantly, unsure if she should tell him.

"Maddie, I think of you as more than a friend. I don't know where our relationship is leading, but I know I would never stop you from seeing Bennie. He loves you so much; I think it would break his heart if he couldn't spend time with you." He reached his hand from the steering wheel and placed it on her small, soft hand. She flushed from her neck up and her palms felt moist, but her mouth was dry.

What is happening to me, Lord? Why am I reacting this way to his touch? She took a gulp from her bottle of water she always carried along. Then she decided that now was as good a time as any, so she began to tell him her story.

"Jim, what I am going to tell you may sound weird or crazy, but it is the truth, ok?" He nodded, not wanting to interrupt her story.

"About four and a half years ago, when on my first teaching job, I was raped by a co-worker." She paused to see his reaction, but he just nodded again, although she could see compassion in his eyes.

"That rape resulted in a pregnancy, and the pregnancy resulted in a child that I gave up for adoption." Again she stopped and looked at him, her heart beating rapidly, her hands sweating and her head thumping. *What must he be thinking of me*? She wondered. But he gave no reaction, said nothing, just nodded again, with moisture glistening in the corners of his eyes.

"That child that I gave up for adoption was... is... Bennie, your son. There, I said it. He was my baby that I gave up and Pastor Tim worked out the adoption for me with you and Suzanne. I didn't know you moved to St. Louis or that you were the ones that adopted him, until I saw Suzanne in Forest Park one day..."

"She used to love to walk him around there..." Jim mused.

"Anyway, when I saw you guys at the Christmas program and saw Ben, and heard his name, I knew, because of the pictures and letters I'd received as updates through Pastor Tim."

"My Bennie is your son." Jim spoke reverently, as if in a trance. He seemed to be trying to come to grips with the idea.

"Yes. I didn't mean to get involved with him. That just kind of happened, but I do love him, and I love the time you allowed me to spend with him." Then Maddie began to weep quietly. She was both embarrassed and scared for Jim's reaction. *Would he think of her as promiscuous ?* She wondered, then she wondered why his opinion should matter to her.

Jim found a spot to pull the car over in the little town of Grafton. Bennie was still sleeping. He turned to Maddie and took her hands in his.

"My dear, you have been through so much. I'm sorry I didn't ask sooner. I was so caught up in my own grief and loss that I lost sight of the suffering of others. Please forgive me." He raised her hands touching them tenderly to his lips, and his compassion reached the innermost depths of her soul. She looked up at him in amazement.

"Maddie, do you know how special you have become to me? How vital you are to both Ben's and my life? I know we haven't talked of romance or anything, but I've truly grown to love you. You have been such a rock for me during the past year, and I can't imagine my life without you in it."

Maddie shook her head in disbelief.

"I don't mean to shock you or to rush into something, so don't feel like you have to reciprocate my feelings. But if you think there is a chance for us, any chance that you might love me…?"

Maddie flushed again, and felt the thudding of her heart up into her neck. She could not believe that the Lord had worked this miracle in her life. Not only had He helped her learn to love her son, despite his origins, He also made it possible for her to be a part of her son's life. And now He was opening a door for love with a man that would include her son. She could hardly believe it; now she understood when people said 'pinch me, so I know it isn't a dream'. The Lord had wrought a miracle especially for her; there was no other way to explain it.

"Jim, there is definitely a chance for us, if you will have me, imperfect as I am. I always wanted to be pure for my husband. Are you sure that isn't important to you?"

"Maddie, there is nothing you could say to change my love for you. When Suzanne died, I thought I had died. Then when I saw you and Bennie hugging at the Christmas program, the ice around my heart melted, and I knew I could love again. Did I tell you that Suzanne made me promise that I would love again? Well, she did. Anyway, if you will have me, I would be honored to be your husband."

He pulled her closer and gently touched his lips to hers, sealing that vow. Then, although he didn't want to continue driving, they had to get home, so he started the car and drove back to St. Louis. All the way back they discussed their hopes and desires. They did not want to rush the wedding, but instead they wanted to spend time getting to know each other even better. Jim wanted to wait until the one year anniversary of his loss before he remarried, and Maddie agreed to that, so they decided an autumn wedding would work.

Spring flowed into summer and Bennie had his fourth birthday knowing he was going to have a new mommy in a few months. He loved the idea of calling Maddie mommy and couldn't wait to be the ring bearer at the wedding. Joy reigned in the Galloway household when Maddie called with the news, and Lizzie was thrilled to be her Matron of Honor. Maddie did not go back to teaching that fall; she wanted time to reorder her life before the wedding in November.

Time flew by and the wedding day arrived with sunshine and golden leaves falling from trees. Maddie's colors for her bridesmaid reflected the glory of autumn as did the theme for their reception. She was a beautiful bride and Jim stood proud to claim her as his life partner. Happiness was palpable at the reception and nobody was happier than little Benjamin Buckley.

Epilogue

Five years later…

Maddie looked down at the tiny, round face of her newborn daughter, Taryn Hope Buckley. Her carrot-red hair was covered with a hand-knit bonnet Mama made, and the matching blanket was wrapped snugly around her. Her long lashes lay on her smooth pink cheeks as she slept. Born prematurely, she was tinier than the other children, and a much quieter baby. She had just finished nursing and was content to be cuddled as Maddie rocked in her rocker/glider.

Maddie lovingly gazed out the nursery window to the backyard, watching her other children at play. At nearly ten years old, Bennie loved being a big brother to his little sister, four-year-old Bethany Joy, and to his two-year-old brother Timothy (named for Pastor Tim). He organized their play, whether they played school or pretended to be animals at the zoo, and made sure they were safe and happy. The swing-set and playhouse were integral to their outdoor play, and Maddie was thankful that Jim had prepared the yard for a large family of children.

Jim would be home soon. He was stopping at the store on the way home for ice cream for Bennie's birthday party tomorrow. He still commuted to Clayton daily, having advanced to a Vice President position in the firm, and was active in the community. He often came home early during the summer months to enjoy the children and relieve Maddie so she could prepare her teaching plans for the next school year.

Maddie was still teaching at the church school, first graders loved Mrs. Buckley, and she was thankful for the nursery at the church where she could leave Beth and Timmy (and, also this fall, Taryn) with trusted caretakers, and she could see them during the day when there was a recess or lunch-break. If they hadn't started the Christian Day Care, she might have given up teaching.

Her children were too important to her to leave with just anyone. Besides, under other circumstances, she would not recommend a mother leave her babies in day care at such a young age. She loved being a mother; it was who she was, first and foremost. Being a teacher took second place in her life, and was not so important that she would give her children to someone else to raise. But she trusted the mothers who volunteered at the Christian Day Care; she knew them all from church. And she saw the kids several times in the day; she would even be able to nurse Taryn on schedule which was important, also.

Life with Jim was definitely an answer to her prayers. Together they volunteered to help unwed mothers work through their options. They were active in Pro-Life movements and in Adoption Support groups. Maddie used her personal experience to help them explore feelings about raising their child versus placing them for adoption; Jim spoke from the adoptive parent perspective, to reassure them of the types of homes available to children. As a couple, they were an invaluable resource in Pastor Tim's work.

She loved the fact that Lizzie lived near enough for them to share in parts of this ministry. Pastor Tim and Lizzie had moved to St. Louis a couple of years ago, and Maddie and

Lizzie enjoyed their renewed friendship. They attended the same church (and, of course, Pastor Tim was the minister) and enjoyed the Women's Bible Study group and the Mother's Fellowship group together.

Lizzie had two little ones of her own now; she also had a Timmy, named for his daddy, who was a tow-headed, freckle-faced, and mischievous six-year-old. He just happened to be in Maddie's class, but he behaved well in the classroom. It was when he was on the playground or at home that his 'Dennis the Menace' personality came out. He quickly received the label of 'typical PK' (Preacher's kid) as if all misbehavior was attributed to the fact that his daddy was a minister.

Lizzie also had a little three-year-old daughter with Down Syndrome, Alyssa-beth. Her angelic face, framed with golden curls, and deep blue eyes that showed her loving nature, stole the heart of all who met her. Lizzie was determined to open every opportunity for her daughter, and refused to see Down as a disability; she called it an 'other-ability'. Aly, as she called her baby, developed motor skills slower than some other children, but once she got going, there was no stopping her from running around the house and climbing on the jungle-gym. Lizzie believed Aly would beat the odds and 'be somebody' someday!

Lizzie received support and encouragement from many corners, not the least of who was Maddie's mother. Because of the bond formed between them before Lizzie married, Mrs. Galloway was like a surrogate grandmother for Lizzie's children. She enjoyed the role, and counted Lizzie's two among her numbering of her grandchildren, now totaling seven. She occasionally made the trip from Nebraska to St. Louis to visit both the Buckley family and the Blake family, spending time playing with the children and crocheting blankets for their beds.

Mama and the Galloway children still live in Nebraska. Simon decided to stay home for college rather than going to a more remote school. He realized that Mama needed him around, and he finally came to grips with his role as the Galloway man of the house. He finished his Bachelor's degree and was now working on a Master's in Counseling. His renewed faith in Jesus, and the powerful examples in his nuclear and extended family, propelled him into a nurturing, healing career path. He wanted to help other families through difficult patches like what his family had experienced.

Samantha was still in college, studying to be a nurse. She, too, had a heart for helping others, but wanted to specialize in pediatrics because of her love for children. There was a time when working with children was the farthest thing from her mind, but watching her nieces and nephews as infants and toddlers helped her realize her calling. She was especially touched by Aunt Lizzie's devotion to Aly. Perhaps, in time, her pediatric work would be with developmentally challenged kids. She would leave that in God's hands.

Jason and Jamie were still in high school, and to Mama's delight, seemed solid in their convictions. They participated happily in youth activities, even taking on projects as leaders on occasion. Together they were strong, but Mama had hopes that individually they would develop unique interests to carry them through life. She knew only too well the twists and turns life's journey can take, and the oceans of tears one often cries. But she had confidence that the Lord could carry her children through those waters, as He had always done for her.

As Maddie sat holding Taryn, she thought over the last few years of her life, and all the paths her journey of faith had taken. On the little table beside her rocker lay an invitation to her college reunion. She thought of all the dreams she had when graduating, all the plans she had and how the Lord had worked everything out for her good. She wondered about Ashleigh, Taylor and Isobel. She hadn't heard from them in years, didn't even know where they were or what their lives were like. She questioned whether they would even want to attend the reunion. They all had such diverse plans for their lives; she was curious about their accomplishments, their careers, but especially their walks with the Lord.

Each graduated with a different emphasis on religion and she wondered if they were walking with Jesus; she hoped they were, and breathed a quick prayer for each one. Then she decided she would attend the reunion. It may be difficult to make the arrangements, but she needed to see them, to be sure they were alright, and if not, to encourage each of them along their journey of faith. Yes, she would find a way to see Ashleigh, Taylor and Isobel once again.

* * *

WATCH FOR THE NEXT BOOK

BY

Jeanne Brooks

ACROSS THE WILDERNESS

NUMBER TWO

IN THE

JOURNEYS OF FAITH

Get to know Maddie's college friend, Isobel,
and watch her grow
in faith as she meets the challenges in her life
beyond college.
Beginning with Isobel's first meeting with her
future in-laws,
it carries the reader through unexpected alterations
in Isobel's well-planned future.

Visit Jeanne's website:

www.jeannebrooks.com

for information on:

Books

Projects in Progress

Book Signings

Availability for Speaking Engagements

CPSIA information can be obtained
at www.ICGtesting.com
Printed in the USA
FSOW01n1028150715
8871FS